By the same author:

Sharon McCone novels

There's Nothing to Be Afraid of
Double (with Bill Pronzini)
Leave a Message for Willie
Games to Keep the Dark Away
The Cheshire Cat's Eye
Ask the Cards a Question
Edwin of the Iron Shoes

Other novels

The Lighthouse (with Bill Pronzini)
Beyond the Grave (with Bill Pronzini)
The Cavalier in White
The Legend of the Slain Soldiers
The Tree of Death

EYE OF THE STORM

EYE OF
THE STORM
MARCIA MULLER

THE MYSTERIOUS PRESS
New York • London • Tokyo

Printed in the United States of America
First Printing: March 1988
10 9 8 7 6 5 4 3 2 1

Library of Congress Cataloging-in-Publication Data

Muller, Marcia.
  Eye of the storm.

   1. Title.
PS3563.U397E94   1988   813'.54   87-19102
ISBN 0-89296-269-0

For Henry J. Muller, Jr.
And in memory of
Annie C. Muller

EYE OF THE STORM

1

California's Sacramento Delta is a strange and beautiful place, decades removed from both the political hustle at the state capital to the north, and the glittering sophistication of the San Francisco Bay Area to its west. If you ask the average Californian about the Delta, he's likely to know little, even though it contains a tangled thousand-mile maze of natural waterways and some of the richest agricultural land in the state. More seasoned travelers may harbor vague images of a summertime paradise of slowly drifting sloughs, islands covered with sun-ripening tomatoes and asparagus and fruit, and marinas choked with pleasure boats. But a person who knows the Delta well is aware of its less hospitable side, of rain-lashed winter nights when the floodwaters rise and the narrow levee roads are no place for the timid or the uninitiated.

The Delta is a constant victim of hostile elements. Every few winters, a disastrous series of storms sweeps through it, smashing levees, inundating entire islands, and forcing hundreds of people from their homes. But come clear skies, the inhabitants—many of whom have lost everything—return to dig mud and debris out of their living rooms and start all over again. That seems to be the way with Delta folk; some overwhelming homing instinct draws them back to the land, even though they know that in a few years the waters will rise again, and that one time the destruction may very well be total.

I was finding out firsthand about the Delta's unfriendly side on this harsh February evening. What I'd principally learned was how unpredictable and ominously changeable the weather could be.

I'd started from San Francisco about three that afternoon, fighting the early rush-hour traffic up the grade to the Caldecott Tunnel and into the Contra Costa County suburbs. By the time I'd gotten beyond the worst of it and was speeding through barren hills that were green from the winter rains, the sky had taken on a high, flat overcast. But it was only a patchy gray, with no hint of an impending storm.

At the town of Antioch—gateway to the Delta—a white arching bridge spanned the San Joaquin River. As I waited at the toll plaza, I checked my watch. It was already close to four-thirty, and I was due at a place called Appleby Island, southeast of the little town of Walnut Grove, by dinnertime. Appleby Island, on the banks of the north fork of the Mokelume River and Hermit's Slough.

The names, like many in the Delta, had an intriguing ring, and I wished I were in better spirits, capable of letting my imagination wander and speculate about my destination. But I was feeling low, and as I started across the span, I lapsed back into a dull, automatic driving mood.

From the highest point on the bridge, I could see land that was radically different from the softly rolling terrain behind me; it was flat farmland, reminiscent of the Midwest, with only the faintest suggestion of mountains on the darkening horizon. High-tension towers linked by massive cable stood in formation across the foreground; beyond them patches in the sky had taken on definition, some still gray, others black and backlit by an eerie white glow.

The temperature had dropped sharply, and the air was crisp with ozone. I turned up the heater of my old MG, thinking about the clothes I'd thrown into the suitcase that rested on the seat beside me. Had I packed that heavy Irish fisherman's sweater? I'd laid it out on the bed, but didn't remember actually putting it in the bag. No matter; Patsy would have things I could borrow. She and I had often swapped clothes in the past.

Then I thought: Patsy. God, what's been happening to her? I had to admit that I was worried about my little sister. And that in itself was strange, because of all us McCones, she was the one whom I'd always regarded as the most stable and self-sufficient.

I tried to figure it out again, went over our conversation at lunch that day, seeking explanations, clues. But I could come up with nothing concrete. All I knew was that Patsy seemed uncharacteristically frightened and had come to me for help. After a while I quit pondering it, let the blandness of the countryside take over, and merely drove.

In less than half an hour heavy dusk had fallen and the character of the land had changed once more. The road narrowed and wound along the top of a levee; to one side was plowed acreage, to the other tule marsh and a wide slough. The wind had risen, and it whipped the branches of the sycamores and eucalypti that grew at the side of the road. Ragged pieces of bark were flung against my windshield, and one caught under the wiper, momentarily blocking my sight. In the distance I noticed the clockwork superstructure of a raised drawbridge, briefly illuminated as lightning flashed across the cloud-piled sky. And then the rain came—a few patters at first, then sheets blowing slantwise across the glass.

I gripped the wheel hard as the wind began to buffet the little car. When I switched the headlights on high beam, the overhanging trees formed a tunnel over the road. The land dropped perilously on either side, and the slick pavement snaked away into blackness. I rounded the curve and braked hard to avoid skidding into the choppy waters of the slough.

"Damn," I said aloud. "Oh, goddammit!" The words sounded a trifle whiny. Well, who could blame me? What was I doing here, anyway? Prior to Patsy's arrival at my house that noon, I'd been tired and irritable, but looking forward to a quiet weekend and an upcoming vacation. Now I was driving along a pitch-black road in a violent rainstorm—all because my heretofore sensible sister had allowed herself to be spooked by some minor and probably harmless events.

Normally I'm not a nervous driver, even under the worst of conditions. But the near-skid and the constant drumming of rain on the MG's roof and hood had set me on edge. I reached over and switched on the radio for comfort, twirled the dial, but got only static. Finally I gave up and put my right hand back on the steering wheel; the fingers of my left were so cramped from the pressure I'd been applying that they ached. I let go and flexed them for a moment. Then I slowed down and turned on the dome light so I could check the directions Patsy had written out. Soon there would be a four-way stop and flashing red light where a drawbridge led left over the Sacramento River to Rio Vista. I was to go straight.

So where is it? I thought. Where?

As if in answer, I saw the red flashes, and then the bulk of the bridge. Across it were the blurred but welcoming lights of the town. Ahead of me the road was once more a dark tunnel. I stopped, even though there were no other cars in sight, shifted into first, and—with a longing look at the bridge—went forward.

After about a mile, the rain began to let up. I was beginning to relax when something appeared in the road only yards from my front bumper. There was a blinding glare as my headlights were reflected back at me, and then a fainter twinkle of taillights. I had to brake sharply to avoid ramming the back of an old pickup truck.

Quickly I geared down and backed off several yards. The truck couldn't be going more than fifteen miles an hour, and since visibility was nil, there was no way of getting around it. The driver must have been aware of my close call, but he didn't speed up. After a few minutes of fuming, I resigned myself to the slowdown. There were worse things, I supposed, than having a pair of taillights to follow along the unfamiliar road.

My headlights shone steadily on the glass at the back of the truck's cab. The glare had an almost hypnotic effect on me. After about half a mile, the truck made an abrupt left turn without signaling or putting on its brakes. Again I almost rammed it. It turned into a shrubbery-choked side lane and disappeared.

I sucked in my breath and drove on. In spite of the near-collisions I still felt less tense than before, and soon the rain stopped, visibility improved, and I was able to put on speed. I passed the town of Isleton, snuggled down below the levee, and then signs bearing some of the picturesque Delta names began to appear: Porkpie Tract, Snodgrass Slough, Dead Horse Island. When I saw one indicating Hermit's Slough, I went slower, watching for the road that led to the Appleby Island ferry. The private ferry, Patsy told me, had been put in by the family who had once owned the island, back in the days when bridge building had been both impractical and uncommon in the area. Although now an outmoded form of transportation, this one—along with a handful of others in the Delta—had not been replaced, and it was the only access to the island.

The road leading to the landing came up quickly, indicated by a weathered board sign with old-fashioned script writing and a more recent crude notation that said DELIVERIES. Deliveries of what? I wondered. Of course—they were restoring the house. Trucks would bring sheetrock and lumber and plumbing fixtures. In a few weeks the interior decorating supplies Patsy had been ordering in the city would arrive. I braked and went in the direction the arrow on the sign pointed, down a steeply slanting gravel drive to the ferry landing. There was a board shack to the left, and as my headlights swept over it, a man in a plaid lumberman's jacket and jeans stepped out and held up his hand for me to stop.

This must be the fellow who operated the ferryboat. Patsy had told me his name, but I'd forgotten. I rolled down my window as he came over to the car.

He was probably around fifty: tall and stocky, with a shock of fine black hair that fell over his forehead. His nose was thin and beaky, and over his left eye he wore a black patch.

A pirate, I thought.

The pirate leaned down to the window of the car. "Miss McCone?"

"Yes."

He extended a rawboned hand through the window. "I'm Max Shorkey. Glad you finally made it—your sister's been calling over here every ten minutes, afraid something might have happened to you in the storm." He patted his side, and I saw he had a walkie-talkie strapped there.

"No, nothing happened," I said. "The rain slowed me down, that's all."

"Well, good. I suppose you'll be wanting to take your car over there. That's what all of them do. Strikes me as stupid."

"Why?"

"No place to go once you're on the island, unless you want to drive around in the orchards. Make more sense to leave the cars and trucks here, closer to the road."

"Why do they do it, then?"

"Search me. Don't understand city ways myself. No offense meant, ma'am."

"None taken."

"Well, you go ahead and drive onto the ferry. I'll take you over."

I watched as he walked to the bargelike vessel waiting at the foot of the ramp. It was about thirty feet long, with room for no more than two cars. Max Shorkey unhooked a heavy chain across its stern and waved me on. I took my foot off the brake and let the MG coast down the ramp and bump onto the boat. In the rearview mirror I saw Shorkey rehook the chain and go into the engine house. Then the motor started grinding and burbling, and we began to move away from the shore.

I got out of the car and went to the front of the ferry, zipping up my navy wool jacket and pulling its hood over my head against the damp, biting cold. Ahead lay a hump of land, and at its top was a white, floodlit house. Not a house—a mansion. It was enormous, stucco, of a style I thought was French Regency, with three stories and oval dormer windows in its mansard roof. How many rooms had Patsy said there were? Forty-five or -six?

I couldn't tell anything about the rest of the island, but the mansion was enough to occupy my attention. Its high lower windows and French doors were surrounded by fancy sculpted decoration and elaborate ironwork. Cypress trees of the sort that look like furled umbrellas stood at regular intervals along the front wall, and at each corner were tall palms, their thick fronds tossing about in the still-strong wind. As I watched, the front door opened and Patsy came out, followed by her nine-year-old daughter, Kelley. She put her arm around Kelley and spoke to her, pointing to the ferry, and then Kelley started to jump up and down.

"I guess the kid's excited to see her auntie." Max Shorkey spoke from behind me.

At first I was startled that he wasn't back there steering the ferry, but then I remembered Patsy had said it operated on a cable anchored to the floor of the slough. "Her auntie's excited, too," I said, feeling glad for the first time that I'd come. "I haven't seen Kelley since she was six."

"Not close to your sister, then?"

"Not so much, these past few years."

"Well, you can make up for lost time now. Staying long?"

"I'm not sure. The weekend, anyway." I looked back at the floodlit mansion; Patsy and Kelley looked small against its mammoth facade. Now that we were closer, details stood out more clearly; I could see deep cracks in the stucco and places where slate was missing on the roof. "They've got their work cut out for them, don't they?" I said.

"Sure do."

"You think it'll be ready for the summer season?"

"Maybe, if everything goes like they plan." But there was a note in Shorkey's voice that said he doubted things would go right. After a moment he said, "*If,*" in that same pessimistic tone, and then started back toward the engine house.

As he walked away, I could have sworn I heard him mutter, "Damn fools."

2

At noon that day, I would have been very surprised had anyone told me I'd be spending the night on a remote island in the Delta. The previous morning I'd given testimony at a child-custody hearing; the rest of the day I'd devoted to paperwork—client reports and my weekly reckoning of expenses. With my desk at All Souls reasonably clear, I felt justified in taking Friday morning off to run some errands and fix a special lunch for Patsy, who would be in town on some business she'd promised to explain later.

The lunch—like many things in my life these last few months—had rapidly turned into a crisis. The last time I'd seen my sister, she'd been in a health-food stage, raising her own vegetables on a farm she owned near Ukiah. I had no reason to believe that had changed, but I know nothing about vegetarian cooking and even hate salads, unless they have ingredients like shrimp or crab or taco meat. Finally out of deference to her, I opted for a salad; out of deference to me, I put plenty of shrimp and crab in it (taco meat seemed inappropriate even to my eccentric gastronomic tastes). A loaf of fresh sourdough bread, a pitcher of iced herbal tea for her, and lots of white wine for me rounded out the meal. When my preparations were done, I set the table on the newly completed back deck (cloth napkins and placemats, no less!) and sat down out there to wait—and to wonder why I was getting myself in a stew over what was really only a simple lunch with my own sister.

Actually I already knew that the problem had nothing to do with not having seen Patsy in three years, or with knowing nothing about vegetarian cooking, or with hating salads. What it had to do with was the strange way I'd been feeling for the past few months, and my increasing inability to deal easily with life's small things.

Small things. Such as when I went to a restaurant and took forever to make up my mind what to order. Or the way I wasted hours when my bank statement came, trying to get it to balance to the exact penny. For years my poor old MG had languished from my neglect; now I'd taken to washing it once a week, and had recently changed my own oil. And every morning I engaged in a painstaking mental debate over which of the items in my never-too-extensive wardrobe to take from the closet; if the garment was wrinkled, I'd spend even more time ironing it to perfection. Small things. I focused on them, fretted about them, and let them sap my energy.

I shifted on my deck chair and looked at my watch. Twelve-fifteen. Patsy was late. I felt like having a glass of wine, but I wasn't sure what she'd think when she arrived and found me drinking alone. Then I thought: Oh hell, what do I care? and went and got the wine. If she wanted to think her big sister had turned into a drunkard, let her. Truth was, I *had* been drinking more than usual lately.

And why? The answer to that seemed relatively simple. I may try to avoid too-frequent bouts with introspection, but I am not unperceptive when it comes to my own motives. The increased drinking, like the fanatical fussing over the small things, was my none-too-original way of not dealing with the big things.

The big things. Such as the fact that everything seemed flat lately, that the world looked gray, as if I were viewing it through a pane of dirty glass. Often there was a leaden lump in my stomach that took my usually overhealthy appetite away. I seemed to dwell on the past—much more nostalgically than the quality of that past warranted. I performed my work mechanically, actually hoping no important case would come along to challenge me. And the sparkle had gone out of my relationship with Don; he'd noticed it, too, and we'd begun avoiding one another. The big things. Things I didn't want to think about now.

As it happened, I didn't have to. The doorbell chimed, and I went to answer it, carrying my wineglass.

When I opened the door, my mild concern about what Patsy might think of her older sister drinking when the sun was barely over the yardarm vanished. The woman standing on my front porch was not the Patsy I remembered. For one thing, she was too thin. Her skin looked dry and pale, and deep parentheses around her mouth made her look older than her twenty-seven years. When I'd last seen her, up at the farm, she'd had a plump earth-mother quality: shiny light-brown hair combed straight from a center part or done up in a fat braid; a glowing, tanned complexion; an inner contentment that was revealed in a slight and constant upward curve of her lips. This new Patsy flashed me a bright, theatrical smile. When we embraced, her bones jutted out, and her perfume smelled too exotic and heavy. The chic cotton aviator's suit she wore was something the old Patsy wouldn't have allowed in her closet. Even her hair—cut short and permed in a halo around her drawn face—reflected a new, brittle personality.

Taken aback as I was, it was still good to see her. At her request I took her on a quick tour of my half-restored earthquake cottage: front parlor (seldom used, but a handsome room with a tile fireplace); bedroom (with a quilt she'd made for me covering the bed); dining room (full of paint and other supplies); spiffily remodeled kitchen and bathroom. Throughout Patsy exclaimed over everything in an artificial, chattery manner; she practically went into raptures when I told her of my plans to enclose the back porch and turn it into another bedroom. I was about to say, "Knock it off, this is your sister you're talking to, not some stranger at a cocktail party," when her eyes rested on the half-forgotten wineglass I was carrying.

She said, "Oh, wine! Can I have some?"

So much for Patsy's health-food stage.

I fetched the wine and took her out onto the deck, where we sat at the table. It was a sunny afternoon, warm for February, and everything had that hard-edged quality that comes from the air being cleansed by rain. For a moment the day's loveliness broke through my dirty glass shield, and I raised my eyes to the sky above the fir trees at the back of the lot and smiled. Then I toasted Patsy and said, "Here's to seeing you again."

She lifted her own glass in return and took a big swallow of wine. For a moment she seemed about to set it down, but then she took another drink.

Good Lord, I thought, she's in as bad a shape as I am. Worse, maybe, because my discontent doesn't show on the surface yet. With her, it's there for everyone to see.

I wondered if her poor emotional state was the cause of her recent lack of communication. Although I hadn't considered it until then—too wrapped up in my own problems, I supposed—she'd been strangely silent for six months or more. Patsy had always been an indifferent correspondent, but every now and then she'd call or I'd find a funny card from her in the mailbox. This past Christmas, however, I'd received no package—nor any acknowledgment of my gifts to her and the kids. Maybe, I thought, I should have been more concerned about my little sister. . . .

Now she set her glass down and looked around, eyes skipping restlessly. The old Patsy had been able to sit deep in her own thoughts for long periods of time, quietly self-possessed without conveying any impression of brooding. But now, while silent, she was intense and nervous; her fingers toyed with the edge of the table and she fidgeted, crossing and recrossing her slim legs. She certainly didn't look like a woman in love—but that was the one thing she'd told me on the phone the day before: She had met the love of her life and was very, very happy.

When it didn't seem she was going to speak, I said, "So how are the kids?" She had three, each by a different father, none of whom she had bothered to marry.

"Fine. Growing. You'd never recognize them."

I waited for her to produce pictures, but none was forthcoming. I said, "And the farm—how are things there?"

"I sold it."

That surprised me even more than her appearance. Patsy had been living on the farm near Ukiah since the late seventies, and had turned it into a self-sufficient operation. She was one of the few people I knew who had been bitten by the back-to-the-land bug and had actually succeeded. "Where are you living now?" I asked.

"In the Delta, at a place called Appleby Island. Evans—that's my new love, Evans Newhouse—and I have gone in with some other people to start a boatel."

It was almost more than I could take in. "A what?"

"Boatel. Where people can rent slips by the night and either stay on their boats or in the bed-and-breakfast . . . what's wrong?"

When she'd said "bed-and-breakfast," my nose had involuntarily wrinkled. "Oh, Don and I stayed in one of those a few months ago."

"You didn't like it?"

"Not particularly. There was no privacy. The johns were down the hall, and you had to share. People kept trying to serve us sherry every time we walked through the parlor. When they turned down the bed at night, they put crummy stale pieces of chocolate on the pillows. There was this bowl of potpourri—smelly weeds, you know?—in the room, and it kept making me sneeze. Finally I stuck it outside the door. The owner acted offended because I'd removed it."

"Oh." She looked thoughtful, as if she were filing away my objections for further consideration. "Well, ours won't be like that. Actually it'll be more like a hotel, with a good restaurant. Evans is going to be chef."

"I see. Do Ma and Pa know you're doing this?"

Her mouth twitched in annoyance. "I haven't told them yet, no."

Of course she hadn't; my mother would have been on the phone to me immediately. "Why not?"

"I just want to wait a while, until we're making a go of it."

"So you don't want me to mention it to them?"

"No."

"Okay." It wasn't unusual for me to keep my knowledge of her activities from the rest of the family. Patsy wasn't estranged from them, but she didn't confide much either. I was the only one she'd ever really been able to talk to.

She'd run away from home when she was fifteen; by the time my father had located her—here in San Francisco, where she was living in a commune and working as a waitress—she'd been pregnant with her first child. Other parents might have forced her to return home, but there had always been a self-sufficiency in Patsy, and after spending some time with her, Pa had concluded she'd be okay, maybe even better off.

And she had been: scraping enough money together to buy her land, establishing herself both as a farmer and a seamstress, raising healthy and happy kids, surviving the ends of the relationships with each of their fathers. The family couldn't understand why she never came home, why she wouldn't get married, why she'd chosen a life-style that was marginal at best. Even I, who knew her best, didn't understand what had driven her away from us at such an early age; but I did sense that it was linked to a deeply rooted need to be independent and alone. She is one of those people who are actually able to be closer to their loved ones at a distance, and in time we'd all come to accept that.

But now she no longer wanted to be alone. Because of this new love, she'd given up the life she'd struggled to build; she'd sold her farm and moved away. She'd entered into a risky business operation, changed her appearance, almost changed her personality. A boatel in the Delta sounded like the perfect dream for an independent and adventurous person like Patsy. But I wondered if she were buying into her own dream—or into this Evans's. Suddenly I felt a little afraid for her.

My ready agreement not to tell the family seemed to have softened her, however. She leaned forward and said, "Look, I just don't want the folks thinking I'm doing something stupid. You remember how they acted when I bought the farm. They never say anything, but I've always known that down deep they think I'm . . . well, a fuck-up, because I don't live their way. This time I have a chance to do something that will make them proud of me."

I hadn't realized she cared that much. But as she spoke, her face had taken on an earnest, almost wistful expression, and behind the makeup and chic facade, I caught a glimpse of the sister I'd always known. I said, "Don't worry, they will be. We'll just wait and surprise them with your success." And then I added, "Now tell me about Evans."

Now, suddenly, she *did* look like a woman in love. Her cheeks flushed and she smiled, and when she spoke her voice had turned husky. "Evans is wonderful," she said. "He's handsome and intelligent and talented and good with the kids. He's just turned forty and has been working as a chef off and on for about ten years. He studied in Paris with some of the top people."

"Where'd you meet him?"

"At a sushi bar where he was working in Ukiah. I'd take the kids in, and he'd give them special little delicacies and we'd talk."

A sushi bar in Ukiah didn't sound like the sort of place a chef who had studied with the top people in Paris would end up. I said, "Is he from Ukiah?"

"No, Michigan, originally. One of those rich suburbs north of Detroit."

"His family has bucks, then?"

"Plenty."

That was good; at least he wasn't after her for her profits from selling the farm.

She added, "Of course they disowned him when he flunked out of Yale Law School."

I said, "Oh."

"Evans just didn't care about the law," she said quickly. "What he cares about is food. You should see the plans for the new restaurant! It's got everything he's ever dreamed of."

"What are you doing—building the hotel?"

"No, we've bought an old mansion, a whole island, actually. We're restoring it. The mansion, I mean."

"And where is it again?"

"Near Walnut Grove. It's called Appleby Island. The mansion was built back in the 1880s by one of the big agricultural barons." She paused, smiling wryly. "It's ironic—he made his fortune in pears."

I smiled, too.

"Anyway," she went on, "the island is about thirty-five acres, all covered with gnarled old pear orchards. William Appleby, the one who built the mansion, got rich and bought up orchard land all over the Delta, but in the 1920s the pear market collapsed and his heirs had to sell off most of their holdings. All they were able to hang on to was the island and the mansion, and they weren't able to maintain it very well. That's why Neal was able to buy it at a reasonable price."

"Neal?"

"Neal Oliver, the guy who's bankrolling the project. He's an old friend of Evans's from Michigan." Patsy drained her wineglass.

I reached for the bottle and filled the glass again. The animation that had suffused my sister's face when she first spoke of Evans had faded; she looked nervous again, and a little sick. I said, "Do you want to eat now?"

"Not yet. Actually, there's something I . . . want to ask you first."

I settled back in my chair. "Okay."

"Shari," she said, using the nickname that nobody but my father has called me since I was a child, "do you think you could come up there?"

"Sure, I have a vacation in two weeks, and I could—"

"No, I mean right away. Today."

I frowned. "Patsy, what is it? Is something wrong there?"

"Yes. Well, I mean, I think so. The others all say I'm blowing it out of proportion, but . . . I don't know, it's all so odd, and I thought since you're a detective . . ."

Aha! I thought. Lawyers' relatives ask them for free legal advice; doctors' relatives want a diagnosis over the dinner table; CPAs get to do the family taxes, gratis. But no one in my family had ever asked for my investigative services before. Most of them perferred to pretend I wasn't engaged in a strange and—to them—inappropriate occupation. Besides, a psychiatrist would have been better suited to their particular brand of problems.

As if she could hear my thoughts, Patsy said, "I'm not asking you to do this for free. We'd pay—or at least I would. I was able to bank most of the proceeds from the sale of the farm."

I made a gesture of dismissal. "Does Evans know you're asking me to come up there?"

"Yes, they all do. He and the others don't like the idea much, but since I had to come down here to the decorator showrooms anyway—"

"Wait a minute—what decorator showrooms?"

"Oh, that's right—you don't know."

"I don't know *anything*. I didn't even know you'd moved." I sounded a little peevish, but I figured I had a right.

Patsy had the grace to look ashamed. "I haven't been a very good sister lately, have I?"

"Stop with that. I won't carp at you if you just fill me in some more about this boatel project."

"Well, all right. There are six of us in on it. Neal and Evans and a couple of other women, one who's going to handle the marina and the other who's business manager. A contractor, and me. I'm in charge of the interior decoration." She said the last words proudly, and in spite of her fashionable, grown-up appearance—which must have been specifically created for her visit to the professional showrooms—she reminded me of a kid who has just landed her first paper route.

"I'd say they made a good choice."

She smiled—her first real smile since she'd been there.

"Okay," I said, "tell me about the problem. If you *are* just blowing it out of proportion like the others say, maybe I can help you put it in perspective."

"Well . . ." She looked anxiously at the wine bottle. I poured us some more, and she continued. "These things have been happening. Things that keep slowing up the project. We had five workers—local people—and after a few weeks they just didn't show up. When our contractor went looking for them, they refused to come back. They seemed . . . frightened somehow."

"And they wouldn't say why?"

"No. Then one night last month there was a storm, and these canoes we'd just bought and had lashed together down by the boathouse all broke free. Most of them sank."

"Could the storm have done that?"

"Both the woman who's to run the marina and the man who operates the ferry—there's a private ferryboat that goes out to the island—say no. She's very knowledgeable about boats, and he's a Delta native, used to what storms can do. If anyone would know, it's them."

"Go on."

"Next was an invasion of cockroaches. In all the cupboards, the food."

"Is that so unusual in an old house?"

"It is if you've never had them before. And we hadn't. It's also not the season for them to be hatching from their eggs. Besides, these were big ones, full grown."

I wasn't so sure about her theory on the growth cycles of cockroaches, but I simply said, "What else?"

"Well, Neal's brother is coming out from Michigan tomorrow to look the place over. He said he'd been warned that Neal might be in over his head, and he wanted to make sure the investment was solid."

"Why should he care?"

Patsy looked uncomfortable, almost embarrassed. "Well, um, Neal's money is inherited. But his parents left it tied up in a trust, to be administered by his brother, who's some sort of financial analyst.

The brother can cut off his funds if he thinks Neal is mishandling them."

"Why did the parents do that?"

"Oh, well. Neal's sort of . . . he's never worked. He inherited some other money from a grandfather, when he was just in college. And he's always lived frugally on that. His parents didn't approve of him not doing anything with his life, so they left his inheritance tied up, subject to Sam's approval."

"Sam is the brother?"

"Yes. All he has to do is *say* the project is shaky, and he can cut off our funds."

"Hmmm. Did you say someone had warned him that the investment might not be a good one?"

"Yes. It was an anonymous letter. Apparently he was really apologetic about taking it seriously, but he feels it's his duty to check it out."

"It sounds to me like someone is trying to put a stop to your project."

"It seems that way to me, too, especially when you take all these things together. The others say it's just coincidence, but I don't believe that for a minute." She was silent, staring into the depths of her wine. When she looked up at me, her gray eyes were troubled— and more than a little afraid.

I said, "There's something else, isn't there?"

"How did you know?"

I just smiled.

"Oh, yeah—family."

"Sometimes we do understand one another, you know."

"*You* understand me, maybe. But not Charlene, and never John or Joey—"

It was the most resentment I'd ever heard her express. "Let's leave off the family for now. Tell me what else is scaring you."

"Oh, Shari." For a moment I thought she was getting up to run into the house in tears, but then I realized she was just fetching something from her purse, which sat on a chair by the door. She came back and held out a small object to me.

It was a doll, a plastic doll, and from the jet-black thatch of hair and dusky cast of its skin, I guessed it was supposed to be an Indian.

It was old and battered, about the same vintage as the toys my parents had brought us all as a reward for not carrying on too much when they took a second honeymoon to New Mexico back in 1962. But there the resemblance stopped.

The doll was dressed in tattered pieces of cloth that were held on by straight pins and looked like they'd come from a yellow dishrag. The head was cocked to one side, and around its neck was a small, intricately tied noose. The eyes had rolled up into the head, leaving the sockets hollow, and the limbs were twisted at torturous angles. In spite of it being only a cheap plastic toy, I felt my flesh ripple.

"Where did you get this?"

"Jessamyn found it." Jessamyn was her five-year-old. "It was hanging—just like that—from a low limb on one of the pear trees."

I frowned, picturing the golden-blond child who had appeared in Patsy's Christmas photo two years ago reaching up to pluck the repulsive figure.

"It was like someone had hung it down low so one of the kids would be sure to find it," Patsy said.

I looked at the doll again. It was gruesome, true, but there was no reason such an aura of horror should emanate from it. . . .

I said, sounding more sensible than I felt, "This doll seems to disturb you a great deal. Why?"

Patsy returned to her chair, picking up her glass with an unsteady hand. I noticed now that her nails had been bitten to the quick. "There's more to the story of the island than I told you," she said. "It's surrounded by the north fork of the Mokelume River and a body of water called Hermit's Slough. The slough is named after an actual hermit who lived there back in the 1850s and '60s. His name was Alf Zeisler. 'Crazy Alf,' they called him. His name was German, but he was mostly Miwok Indian. There used to be a lot of Indian tribes in the Delta, but most of them were killed off in a malaria epidemic in the 1830s. Anyway, Crazy Alf had survived that, and he lived alone on the island, raising potatoes and other vegetables."

She paused to sip wine, then went on. "When William Appleby arrived on the island, he tried to drive Alf off. Alf was clever, though. He hid, and sabotaged Appleby's orchards and farm buildings. He crept around and tried to frighten the family, and did whatever he could to drive them off in return. The Applebys more or less just put up with him, until one night in the late 1860s, when he did something so outrageous that William Appleby and his sons murdered him—hanged him in the orchard where Jessamyn found that doll."

"Good Lord. What was it Crazy Alf did?"

"No one knows. The Applebys never would talk about it. There wasn't much law in the Delta in those days, and certainly none that would protect an Indian squatter, so the Applebys were never charged with the crime."

I looked down at the hideous doll in my hands.

Patsy went on, her words spilling out now. "Ever since Crazy Alf's murder, the island's been said to be cursed. Indian spirits taking their revenge or something like that. William Appleby was mysteriously drowned in Hermit's Slough in the 1880s, shortly after the mansion was completed. Other members of the family met with tragedy—I don't know the exact details. The last Appleby—Stuart—shot himself in the library of the mansion two years ago. Neal bought the place from his estate."

"So what do you think this doll means?"

"I think it means someone who realizes we know the history of the island is trying to frighten us—much like Crazy Alf tried to frighten the Applebys. Someone wants us off there."

I examined the doll more carefully—turned it over, shaking it a little. When I turned it so its face looked up at me again, there was a clicking inside, and its black eyes rolled back into their sockets. They stared at me, curiously compelling in spite of their glassy blankness. I thought unpleasantly of a voodoo fetish.

When I glanced at Patsy, I saw she was staring at the doll, too, her face drawn. Quickly I said, "So you want to hire me to find out who's doing these things?"

She nodded, her gaze still fixed on the doll. The fear in her eyes shocked me enough to force a quick decision. Besides, in the McCone family we had always operated on the principle that when a sibling called for help, you galloped to the rescue.

"Then I'll be up there by dinnertime," I said. "And speaking of food"—I got up and placed the doll on the chair by the door, out of sight behind her purse—"what do you say we eat, before we get swacked?"

Patsy grinned in relief. "I'd rather get swacked," she said, "and then eat."

3

When Patsy left at a little after two—slightly unsteady but insisting she was okay to drive—I piled the dirty dishes in the sink, packed my weekend bag, and went to whistle up my cat, Watney. As usual, the fat black-and-white creature was nowhere to be found. During the two years I'd owned the house, he had absented himself for longer and longer periods of time, preferring to sleep in a nest he'd made for himself under the back porch and spend his waking hours prowling the overgrown yard. Finally I'd become resigned to his new habits and installed a cat door. But I missed his friendly presence, which had been so readily available at my former studio apartment, and every now and then I thought I should get a kitten to keep me company. But kittens were trouble, especially when you were fixing up a house, and besides, I wasn't home much anyway. . . . Another small thing to incite endless mental debate.

Finally I gave up on the cat and left a note on the neighbors' door asking them to please feed him outside if they saw him. Then I threw my bag in the MG and headed for my office. I wanted to check my in-box and speak with my boss before I left town.

All Souls, the law cooperative where I am staff investigator, is housed in a big brown Victorian on one of the steeply slanting side-streets of the city's Bernal Heights district. The area is largely working class, full of run-down houses that are gradually beginning to be upgraded. The freeways skirt roughly two sides of the hill, and the west side is bordered by Mission Street with its taquerias, small neighborhood stores, sleazy bars and discos. To the north is Army Street, and the public housing projects. While the location would not be particularly desirable for the average law firm, it suits us perfectly; we're an outgrowth of the poverty-law movement of the 1960s and '70s, and exist to serve people with low-to-middle incomes and a desire for quality legal assistance. Our sliding-fee scale attracts both the rich and the poor, however, because in the nearly fifteen years we've been in business, we've acquired a solid—often outstanding—legal reputation. I like to think my investigative services have also helped in that department.

I arrived to find the front door of the house standing wide open, and when I stepped inside, there was Ted, the secretary, sitting with his bare feet propped on his desk and a blank stare on his face.

"Hey, real class," I said, pointing at the feet.

"Fuck class," he replied.

The ambience, I thought as I went down the hall to my office. That's why I work here—the ambience.

Until recently, Ted's cavalier attitude would merely have amused me. Now it gave rise to the thought that I was in my mid-thirties and making a mediocre salary at an establishment where the first thing you saw when you walked in was a pair of big, bare, callused feet. Quickly I pushed the notion aside (it was a Big Thing) and rooted through the messages on my desk, separating them into what could wait and what could not. When I got to one that said, "Don called to say hi," I hesitated, then put it in the wait pile.

There were two calls that needed to be returned immediately, from clients whose reports were already in the mail. I knew they were anxious for my findings, so I briefed them and said they should call if they had questions after the reports arrived. That done, I fussed with my already neat desk for a few minutes and went down the hall to my boss, Hank Zahn's, office.

A surprise awaited me there. Hank sat at his cluttered desk, looking characteristically rumpled in spite of his three-piece suit, his wiry hair sticking up in tufts as if he'd been clawing at it. He was going over a contract, and Anne-Marie Altman, our tax attorney and my best woman friend at All Souls, stood behind him, pointing out one of the clauses in the document. She was leaning against his shoulder, her long blond hair brushing his cheek in a most unbusinesslike manner, and the look on Hank's face expressed more pleasure than even he could get from tearing a contract apart. When she saw me in the doorway, Anne-Marie straightened, flushing slightly. Hank just looked up and said, "Oh, it's you."

I came all the way into the office, trying to act as if I found nothing strange about their literal *tête-à-tête*. "It's nice to be made to feel so welcome," I said. Then, to cover my discomfort, I turned to the bookcase where Hank's collection of *National Geographics* was housed—an odd thing to find in a normal lawyer's office, but perfectly in character for one of Hank's eclectic interests—and began looking through them.

His voice tinged with amusement, he said, "You after anything in particular?"

Actually I was. "Has the *Geographic* ever done anything on the Delta?"

"I think so. Try around 1976. Volume a hundred and fifty or so."

His ready answer didn't surprise me. Hank not only collects newspapers, magazines, reports, and statistical studies, but he also devours their contents and commits most of them to his photographic memory. It didn't take me long to find the right issue—November, 1976. "Can I borrow this?"

"Sure. I think there's a whole book on the Delta in that bookcase in the upstairs hall—bottom shelf, toward the right."

"Thanks. I'll check it out." When I turned, I saw that Anne-Marie had come around the desk and sat down in one of the clients' chairs. I took the other.

Hank asked, "So what's with the Delta?"

"I'm going up there for the weekend." Briefly I explained about Patsy and her friends and the boatel, neglecting to mention the strange goings-on. Hank has often accused me of taking too many busman's holidays, and I didn't want to get him started on that again. When I'd finished, I added, "Anyway, it sounds like an interesting place and I wanted to read up on it while I'm there. I wonder—if I call in to make sure nothing important's come up, could you spare me for the early part of the week?"

"I take it your desk's clear?"

"Yes."

"Take a few days, then."

"Thanks."

The trouble with Hank is that he never knows where to stop—not where I'm concerned. He regards me as a cross between employee, friend, and little sister—which makes him feel he has free rein to pry into my personal life. He said, "Frankly, I'm glad you're getting out of town. You need a change of scene. You've been awfully cranky lately."

Anne-Marie sank down lower in her chair, rolling her eyes at me.

Hank went on, "What the hell's the matter with you, anyway? Trouble with Don?" He looked almost hopeful. Hank had never approved of my boyfriend, Don Del Boccio—partly because he considered Don's occupation as a disc jockey lightweight and frivolous, but mostly because Don had supplanted his friend, Greg Marcus of the SFPD, in my life.

I stared rigidly at him, not saying a word.

Anne-Marie covered her eyes with her hands.

"I thought as much," Hank said. "I knew you'd get bored with him eventually. Actually, Greg mentioned that he'd had dinner with you lately—"

Anne-Marie said, "Hank."

I made something akin to a growling noise.

Hank looked confused.

Anne-Marie said, "Hank, I would like a glass of wine."

"A what? Oh, sure. I'll go see what's in the fridge."

"There isn't any. We drank it all."

"Well, why don't we wait until we've finished with this contract, and then all three of us can go down to the Remedy Lounge—"

"I do not *want* to go to that sleazy bar. And I would like some wine *now*."

"Jesus, that means I'll have to run out to Safeway and stand in line forever—"

"Good."

"Oh." Comprehension touched his face and he glanced guiltily at me.

Anne-Marie smiled at him, and he exited the office as gracefully as possible for an embarrassed, clumsy, meddling pest.

After he left, she said, "He means well."

"So, they say, did Nixon."

"Shar . . ."

I sighed and sank down in the chair in a posture that matched hers.

"All right, he always *means* well. He's my friend. He's been my friend since I was in college. He gave me a job after I'd been fired and no one else would even interview me. He's the reason I've stayed at All Souls all these years. In my way, I suppose I love him, but dammit—"

"So do I."

I just looked at her.

"I think we're going to get married."

That was a real jolt. For a moment I couldn't think of anything to say. Hank and Anne-Marie had known each other almost as long as he and I had. She'd been one of the people he'd founded the co-op with. They'd always joked, laughed, worked well together. When there had been a takeover attempt last year, she'd been his staunchest ally. But Hank and Anne-Marie in love? Married? It was unimaginable.

"How long has this been going on?" I asked.

"A few weeks. It started when there was that revival of western movies at the Castro. Hank loves westerns, and nobody would go with him except me."

"You *must* be in love." Anne-Marie and I shared a passion for late-night horror films, but we'd always considered westerns beyond the pale.

She nodded.

"Are you sure, after only a few weeks?"

"As sure as I need to be."

"Good Lord." For a moment we were both silent. Then I realized I was being rude and said, "I'm happy for you. Really I am."

"I know it's a shock. I'd planned to tell you soon. I didn't want to just blurt it out this way. I know a lot of people are going to be unsettled by this, and I didn't want you to be one of them."

"I'm not. It's just that it's . . . so unsettling."

We both laughed, the kind of deep, sharing laughter that is possible only between old and good friends.

Finally I said, "Look, I've got to leave or I'll get stuck in traffic on the bridge. We'll talk more about this when I get back. I want to know all your plans."

"Don't you want to stay and share some of the exquisite jug wine Hank will buy at Safeway?"

"No, I don't think so. Maybe after you're married you can

improve his taste in wine. But when he gets back, give him my best wishes."

I meant it. I really did. I was happy for both of them, would be happier still when I'd had time to get used to the idea.

I only wished that something half as good would happen to me. . . .

4

When I stepped through the door of the mansion on Appleby Island, I momentarily forgot it all: my recent personal problems; my wandering cat; Anne-Marie and Hank; even the torrential storm I'd just driven through. The reception room I was standing in was that impressive. And the people assembled there to greet me were that ill assorted.

I was facing a blue-carpeted staircase that curved gracefully up to the second story, its polished mahogany banister gleaming in the light from an ormolu-and-crystal chandelier. Beneath it a second staircase, edged by a gilt-and-mahogany rail, descended to a lower level. The walls were papered with embossed blue-and-silver *fleurs de lys*; the floor, where it was not covered by a royal-blue Chinese rug, was white marble. There was no furniture, save for a delicate table that held a guest-register book; no pictures or clutter detracted from the room's elegant proportions and color scheme. If this was an example of Patsy's decorating skill, she had found her true calling.

Of course I had only a few seconds to take all this in. Kelley was bouncing around and yelling something about Aunt Sharon finally getting there. Patsy was trying to take my jacket. I couldn't get it off because five-year-old Jessamyn had attached herself to its hem and was staring up at me, her round face—so much like Patsy's before she'd gotten so thin—screwed up in a grin. Even Andrew, the eleven-year-old whom my sister described as withdrawn and often hostile, was there, hanging back in an archway, smiling tentatively. I was struck by his strong resemblance to our father, for whom he'd been named.

I wasn't so sure of a welcome from the others. Two men and a woman, they stood in a tight little group behind Patsy, arms folded, expressions blank, obviously sizing me up. For a moment they seemed frozen in that pose, but then Patsy wrenched my jacket free, Jessamyn grabbed my purse, and they broke ranks and stepped forward.

Patsy draped my jacket over her arm and moved closer to me, almost as if seeking protection. Her face was the same sickly pale I'd noticed at lunch, except on her cheekbones, where bright patches of color burned. I felt a flash of concern, followed by relief; I'd done the right thing in coming here. With a sudden surge of affection, I squeezed her elbow. She smiled weakly in return and began the introductions.

"This is Neal Oliver." Neal was short and potbellied, wearing cords and a lumberjack's shirt that screamed the name L.L. Bean. His face was moonlike, his hair gray and wispy, and when he came closer and shook my hand, I saw his teeth were crooked and badly in need of cleaning.

"And Angela Won, our business manager." Angela was tall for a Chinese woman, approaching my own five foot six, and even thinner than Patsy. Her black jeans and turtleneck seemed calculated to emphasize her slenderness, in much the same way as the hair piled on top of her head added to her height. She nodded and smiled at me, but her eyes remained wary.

"And this," Patsy said, reaching out to take the other man's hand, "is Evans Newhouse."

I turned my full attention to my sister's new love. Evans was well over six feet tall, and when Patsy pulled him forward, he moved with a lazy athletic grace. His hair was a thick dark brown with only a touch of gray, and it curled where it fell over his collar—a stubborn wave that would have been the despair of a member of the styled-and-blow-dried set. But apparently their ranks were nothing Evans aspired to. From the looks of his clothes he'd never given a thought to fashion: He wore a green-and-blue-striped rugby shirt with one shoulder seam unraveling; his jeans were ripped out at the knee; and his tennis shoes—not trendy Reeboks or even Adidas, but an off-brand called Vigor, usually found at flea markets—had holes in the toes and broken and knotted laces. He took my hand, mumbling phrases appropriate for a first meeting with a lover's sister, and flashed me a genuinely boyish grin. When he smiled, his regular features just missed being handsome.

I had been prepared to dislike Evans on principle—"What have you done to my little sister, you swine!"—but this unprepossessing character had me somewhat nonplussed. He certainly didn't appear to be the paragon she had described; he also didn't appear capable of exerting the evil and powerful influence I'd been imagining. My reaction verged on the positive, tinged with a vague uneasiness. And the uneasiness might be more of a response to the situation here than to the man.

Patsy began herding all of us through the archway where Andrew was standing. Beyond it was an enormous living room. Its hardwood floor was covered with the same type of blue Chinese rugs as in the reception area, and white brocade curtains screened the high windows on two sides. On the interior wall was a fireplace with an ornately sculpted mantel; a cherub, whose beatific face looked curiously like Jessamyn's, stared down at the formal arrangement of couches and chairs and tables. To the right of the fireplace was a closed door whose wooden surface was covered with elaborate carvings.

Kelley pulled me down on a pale-blue cut-velvet sofa in front of the fireplace. Immediately she and Jessamyn began to squabble over who got to sit next to me, and I had to slide over onto the middle cushion. As the girls arranged themselves on either side of me, I caught Andrew watching us with a sneer. When he saw me looking at him, he quickly took himself off to the far side of the room, where he perched on the edge of a spindly bench in front of one of the windows. Patsy shook her head at me and muttered wryly, "What's a mother to do?" and the adults distributed themselves on the various other pieces in the grouping in front of the fireplace.

An awkward silence fell. The rain had been over for half an hour now, so we didn't even have its drumming to break the stillness.

Finally Neal Oliver coughed nervously and said, "Well, Sharon, we certainly appreciate your coming."

Patsy and Evans exchanged looks and then smiled at me. Their expressions seemed to say, "Uh-oh, we're in for a speech."

Neal went on, "We hope you'll be comfortable during your stay, in spite of the house being in a state of chaos—it's not all as finished as the public areas would indicate, these are to impress . . . Patsy, did you put her in a nice room?"

"Yes, Neal."

"Well, we don't want her in just any room."

"Neal, she's in the Rose Room."

"The—?"

"Rose Room. The one with the rose wallpaper, next to where you plan to put your brother."

"Oh! The Rose Room." He looked at me again. "Well, as I was saying, I hope you'll be comfortable. If there's anything you need, just let one of us know, because we want you to be—"

"Neal," Patsy said.

"Huh?"

"Maybe we should serve drinks now. After all, Sharon's had a long drive through the storm. Do you want a drink, Shar?"

"Sure, as long as it's not sherry."

She smiled, obviously remembering my description of the bed-and-breakfast where Don and I had stayed. The others merely looked puzzled.

"Oh, right. I'll go get the bar cart." Neal jumped up, his fussy, mother-hen manner—which I was sure would quickly become wearying—more pronounced. After he had left the room, another silence fell. It was as if everyone wanted to apologize for him, but no one wished to be the first to do so.

Finally Angela Won said, "So, Sharon, tell us about being a private detective. It must be exciting work."

God, how I hated that sort of probing comment! I'd heard just about every variant on it that ever existed, and had become so sick of giving my stock reply that lately when people asked me what I did for a living, I'd taken to telling them I was a researcher. *That* generally made them hunt for a more interesting topic of conversation.

I said, "From time to time it's exciting, but mostly it's pretty routine. I ask a lot of questions, take a lot of notes, and write a lot of reports."

"What, no peeking through keyholes at adulterous couples?"

I studied Angela as she lounged in her chair, legs crossed, one foot flicking rhythmically up and down. Was the woman baiting me? If so, why? Finally I said, "I've done divorce work, yes, and I don't like it much. Fortunately, with the no-fault law, there's not the call for it there once was."

"Well, what about murders? Patsy says you've solved some."

I glanced at my sister. She was frowning, aware I didn't like to talk about my work to relative strangers. "Some."

"It must be dangerous. Do you carry a gun?"

"Occasionally."

"Have you ever killed anyone?"

Now she was treading onto territory where my closest friends didn't dare to venture. In my years in the business I'd seen too many violent deaths. Most had been caused by others; two were accidents I might have prevented; and for one I had been directly responsible. After many sleepless nights I'd come to terms with each of those deaths, but I'd never taken them lightly—nor fully accepted them. And they were certainly not a fit subject for cocktail-hour chatter.

I said, "I'm sorry, it's a subject I don't care to discuss."

Angela Won shrugged. She didn't appear to be a woman who was easily offended. Probably, I thought, she was just insensitive.

The tension that had been building in the room was broken by Neal wheeling in a large bar cart complete with glassware, ice buckets, and a full assortment of liquors, mixes, and wines. The others grouped around it, helping themselves, but he insisted on bringing me my drink. I asked for a straight bourbon in hopes of warming myself, and soon it began to have the desired effect. The huge room suddenly seemed cozier, the company more friendly. After a refill, I even smiled at Angela, forgiving her the earlier prying. And when Evans announced that he was going to put the finishing touches on dinner, I found myself liking him very much. I nodded approval at Patsy, and she flushed with pleasure.

Dinner—leg of lamb with mustard sauce, new potatoes, and fresh asparagus flown in from Mexico—was served in a cavernous dining room that had yet to be restored. The hardwood floors were scarred, tiles were missing from the hearth, the only light came from twin candelabra on the long Salvation Army table, and the air that radiated off the uncurtained French doors was chill. Beyond them I could see cypress branches being lashed about by the wind. Soon the rain started again, spattering the panes and smacking down on the terrace outside.

In spite of the surroundings, it was a cheerful meal, with plenty of an excellent zinfandel which Neal felt compelled to drone on and on about. The children were elated at having been allowed to eat dinner at the adult hour of nine o'clock, and the room echoed with their giggles and mercifully occasional shrieks. No one seemed to want to talk about the reason I was there or the unsettling happenings on the island—which was fine with me—and even when Patsy had bundled the kids off to bed, the conversation was confined to neutral topics: the proposed menu for Evans's restaurant, the purchases Patsy had made at the decorator showrooms, the Giants' and A's' prospects for the upcoming season. Finally, when we had drunk all the wine and put a sizable dent in the supply of brandy, we rose and snuffed out the candles. Evans went to fetch my bag from the car, and Patsy— leaning on me and weaving a little—guided me up the elegantly curving staircase to a room on the right front corner of the second floor.

It was only after I'd brushed my teeth in the adjoining bathroom— no sharing at *this* B-and-B—and had gotten into my warmest flannel nightgown that I noticed the smell. I sniffed. Sniffed deeper. And sneezed.

"Goddammit!" I said. "Where is it?"

I prowled the room, moving aside little decorative pillows in the wicker rocker, opening drawers in the antique oak bureau, even lifting the dust ruffle and peering under the bed. Finally I found it snuggled securely under one of the goosedown pillows on the four-poster bed.

It was a little basket of potpourri, lovingly purchased and left there for me by my devoted little sister.

5

I was dreaming about sheep, dozens of them. Not the woolly kind you generally think of, but the naked kind—all skinny and wrinkled and embarrassed looking, like they are after shearing. It was one of those sequences just on the edge of waking; I knew I was dreaming, but I couldn't quite shake off sleep. So I remained half conscious, watching the sheep mill around and thinking how stupid they looked without their fleece, and how stupid it was to be dreaming about them. And then their bleating, which had been soft at first, became louder and more staccato: *Baa, baa, baa, tap, tap, tap.* . . .

I opened one eye. The tapping continued. Hammering.

Sitting up in bed, I stared around the sun-washed room, then flopped back against the pillows. Of course—I was on Appleby Island. And the hammering came from somewhere outside the mansion.

The room was chill, the bed soft, the quilts warm. I pulled them back up to my chin. The hammering was the only sound I could hear. There were none of the morning noises I was used to in the city: cars starting, people talking in the street, kids yelling, the J-Church streetcar making high-pitched moaning noises as it rounded the curve where its tracks ended half a block from my house. There were none of the other morning noises you might expect, either. No voices, no water running, no clattering of pots and pans in the kitchen. I turned my head until I could see the small electric clock on the bedside table. Eight-fifteen. These people were either incredibly early and quiet risers, or downright sloths.

I lay there for a moment, contemplating the room. It was freshly painted and papered, and I remembered the furniture from Patsy's guest room at the farm. Last night Neal had told me that they'd restored only the reception area and the living room, to create a good initial impression on his brother, Sam. They'd also done over a couple of rooms on the second floor, so Sam could see how the accommodations would be when finished. This must be one of those, and I wondered if a lived-in appearance (such as I tend to create) might not detract from the desired effect. Maybe I should suggest they give me one of the unrestored rooms instead.

But I'd worry about that later, I decided. Right now I had to formulate a way to proceed with my unofficial investigation. I wanted to meet the other partners in the business venture—the contractor and the woman who was in charge of the marina, neither of whom had been home the night before. And then I wanted to track down the workers who had quit and seemed afraid to come back, to try to find out what had frightened them. At least the weather had improved— that really was sunlight shining around the flowered curtains—so I wouldn't have to run around looking for the workers in the rain.

Finally I got out of bed, padded over to the window, and pulled the curtains aside. The room overlooked the weedy front lawn, strewn with branches that had broken loose in last night's storm. I got up on my knees on the cushioned window seat and took my first daylight look at Appleby Island.

The lawn sloped away from the mansion, which was set on a rise; a semicircular asphalt driveway curved up from the road leading to the ferry landing and then connected with the same road further to the left, where it disappeared into a grove of regularly planted, gnarled trees. Probably the pear orchard where Jessamyn had discovered the gruesome hanged doll.

Around the edge of the island to my right, where it was nothing but lawn, was a levee—a four- or five-foot earth embankment that protected the land from the often-encroaching waters of the slough. Over its top I could see a tangled tracery of bare branches— sycamores and willows and live oaks that grew along the shoreline— and beyond them were the still, glassy waters of the slough itself. Mist rose from it, stained pinkish-gold by the early morning sun. The ferry landing was obscured from my view by a thick stand of evergreen, dark and somehow forbidding, compared to the pastel-pretty scene to its right.

I opened the window and leaned forward on the casement, breathing in the crisp air. The hammering seemed to be coming from somewhere beyond the levee. I peered over there, but was unable to see anything but a flat corrugated-iron roof that must be the boathouse.

I remained on the window seat for a while, unwilling to start the routine of getting ready for the day. After a few minutes the hammering stopped, and then two figures—a man's and a woman's—appeared, climbing on top of the levee from the slough side.

The woman was tall and lanky, wearing a red scarf tied over her hair and baggy olive-drab work clothes that didn't hide the angularity of her body. The man was even taller and very heavy, at least six foot four and maybe three hundred pounds. His hair and beard were carrot red, wild and curly, surrounding his head like the fleece my naked sheep should have been wearing. In spite of the belly that bulged over the tool belt slung low on his hips, he carried himself well.

The pair walked along the top of the levee for a ways, then descended it and started across the lawn toward the mansion, skirting a giant sycamore tree. They seemed to be arguing, or at least the woman did: She waved her arms in the air, speaking rapidly, and occasionally shaking a finger for emphasis. The man basically ignored her, walking with his red head down, but every now and then he would look up and make a reply. As they drew closer, I caught the tenor of their voices—not exactly angry, but clearly irritated. They went around the house to my right, and a few seconds later I heard a door slam somewhere near the rear.

The tool belt indicated the man was probably the contractor, Denny Kleinschmidt. And since they were coming from the general direction of the future marina, I guessed the woman was Stephanie Jorgenson, who would be in charge of the boating facilities. If I hurried, I could catch them while they were in the house.

I took a quick shower in the newly remodeled bathroom, then put on jeans, tennis shoes, and a long-sleeved shirt. After testing the outside temperature by sticking my hand through the window, I added my favorite bright-green pullover sweater. Applying minimal makeup and tying my hair in a knot at the nape of my neck took only a few minutes more, and then I went downstairs to the reception area.

No one was there or in the living room, but as I stood in the archway, the carved door in the wall next to the fireplace caught my eye. No one had gone in or out of there last night, and now I wondered what it might lead to. I crossed the hardwood- and oriental-carpeted expanse and tried to turn the door's heavy brass handle. It was locked, which seemed puzzling.

It could, I supposed, lead to someone's private living quarters, but given its location, that seemed unlikely. And then I remembered Patsy saying something about the last of the Applebys shooting himself in the library two years ago. If this was that library, that might account for keeping it off-limits. I'd have to ask someone.

But right now I wanted to meet the pair who had crossed the lawn earlier. I left the living room and went through the drafty dining room and the swinging door to the kitchen. It was another room that hadn't yet been restored, although Evans had told me all his sophisticated new equipment was on order, and even in the morning sun it was drab and cheerless. The floor was speckled black linoleum, the walls an institutional green, the counters dingy yellow tile. And the man and woman seated at the metal table drinking coffee wore expressions that matched their surroundings.

They were the pair I'd seen outside, and their discussion had grown more heated. As I came through the door, the man said, ". . . don't care what you say. It's dangerous and I won't—" He broke off, and they both turned to look at me.

The man's complexion was ruddy, and his eyes dominated his face: sky-blue orbs whose roundness created an expression that was peculiarly innocent for one who must be in his early forties. By contrast, the woman's eyes were so dark I could barely distinguish their pupils from their irises. Medium-length black hair hung out from under her red scarf, and her features were as harshly angular as her body. Her skin had a tanned, leathery-looking texture, and deep lines at the corners of her eyes gave her a slightly aged look, even though she couldn't have been much older than her companion.

The two merely stared at me until I explained who I was. Their own introductions confirmed my earlier guess: They were Denny Kleinschmidt and Stephanie Jorgenson. My arrival had dissipated the tension between them, so I got a cup of coffee from the pot on the old gas stove and joined them.

"Sorry I couldn't be here to meet you last night," Stephanie said in a deep-timbred voice that suited her appearance. "I had to go up to Sacramento to see an old boy I know there." She laughed then, harshly, as if at some ironic private joke, and lit a filtered cigarette.

I studied her with interest, wondering if—like me—she had Indian blood. The name Jorgenson didn't indicate that, but then, neither did McCone. My own Indian ancestry is only one-eighth, and no one else in my family shows it, but some long-recessive gene has surfaced to make me look distinctly Shoshone.

When I asked her, though, she looked startled, then shook her head. "No, I'm Italian and Scandinavian, with a little Irish and French thrown in. A real mongrel, you might say."

Denny Kleinschmidt said, "A nice mongrel, though. Hardly ever gets vicious, except at me."

Stephanie sniffed in a derisive manner.

"So," Denny went on, "you're here to check out the little problems we've been having."

"From the way you say that, I gather you don't think they're very serious."

He held out one big hand and waggled it from side to side, like a model airplane in uncertain flight. "I think they've been blown way out of proportion."

"By my sister?"

"Well, yeah. And Steff here hasn't helped people stay cool, either."

Stephanie blew out smoke and regarded him with narrowed eyes.

"Well, you know you haven't, dear."

"Don't 'dear' me! I haven't done anything to upset anybody. But if you had any sense, you'd think twice about the stuff that's been going down. Damned island. It's spooky."

"You can always leave."

"You'd like that, wouldn't you."

"Nope." To me, Denny added, "Steff gets kind of touchy at times, but I like her. Can't convince her of that, though."

Stephanie was silent.

I said, "Let's take the things one at a time. What about the workers who quit? Patsy tells me you went looking for them and they seemed afraid to come back."

"The workers who quit were five local people. Chinese. Two from Walnut Grove and three from Locke."

"Locke's the historic Chinese town, isn't it?" I hadn't been able to sleep right away the night before—a consequence of having had too much to drink—so I'd sat up reading the *Geographic* article and the book on the Delta that I'd borrowed from Hank. Locke was one of the places that had particularly interested me. Although I'd been to the Delta several times on boating excursions with friends, I'd never managed a visit to what was called California's only rural Chinatown.

Denny nodded. "So you see, we've got two things working against us where the workers are concerned. First, the folks in this area have been hearing about the curse of Appleby Island all their lives. They've got their superstitions and legends all mixed up with their facts. Something minor spooked the workers, and they took off. It's as simple as that."

"And what's the other thing?"

"The Chinese community, particularly in Locke, is closed and suspicious of strangers. They've got good reason to be: Tourists are always poking around their town and treating the Chinese as if they're curiosities. Developers keep trying to take it over and turn it into some sort of Asian Disneyland. They seem to look at the people as stage props; one of them said in a newspaper interview that she hoped the Chinese would stay after redevelopment because they 'need these people for local color.' Anyway, as a result, they don't want to have much to do with outsiders. And that includes us."

"When did the workers quit?"

"Let's see." He looked at Stephanie. "It wasn't long after you came, was it?"

"January. The second week, I think."

"And exactly what happened when you went and tried to get them to come back on the job?"

Denny said, "I never was able to contact the two guys in Walnut Grove, and the three in Locke wouldn't talk to me. They saw me coming and just melted into the woodwork—which is easy to do there. From the looks on their faces, you'd have thought I was the ghost of Appleby Island himself."

Stephanie glared at him. "Don't talk that way!"

"Why not? You think by mentioning him I'll conjure him up?"

"I just don't like to hear you go on that way, like it's some kind of joke."

"Isn't it?"

"Denny!"

"Sorry, dear. I won't do it again."

I expected Stephanie to make some retort, but all she did was drag on her cigarette. I asked Denny, "Can you give me the names and addresses of the people who quit?"

"Not offhand. But Angela—you've met her?"

"Yes."

"Angela will have them. Her office is on the lower level, next to the bar. You want her, she'll be there." His tone implied that he found Angela's work ethic mildly annoying.

"Okay," I said. "What about the canoes, Stephanie? Patsy says neither you nor Max Shorkey thinks the storm could have set them adrift."

She snorted and stubbed her cigarette out. "She didn't need to quote Shorkey on that. I've worked around boats all my life—my dad had a charter business in Seattle—and I know what a storm can do, and what it can't do. Besides, I checked the ropes that I'd lashed the canoes together with, and they'd been cut."

"Any idea by who?"

"No, but if I find him—"

"Calm, Steff," Denny said.

"Don't 'calm' me. They weren't your canoes."

Denny looked as if he was about to say they weren't *her* canoes either, but then he just rolled his eyes and scooted his chair back, out of range of the smoke from the fresh cigarette she was lighting.

I thought about bringing up the anonymous letter that had provoked Neal's brother's imminent visit, but decided it would be better to talk to Neal himself about that. I said, "Now we come to the cockroaches."

"Shit," Denny said, "every old house has roaches."

"Full-grown ones that appear overnight?"

"So they were in a cupboard that nobody had opened before and somebody did and they got loose. Or they hitched a ride on one of the deliveries."

"Or they were *brought* in," Stephanie said.

"You're borrowing trouble, Steff."

"Dammit, Denny, Patsy and I helped Evans clean that kitchen before he would so much as move a dish in there. We scrubbed every cupboard, and there were no roaches, no eggs, no nothing."

"So maybe you missed one; that kitchen's got a million little hidey-holes."

It sounded like a debate they'd held before, and it wasn't going to get us anywhere. I said, "Let's forget the roaches for now and talk about the doll Jessamyn found."

My words had a curious effect on them. Denny looked uneasy, his earlier cavalier attitude stripped away. Stephanie lowered her gaze to a chipped saucer on the table and busied herself with shaping her cigarette ash against its edge. Finally she said, "What about it?"

"It's what you meant earlier by 'spooky,' isn't it?"

A pause. "Yes."

"Bothers you too, Denny, doesn't it?"

The big man merely nodded.

I thought of the doll, a piece of plastic junk like you might pick up at any garage sale. And the rags it was dressed in—simply someone's discarded dishtowel. It had no intrinsic frightening quality, but it certainly had set everyone on edge. The whole thing had been so coldly calculated to frighten.

Denny had been thinking along the same lines. "Awful thing for a kid to come across."

I said, "I didn't get to ask Patsy—she didn't seem to want to talk about it—but what was Jessamyn's reaction?"

Denny said, "It scared the hell out of her. She came roaring up here, yelling and crying. Seemed to think it was some trick of Andrew's. She kept saying, 'Mom, Andrew's being weird again.'"

Andrew. I considered my nephew. Patsy had complained that he'd been withdrawn and angry ever since their move to the island. But *weird*? "Does he often play tricks on his sisters?"

"Well . . ." Denny looked away from me. "The kid's kind of . . . strange."

"What do you mean, 'strange'?"

"Maybe you better talk to his mother about it."

I definitely would. "Any ideas about who hung the doll on the tree? *Could* it have been Andrew?"

"Hey, I didn't mean for you to think the kid actually did it! He says no, and everybody believes him. Besides, it wasn't a kid's kind of prank. It was too . . ."

"Ugly," Stephanie finished for him.

"Yeah, ugly."

"Do either of you have any other ideas about it?"

Now neither of them would meet my eyes. Finally they both mumbled, "No."

My coffee and my questions were finished. I thanked them, rinsed my cup in the sink, and set out to find Angela's office.

The lower story of the mansion was also impressive in its way— much as the stage set for a B-grade horror movie would be. The staircase that led down there was carpeted in the same royal-blue as the one that led up from the reception area, but at its foot all pretense of elegance stopped. The hardwood floors were even more scarred than those in the dining room, and near the archway that led to the bar, the boards were warped and buckled. A variety of buckets and dishpans stood there, half full of water. When I looked up I saw part of the ceiling had caved in, exposing old cast-iron piping from which drops of water fell in a regular rhythm.

I stepped around the receptacles and went into the room with the bar. It ran almost the length of the main wing, and the only light came from French doors similar to the ones upstairs. Because of the slope of the land, the lower story was at ground level here in the rear, and the doors looked out on a flagstone terrace like the one off the dining room. At one end of the shadowy space was a massive carved back-bar with a badly shattered mirror. The bar in front of it was made of a slab of laminated redwood. A lone pool table with ripped felt and a fifties-style jukebox with no glass or records were the only other furnishings.

I crossed to the French doors and looked out. Beyond the terrace were steps leading down to a formal garden. At least that was what it was supposed to be: There were flower beds—square, oval, and rectangular—laid out in a regular pattern, and hedges separated it from the rest of the lawn and surrounding orchard. A pedestal that might once have held a birdbath or statuary stood in the center. But everything was choked with weeds, overrun with blackberry vines and tough clumps of Bermuda grass. The hedges had grown wild and were at least four times as tall as they should be.

The enormity of the job my sister and her friends had taken on filled me with an almost physical weariness. I wondered if they really had any idea of the sheer volume of work and money that would have to go into the place. The kitchen alone would eat up many thousands of dollars; I had recently remodeled my own, so I knew what these things cost. And what I'd seen down here indicated there were serious problems with the plumbing. Probably the wiring was also faulty. God knew what condition the roof was in; it didn't look good, even at a distance. And the garden . . . did any of them have expertise with clippers, pruning shears, hoes? Did they realize how persistent blackberry vines and Bermuda grass were? Did they even own a *lawnmower*?

And they were determined to take care of all these problems by the start of the summer boating season. Rectify everything, while someone was apparently equally determined to stop them.

Damned fools, I thought, recalling Max Shorkey's comment. Damned fools. . . .

Quickly I left the bar and went down the wide corridor until I found a door marked OFFICE. I knocked, and Angela called out for me to enter.

She was sitting behind a metal desk, a computer printout spread before her. The desk was well organized—papers filed in stack trays, pens and pencils and paper clips in holders, Rolodex and telephone within reach. Behind her, on a separate table, was a computer keyboard, screen, and printer. The office was such a contrast to the room I'd just left that I stood in the doorway and stared.

The Chinese woman looked up. "From your expression, I'd say you expected to find me adding on an abacus." She smiled ironically. When I didn't reply immediately, she motioned for me to come all the way in and sit down, then folded the printout and placed it in the bottom stack tray.

"It surprises me that you have a computer," I said, "given all the other things you obviously need more."

"Neal's a technology freak. One of the first things he insisted we get was a computer."

"And you went along with it? It strikes me as not a very smart business decision."

"It isn't, but I wasn't about to protest it." Angela leaned forward on her elbows, folding her hands on the blotter. I had the sensation I was about to hear an outwardly candid but essentially self-serving and insincere recitation.

"I must admit, Sharon, Neal's a lousy businessman. His brother has every right to be concerned and come snooping around because, frankly, this investment is damned risky."

The content wasn't quite what I'd expected, but the tone was right on key. "So what do you think he'll do after he sees the place?"

"He'll continue to allow Neal access to his funds."

"Oh?"

"You have to know Sam Oliver to understand. He's got the rest of them terrified with this impromptu visit, but not me. Sam's astute financially, but I'm even smarter. And I also know how to manipulate people, make them believe an investment's sounder than it is. By the time Sam leaves here, he'll want to put money of his own into the project."

"You know Sam, then?"

"We went to school together, got our MBAs from the University of Michigan the same year. In fact, Sam recommended me to Neal for this job."

"Job? I thought everyone here was a partner."

"I use the term loosely. In exchange for my expertise, I get room and board, a small salary, and an investor's position."

"I see." I was beginning to wonder about Angela's relationship with Sam Oliver, and where her loyalties lay in terms of the venture. "Are you and Sam friends?"

"Friendly adversaries. Nothing would please me more than to see this project succeed, in spite of Neal's quirks or Sam's opposition."

"What do you mean—Neal's quirks?"

"Obviously you've observed that he's quite peculiar."

"Well . . ."

"He is. On the one hand he delegates authority left and right, without any thought as to whether the person's qualified for the responsibility. On the other, he's fanatically possessive about this island. I suppose you noticed that the door to the library is kept locked?"

"Is that the one next to the living room fireplace?"

"Yes. It's Neal's private domain. He claims he keeps it off-limits to the rest of us because there are valuable books in there—they came with the house—and he doesn't want people handling and damaging them. Fancies himself a book collector, you see."

"But you don't believe that's the real reason?"

"No. I think—" She bit the words off and compressed her lips. "It doesn't matter what I think. My only concern is to keep the cash flowing."

I was disappointed that she wouldn't go on about Neal, but I followed her new train of thought. "How do you intend to do that, given the magnitude of the problems here?"

"Oh, a little creative accounting. Salesmanship, public relations."

"Well, I hope it works. Tell me, Angela, do you have any thoughts on who might have sent Sam that letter—the one that prompted this visit?"

She shook her head.

"Who would benefit if the project fails?"

"No one that I know of."

"Perhaps there's someone who wants the land for some other use."

"I doubt it. But if there were, I'm sure they'd go about it in more direct ways than hanging dolls in trees or setting cockroaches loose in our food."

"Has anyone approached Neal about selling out?"

"No. There was another offer on the island before Neal made his, but it was much too low and the Appleby estate rejected it."

"Can you find out about it for me?"

"Sure." Angela pulled a scratch pad toward her and made a note on it.

I said, "I need some other information, too. Can you give me the names and addresses of the workers who quit?"

"Yes, but why?"

"I want to talk with them, see if they'll tell me why they left."

She reached for her Rolodex. "I'll be glad to help you, but I doubt you'll learn anything."

"Why not?"

"How familiar are you with the Delta, particularly the town of Locke?"

"Not very."

"Well, I know it intimately. My grandfather lives at Locke; that was one of the reasons this position was attractive to me—I wanted to be where I could keep an eye on him. Anyway, it's a closed community. Most of the people are old and don't like to talk with strangers. Even the younger ones, the ones who were employed here, pretty much keep to themselves."

"I have to try anyway."

"Of course." She tore a second piece of paper off her scratch pad and began writing down names and addresses.

"Would you also include your grandfather's address?" I asked. Her pencil paused. "Why?"

"I'd like to have a friendly contact in Locke. He might be able to persuade the workers to talk to me, if I can't convince them myself."

"Oh. All right." She went on writing.

To her bent head, I said, "By the way, have you seen my sister this morning?"

She raised her eyes to mine, surprised. "No one told you?"

"Told me what?"

"There was an accident this morning. Nothing serious," she added at my look of alarm. "Andrew was out wandering, about seven-thirty, when it was just getting light. He took a nasty fall on those steps leading down into the garden, and Patsy and Evans took him into Rio Vista to the doctor. They think he may have broken his arm."

"Why didn't I hear any commotion?"

"Sound from the rear of the house doesn't travel to where you're sleeping. And Patsy didn't want to wake you. She told Neal to let you know what had happened when you got up, but he obviously forgot. That's Neal for you."

In spite of her minimizing the accident, I was slightly shaken. "What was Andrew doing out at that hour, anyway?"

She handed me the list of names. "Andrew's a little . . . well, he wanders, and he's hard to control. This morning he claimed he was playing detective, just like Aunt Sharon." For the first time since I'd met her, Angela seemed unsure of herself. A shadow passed over her delicate features—indefinable and vaguely haunted.

"What did he mean by that?"

"He claimed he was following something, and that it got away."

"Something? What?"

She hesitated. "I'm not sure. All I know is what he kept repeating while Evans was carrying him to their van."

"*What?*"

"He said, 'Crazy Alf is going to get us.' "

6

Angela claimed to know nothing more than what she'd already told me about Andrew's accident, so I got into my car and drove down to the ferry landing. When I beeped the horn, Max Shorkey—who looked even more like a pirate in the morning light—came out of the rough-board building on the other bank and brought the barge over to get me. On the return trip I asked how Andrew had seemed when Max took Patsy, Evans, and the kids over earlier. He said that Andrew had been quiet, probably in shock, but that the girls "more'n made up for it, shrieking like a couple of little banshees." Patsy and Evans had seemed upset, but in control of the situation.

It made me wonder if Angela's report about what Andrew had said was really true. Given Patsy's anxiety over the hanged doll, she'd probably have gone into hysterics upon hearing her son raving about Crazy Alf. Of course, it was possible she hadn't been within earshot at the time; and Evans struck me as the protective type who wouldn't mention it to her—at least not until she was assured Andrew would be all right.

When I'd driven off the ferry Max fetched a road map of the Delta from his pickup truck and marked out the route to Walnut Grove and Locke. I thanked him and started off along the levee road, dismissing my anxiety about my nephew and concentrating on the interviews ahead. The road wound along on the edge of the slough; tule grass and other scrub vegetation grew on either side. In places the levee was shored up with sandbags—grim reminders of the disastrous floods of two years ago.

But on a sunlit morning like this, it was easy to ignore such signs of destruction. The road took me through farm and orchard land—possibly some that had once belonged to Appleby the pear czar—and into thick stands of sycamore and willow, and finally over an old humpbacked bridge. Nestled at a bend downstream were four white cottages with wide lawns and shade trees and their own docks, and I thought how pleasant it would be on a summer afternoon, to get into my own boat and set off through the interconnecting waterways.

The idea took hold of me, and soon I was picturing myself living in a cottage at the water's edge. There would be no noise, none of the distractions of city life. The days would pass at a lazy pace, a pace that was healthful and sane. I began to wonder if I could establish a clientele here. Surely there must be Delta folk in need of investigative services. And while the volume of business would not be high, the cost of living would be lower. I would be free of the exorbitant monthly payments on what was really a very small house. Free of the everyday hassles of parking and traffic. Free of the anger and hostility that seemed to have become so much a part of urban life. If I left the city, it would be easy to escape the clutch of the past: memories of the violence I'd witnessed and been a part of; friendships I'd outgrown; my unsatisfying relationship with Don. . . .

I dismissed the idea as ridiculous, decided it was another way of not coming to grips with what was really wrong in my life. And began looking for the turnoff for Walnut Grove.

The town, a prominent agricultural port before the advent of hopper trucks, nestled below the high levee road and spread to the banks of the Sacramento River. As I drove down the main street, I was struck by the quiet, old-timey feel of the place. The buildings were concrete or frame, many of them with the second-story balconies favored by the Chinese. Even the most modern structure—the Bank of Alex Brown, founded, I had read, by the town pioneer—seemed something out of a distant era. The narrow sidewalks were sparsely populated, but what few pedestrians I saw turned to stare at my red MG, as if they'd never seen a foreign car. I was glad when I found one of the addresses on Angela's list and was able to park; on foot I felt less conspicuous.

The address was one of the Chinese-style frame houses, sitting right at the edge of the sidewalk, its balcony jutting out overhead. Ugly dark-green shades were pulled over the street-level windows, and the paint had long ago peeled from the boards, leaving them a soft, scoured gray. I knocked on the door, rattling it in its frame. Within seconds it was opened by a youngish Chinese woman in jeans and a T-shirt that said, "I heart my cat head."

The inscription on the T-shirt made me smile, and the woman, who had initially looked suspicious, smiled back. When I asked for Jim Loo, she said, "He's working up in Carmichael this week. Can I help you? I'm his wife."

"I'm from the boatel on Appleby Island," I said. "We were wondering if he might be interested in coming back to work."

Her smile faded. "I doubt it."

"We never did get the full story on why he quit. Can you tell me what happened?"

She bit her lower lip and her fingers tightened on the doorknob. For a moment I thought she might shut the door, but then she said, "It had to do with one of the other guys he was working with, Eddie Huey."

Eddie was one of the three men who lived at Locke. "What about him?"

"Well, Eddie was the guy doing the driving. Jim's truck was busted—this job in Carmichael, he got an advance that paid for the repairs—and none of the other guys owned cars, so when Eddie said he wouldn't go there anymore, Jim didn't have transportation."

"Why wouldn't Eddie go back?"

"Something scared him, something he saw there. That's all he said. But he told Jim he wouldn't go back if his life depended on it, and Jim figured if Eddie was that scared, it wasn't worth *his* life either. Besides, he didn't have no way of getting there, so what was he going to do?"

"And Jim had no idea of what it was Eddie saw?"

"No. I think Eddie might have told Dan and Charlie, they're his friends, they all live at Locke. But he didn't tell Jim—or Chuck, the other guy on the crew, who lives here." She shrugged. "Probably it wasn't much of anything. Eddie might have been smoking, or tripping out on something. Besides, they're all crazy up there at Locke. I don't even know what those guys were doing there. I mean, everybody else there is so *old*. I'd freak out, too, if I never saw anybody under ninety."

It was a psychological profile I couldn't quite buy, but I thanked her for the information and asked her how to get to where Chuck Hong, the other worker she'd mentioned, lived. She stepped out onto the sidewalk and pointed down the main street. "You turn at the drugstore. It's the three-story rooming house just behind there. When you see Chuck, tell him to stop by on the weekend when Jim'll be home. We haven't seen him in a couple of weeks now."

I said I'd tell him, but I wasn't able to deliver the message. The rooming house she'd directed me to was the address given for Chuck Hong on Angela's list, but the door to his room—off an open gallery and up two flights of a rickety outside staircase that clung tenuously to the rear of the building—stood open, the premises deserted. The iron bedstead was stripped, exposing the sagging, stained mattress, and the only signs of previous occupancy were a couple of twisted hangers on the dusty floor beneath a clothes rack. Hong had moved, but how long ago and to where I couldn't begin to guess. I went along the gallery, knocking at other doors in the hope of finding someone who would know, but the only resident I was able to rouse was an old Japanese man who didn't speak English. Finally I gave up, retrieved my car, and went on to Locke.

California's last rural Chinatown fronted the road and extended down below the levee less than a mile north of Walnut Grove. It reminded me at first of a set for a western movie: board sidewalks and stairways, railings where you could hitch horses, frame buildings weathered to deep browns and dark grays. There were subtle differences, however: the curving archways between some of the buildings, the overhanging second-story balconies, the Chinese characters on dusty store windows. A few of these stores had been spruced up and painted; two offered antiques. Redevelopment, on a major scale, had yet to come to Locke, but I wondered how much longer the stubborn and reclusive townspeople could hold off the advance of what is nowadays termed progress.

Locke, I had read last night, was a true child of the Delta, born of disaster. In 1915 fire had engulfed Walnut Grove, destroying most of the town. Rather than rebuild there, many of the displaced Chinese residents, led by a merchant named Lee Bing, had moved north and leased this land from the estate of a rancher named Locke. The Chinese community—initially comprised of male laborers who had come to California to make their fortunes as sojourners and then retire to a life of luxury in their home villages—was a tightly knit one, often exploited and prevented by law from either attaining citizenship or owning their own land. Locke became a haven for them; in its heyday, it could brag of schools, a theater, restaurants, shops, saloons, a hotel, and the ubiquitous gambling dens.

But prosperity had abandoned the town decades ago. From a permanent population of around four hundred—which swelled to several times that number during the harvest season—the number of residents had dropped to a mere fifty-two by 1981. Young people had drifted away, lured by better jobs and pay, and more stimulating lives in the city. As Jim Loo's wife had pointed out, most of those who were left were very old. And now developers wanted to "revitalize" Locke and turn these elderly residents into objects of curiosity.

As I drove along the road, I studied the town, then turned the MG and drove back to a gravel lane I'd passed. It descended the side of the levee, bypassed the village's main section, and ended in a muddy, rutted area beyond which I could see a number of small frame houses. They were squat, with raised front porches and corrugated-iron roofs. Those near me had small garden plots marked off with string; their hills and furrows were crowned with bright-green shoots. Elsewhere wild nasturtium trailed, its orange blossoms scattered and smashed from the force of last night's storm. Clothes hanging on washlines and chairs on the porches gave evidence that the houses were inhabited, but the shaded windows sheltered whatever life went on inside. A small brown-and-white dog stood in one muddy yard observing me as I stopped my car. When I got out, he barked once—for form's sake—and then squeezed under the porch and disappeared.

I locked the MG—a gesture as unnecessary as the dog's bark—and turned away from the little homes. No reason to snoop about; their owners had been bothered enough by probing tourist eyes and cameras.

Given my luck in Walnut Grove, I decided to pay a call on Angela's grandfather before tackling the former workers. He lived in a house on the main street, known as the "Street of Tales," because of the many strange and unbelievable stories it had spawned. She had told me I could find his place by its proximity to a restaurant called Al's Place, known more familiarly as "Al the Wop's," after the

Italian who had founded it during bootlegging days. Another of the Delta's ironies, I thought: The best-known restaurant in Chinese Locke—until the developers bring in McDonald's—was started by an Italian.

I walked along the Street of Tales in the shadow of the overhead balconies. The sidewalk here was concrete, and utility poles ran along one side, but the buildings were still old and sagging. Cars were parked here and there, and a group of elderly men standing around one eyed me with open hostility. Two others, who had been talking on the sidewalk, stared at me and then stepped inside a nearby liquor store. I ignored them, found Al's, and counted doorways until I located the one belonging to Tin Choy Won.

Mr. Won was a diminutive man, made frail by age. He wore a plaid wool shirt and jeans that were held up by suspenders—simple country garb befitting the former farm laborer Angela had said he was. His face was an oval browned by decades of Delta sun, and the web of lines that radiated from his mouth and eyes was curiously beautiful. He smiled when I introduced myself and mentioned Angela, and then he invited me inside.

The room beyond the door was a plain one, extending the width of the house. Its wood floors were clean and bare, and the furniture was of the cheap plastic-and-imitation-wood variety that had been popular in the fifties. The only wall decoration was a poster from the Mainland Chinese art exhibition that had been held at the de Young Museum in San Francisco over ten years before; I suspected Angela had given it to him. Mr. Won seated me in an armchair and offered me a grape soda, which I accepted. As he walked unsteadily toward a door at the rear of the room, I thought once again of irony: Instead of a man in a smock who would give me traditional tea, I had found a man in jeans who drank grape soda pop.

When he returned with the drinks and was settled in his chair, Mr. Won asked, "How is my granddaughter?"

"She's fine. And she sends her love."

He smiled—somewhat wryly, I thought. "You may tell her that I, too, send my love."

He didn't sound totally sincere, so I decided to probe. I said, "You must be a very close family. Angela told me she came all the way back from Michigan so she could be near you."

"Yes."

"Then you must be happy to have her so close by."

"She is a good granddaughter. She visits often and brings me things—candy and pastries and sweet wine." He paused. "I think she is trying to kill me."

"What!"

He nodded earnestly, but his twinkling eyes gave him away. "That sweet stuff isn't good for me. I drink the wine, but I give the candy and pastries to a neighbor lady who is already fat."

I decided to play along with the game, since he was obviously enjoying it. "Why does Angela want to kill you?"

"For my money, of course. There's a family story that I've saved a lot of money. It's supposed to be buried under the porch. When I die of too many sweets, my granddaughter thinks she will dig it up and get rich."

"And *is* it under the porch?"

"No." He leaned forward, grinning now. "It's in the Bank of Alex Brown, invested in a long-term, high-yield C.D."

"Angela will be very disappointed—after the sweets take effect and she digs, I mean."

"Yes." He sat back, pleased with our repartee. "You must remember this, and when I die, have her arrested for my murder."

"I'll remember." I decided Tin Choy Won was probably a little cracked, but pleasantly so. I liked him a lot more than I did his granddaughter.

But now he got to business, sounding very much like Angela. "You're the private detective. Angela told me you might be coming to the island. Why?"

"The problems there. The workers who quit. The other . . . pranks someone's been playing. They need to be looked into, especially since Neal Oliver's brother is arriving from Michigan today."

"The brother, my granddaughter's friend? What for?"

"He's going to go over the books and see if everything's all right. He has control of Neal's funds, you know."

Mr. Won was very still, probably worrying about Angela's job. After a moment he said, "Have you found out anything?"

"Not yet. I'm here to try to talk to the three men from Locke who quit working at the island. Angela told you about that?"

"Yes."

"Do you know them?"

"Yes."

"Can you put me in touch with them?"

"No."

"Why not?"

"They are no longer here. All three received offers of work—in Sacramento, I believe. They left last Sunday."

"Does Angela know this?"

"I think I told her about it."

Damn! She had known the men were no longer in town, but she had sent me here anyway. Why? To get me off the island, maybe. To slow my investigation. Or had she merely done it in a fit of pique because she thought I was upstaging her efforts to handle Sam Oliver's visit in her own way?

Tin Choy Won was watching me, a troubled expression deepening the wrinkles around his eyes. "I see my granddaughter has been playing her tricks on you."

"Does she do that sort of thing often?"

"It has happened." He was silent for a moment, still troubled. I could read disapproval of Angela's behavior into his words, and something more as well. Worry? Yes, certainly. Anger? Not really, but something close to it.

He said, "I will tell you about the young men, so your visit will not be wasted. They did not belong here. All three had family ties in Locke, but they came from Stockton. I heard there was some trouble with the law there. Nothing serious, but enough to make them leave town for a while. Here they lived with relatives in the block where the old Star Theatre is. When they got the chance to work at Appleby Island—through my granddaughter—the family was relieved. This is no place for idle young men."

"But then they quit their jobs. Why?"

"What do you know of the island?"

"I know about the supposed curse."

He nodded slowly and sipped at his bottle of soda. "You say 'supposed.' You don't believe in it?"

"No, I don't."

"Well, you are young yet."

"I don't understand."

When he spoke, his tone was patient. "You are young. You think you have seen much, and there is something about you—your eyes, I suppose—that tells me this may be true. But what you have seen is nothing to what I have seen in my eighty-one years. And *I* believe in that curse."

The way he said it gave me a faint chill. I thought about Denny Kleinschmidt's comment that the local people had their facts and their superstitions all mixed up, but it still didn't banish the coldness.

Mr. Won said, "Never mind. You have time to learn—and to believe."

"I take it the young men—the workers—believed?"

"Initially they knew nothing of the curse. But people here talk, there is not much else to do. And when the three went to work there, they had been warned."

"And?"

"And the warnings proved correct."

"In what way?"

"The ghost of the hermit still walks that island."

"The ghost of Crazy Alf Zeisler?"

He nodded.

"What did they base that idea on?"

"They saw him. In the pear orchard. They saw the hermit's ghost. And it is not a benign one."

7

didn't believe it. Not for one minute did I believe that a malevolent ghost was stalking Appleby Island.

So why was I gripping the wheel of the car so hard? And feeling so uneasy?

Nothing about the story Tin Choy Won had told me was frightening in and of itself. While framing in a bathroom at the left front corner of the second story of the mansion—the opposite end from where I was staying—Eddie Huey had glanced out the window and seen a man watching the house from the orchard. A big man, he had said, with long hair. Because he knew the legend of Crazy Alf Zeisler, the sight had made him uneasy, and he had asked around about other men working on the island. There weren't any. Then, two days later, he'd seen the same man again, dressed in rags like the hermit must have worn, standing at the edge of the first row of pear trees. When the man saw Eddie watching him, he raised his hands; in it was a hangman's noose. The "hermit" gestured angrily with it and then disappeared into the trees. That was enough for Eddie Huey; he drew his pay and quit, convincing his friends to do the same.

When I'd pressed Tin Choy Won for more details about the hermit, he'd become evasive. The hermit had been hung by the Applebys in their own orchard, he'd said. But why? I'd asked. Tin Choy Won claimed not to know. The Applebys had kept their reasons to themselves, and it was not for lesser individuals to question them. Besides, things like that were best left forgotten. Bad enough it had happened at all.

I was certain he knew the whole story and was keeping it from me.

But whatever the reason for the Applebys' actions, there was nothing eerie to me about what the workmen had seen. As I'd suspected, some flesh-and-blood person had been trying to frighten the men off—and had succeeded. What *was* chilling was the conviction with which Tin Choy Won had told his tale. Listening to it, I could feel the power of more than a hundred years of superstition. There were dark currents running through the minds of Delta folk like Tin Choy Won, and they were too strong for me to contend with.

What I *could* contend with was the person behind the alleged ghostly happenings—as soon as I figured out his identity.

When I arrived at the ferry landing, Max Shorkey was sitting on a folding chair in front of the shack, looking grouchy and out of sorts. A couple of T-shirts and a pair of jockey shorts were spread out to dry on a nearby sawhorse, and I realized the ferry operator must live in the makeshift structure. After I'd driven onto the barge and we'd moved away from shore, I got out of the car and asked him. He nodded and muttered something about it being only temporary "until the wife comes to her senses and lets me back in the house." Then he added darkly, "And nobody better give me any more crap about taking in my laundry. Man's got a right to dry his clothes, no matter who's coming." By expressing the proper sympathy, I got out of him that Neal had left a couple of hours ago to pick up his brother at the San Francisco airport; before he'd driven off he'd taken Max to task because the laundry on the sawhorse made the place look "like a slum."

"Neal's a real mother hen, isn't he?" I said.

"Damn right. I know his brother's some kind of rich asshole, but you can't tell me he hasn't seen underwear before!" Max turned and stomped back to the engine house.

At the mansion I found that the "rich asshole's" imminent arrival had spawned further bad tempers. Patsy was running around with a feather duster, scowling and looking like a maid in a French drawing-room farce. Evans and Denny were rearranging the living room furniture. Evans kept yelling at the contractor to pick things up so they wouldn't scrape the floor. Angela was criticizing the way Stephanie was arranging a vase of flowers. Stephanie looked as though she wanted to hit her with it.

I said to Patsy, "How's Andrew?"

She looked distracted, as if she couldn't quite remember who that was. "Oh—broken arm. But not a bad break. I think the cast makes him feel important."

"Why the last-minute rearranging?" I motioned at the living room.

"Neal's idea. Honest to God, I could kill him."

"Why?"

"He spent the whole goddamn morning in his room, making sure everything there was shipshape and deciding what to wear. Angela told me he didn't even bother to come out and let you know about Andrew. And then right before it was time for him to leave for the airport, he decided he didn't like the way the living room looked and told us to change it. We've been so busy cleaning that we never even got to it until five minutes ago. Evans and Denny will probably have to meet Sam with a couch in either hand."

If she hadn't been so agitated, it would have been comical. As it was, I forced back my smile and simply said, "I need to talk to Andrew. Where is he?"

"In bed, acting the prima donna."

"And Kelley and Jessamyn?"

"Down there, too. And if they jump on the bed and bump his cast, I'll kill them along with Neal."

"I'll check them out." Patsy gave me directions to the former servants' quarters at the rear of the lower level, and I went down there, glad to escape the turmoil.

The servants' quarters were in a wing that extended at a right angle from the main body of the mansion. There were at least ten rooms, enough to house a full staff, and the ones Patsy, Evans, and the kids shared were at the far end, overlooking a yard that contained clothes poles and a plot that might once have been a vegetable garden. The rooms were small and dark, but my sister had brightened them with decorative quilted pillows and rag rugs, and high-wattage bulbs in the lamps provided additional light. The advantage of being far away from the others—and thus not liable for criticism because of the kids' noise—greatly outweighed any disadvantages, Patsy had told me. Besides Angela, who slept next to her office at the far end of the main wing on this floor, everyone else had rooms on the second story.

I found Kelley and Jessamyn curled up on the couch in the sitting room watching an old TV movie. They seemed uncharacteristically subdued. Jessamyn barely looked away from the screen when I came in, merely waved and then folded her round arms across her chunky body. Kelley turned her thin face, and I was faintly surprised that this child bore a resemblance to me, mainly in the prominent structure of her nose and cheekbones. Her eyes were mine, too: heavily lashed and far too serious for the tender age of nine.

She said,"Did you hear about Andrew?"

"Yes. I came to see him. Where's his room?"

She looked vaguely disappointed that I wanted to see her brother, and motioned to a door to the left.

It was a typical kid's room—meaning there were dirty clothes and toys strewn all over the floor. My nephew was propped up in bed, his left arm in a cast to the elbow, reading a comic book. The comic's cover showed weird futuristic structures and people with purple-and-green faces. I sighed inwardly, wondering whatever had become of Donald Duck.

I perched on the bed carefully, remembering Patsy's comment about killing the others if they bumped his cast. "So how's it going?" I asked.

"Okay." He looked back at his comic, clearly more interested in it than in me.

"What's this I heard about you playing detective?"

He looked up guiltily, eyes evasive behind his brown-rimmed glasses. Again I was reminded of family resemblances: His face, when it rounded out and developed laugh lines, would be like my father's. His hair was the same wheat color Pa's had been before it got white. He said, "What do you mean?"

"Angela told me you were out playing detective, following something, when you fell."

He was silent.

"Would it have anything to do with the hermit they think haunts this place?"

"What hermit?"

"Come on, Andrew, you know about Crazy Alf. Angela says you were talking about him when Evans was carrying you to the van."

"Well, she's full of shit."

"What!"

His lips curved up with pleasure at shocking me. "I said, she's full of shit. I didn't say nothing about no hermit." He stared at me defiantly.

I knew that look. I'd never seen it on Andrew's face before, but I'd been on the receiving end of it plenty of times from my sister Charlene's oldest boy. It was the old "fuck you, Aunt Sharon" look, and it meant—for whatever reasons—that I wasn't going to get anything out of Andrew. Not until he was good and ready to tell me.

I returned the look with a steady gaze that finally made him drop his own to the comic. "I'm tired," he said in a whiney voice.

"I'll leave you to rest, then." I got up and went to the door. "But, Andrew, here's something you should think about: Good investigators cooperate with other detectives. They know it's easier to solve a case if they pool what they know."

Andrew kept reading as if he hadn't heard me.

I went into the sitting room. A commercial for fake nails that you were supposed to glue over your own was playing. Kelley looked at me and said, "Andrew's being a poop."

"I know."

"Sometimes I hate him."

"Me too."

Jessamyn glanced up. "Mama says you're not supposed to hate."

I wasn't about to explain to a five-year-old that "supposed to" and "what is" very seldom mesh. Instead I said, "Why don't you two come for a walk with me?"

They both jumped up as if the recess bell had rung. Kelley turned the TV off, and Jessamyn led us down the hall and through the door that led to the yard with the clothes poles. There was an opening in the hedge that looked as if it had been created by the frequent passage of small bodies. Beyond it was the formal garden. We toured it, and then Kelley grabbed my right hand, Jessamyn my left, and we wandered around the mansion to the front yard. I felt slightly lopsided because of the difference in their heights.

I don't mind kids—as long as they're someone else's. God knows I'm used to them: My older brother John has two; my younger sister Charlene has recently given birth to her sixth; I suppose if my brother Joey ever settles down, he'll have a passel of them, too. Therefore, I consider it up to me to make certain the McCones don't completely overpopulate the world.

I probably would make a lousy mother, anyway. I can't seem to sentimentalize kids the way a lot of parents do. To me, they're just small adults, simply lacking the skills and worldly knowledge to do the truly terrible and vicious things to one another that the rest of us do. Not that they don't try, in their own crafty ways. Maybe that's why I get along so well with other people's kids. They seem to sense I'm on to them, so they don't have to bother to put up a facade. Such candor is probably not a very good basis for a parent–child relationship, however.

I began to steer us toward the pear orchard, thinking to have Jessamyn point out where she found the hanged doll. She didn't want to go there, though, and she squealed a protest and let her knees buckle, nearly wrenching my arm from its socket. I jerked her to her feet and said, "Okay, let's go see the marina." That pleased them, and they dropped my hands and took off, making the bansheelike noises Max had commented on earlier. I followed at my own pace.

The boathouse was a flattopped corrugated-iron building resting on a concrete foundation at the edge of the slough. At one end of it was a fueling dock with gas pumps; a boardwalk ran the length of the structure and then extended out in a finger pier. To the right of that a few new pilings had been sunk, presumably for the boat slips, but otherwise the place looked run-down and neglected. As I stopped at the top of the levee to take in the scene—and yell at the kids to wait for me—I saw a lone figure slumped dejectedly at the end of the pier. Stephanie.

She turned at the sound of our voices and waved lackadaisically. I waved back and started down the side of the levee toward her. Jessamyn was already racing along the boardwalk by the boathouse. I told Kelley to watch her and then went to join Stephanie.

"Sorry we disturbed you," I said, sitting down next to her and dangling my feet over the edge. "I guess you couldn't take the chaos up there any more than I could."

She reached into her shirt pocket for a cigarette and lit it. "Jesus. They're running around like crazy people anticipating the Second Coming, and nothing's getting done. And then that bitch Angela didn't appreciate my efforts with the flowers."

She fell silent, dragging on her cigarette. Its acrid smell mingled not unpleasantly with the brackish odor of the water. There was very little current here, and wavelets rippled among the pilings below us. Kelley and Jessamyn had climbed down to a small beach on the other side of the boathouse and were hurling clods of earth into the slough. Even their shrieks and laughter seemed far away.

I said, "You and Angela don't get along?"

"Let's say there's not much rapport there. She's a cold fish."

"Denny seems nice, though."

"Yeah, he is. He and your sister."

"You don't care for Evans?"

"Evans is hard to know. He's always got his nose in a cookbook or a kitchen equipment catalog. He's all right, I guess."

"And Neal . . . ?"

"Neal is just plain weird."

"Let me see if I can get this straight. My sister said Neal and Evans were friends in Michigan, where they grew up."

"Right."

"And Angela went to school with Neal's brother, who recommended her for the job."

"Yes. And Denny was the contractor who remodeled a building Neal used to own in San Francisco. He's told me about *that*. Neal drove him absolutely crazy because he was always changing the plans—after the basics like plumbing and wiring and framing were done."

"I'm amazed Denny would want to take on this job."

She shrugged. "Denny needed to get out of the city—a busted marriage, I think."

"And where do you fit in with the group?"

She laughed in the same harsh, ironic way she had earlier when she'd mentioned her friend in Sacramento. "I don't. The way it went down, I was in the bar at the Ryde Hotel—you know the place?"

I nodded, picturing the old stucco structure with its prominent water tower, several miles west of Walnut Grove. It had been the Delta's most popular blind pig during Prohibition and still functioned as a roadhouse.

"Well, it was one afternoon last December," Stephanie went on. "I was sitting at the bar having a beer and trying to figure out what to do next. About my life, I mean. I'd come down from Seattle—like Denny, I needed to get away—hoping to do something with boats.

They're really all I know, but I hadn't been able to find work. And then I heard these people talking at one of the tables, all excited because they'd bought this island and were going to turn it into a boatel. They looked okay—Neal doesn't seem so bad until he opens his mouth and gives one of his speeches—so I went over and said, 'Hey, you need somebody who knows boats?' It turned out they did, so here I am."

"Did you invest any money in the project?"

"Are you kidding? No, ma'am, this project is Neal's baby—and he's welcome to it."

"You think it's risky, then?"

"Yeah, I do. Even Ms. Moneybags Won will tell you that. But it's Neal's life's dream, and he's determined to sink everything he has into it."

"Why, do you suppose? I mean, why's it his dream?"

She flipped her cigarette butt into the water and watched it bob for a moment. "The way I read Neal is this: All his life he's wanted desperately to be liked. Trouble is, he's not particularly likable, so he's always been frustrated. So he's going to use this project and his money as a way to get friends. He figures he can gather a bunch of people together and more or less hold them captive until they damn well *do* like him. Or tolerate him, at any rate. Toleration he might manage, because you can get used to anybody, given enough time and isolation."

It was a theory worth considering. "Well, he's certainly got isolation working for him."

"Natural isolation, yes. And Neal tries to impose psychological isolation as well. He hates for anyone to leave the island for more than a few hours. Last night, for instance: Denny had to go to San Francisco and I had to go to Sacramento. Plus Patsy had been gone all day. Neal was in a snit because his chicks were scattered."

"That's not normal."

She shrugged again. "What's normal? Besides, when you don't have much, you protect what you've got. And we, my friend, are *all* Neal's got."

"Except his money and this island."

"Yeah, and I wouldn't count on brother Sam letting him have either too much longer."

"What's Sam like, do you know?"

Stephanie had raised her head, listening. "No, but I think we're about to find out. That sounds like the ferry coming over."

I could hear it, too. Quickly I got up, dusting off the seat of my jeans, and waved to Kelley and Jessamyn. "You coming?" I asked Stephanie.

"Why not?" she said. "I like to take my bad news quick and neat."

8

Sam Oliver was the antithesis of his brother Neal. Although he was also short, his body was compact and well muscled, indicating that he probably ran or worked out. His hair was thick and sandy, and he sported a luxuriant mustache that he patted occasionally, as if to make sure it was still there. He dressed casually but well—in newish jeans, a cable knit sweater, and a tan suede jacket. His eyes, behind gray-tinted wire-rimmed glasses, were lively.

We all stood around the reception room acting formal while Neal—dithering even more than usual—made the introductions. His explanations of who everybody was and their functions at the mansion became so convoluted that I began to feel embarrassed for him. Glancing around, I could see the same discomfort on the others' faces. Patsy's was that unhealthy pasty color again, and there was a sheen of sweat on her forehead and upper lip. Sam, however, saved the moment by saying—just as Neal was about to start on me—"I'm never going to remember all this. Just the names, Neal. I'll pick up on the rest later."

Neal looked slightly put out. He said, "Sharon McCone, Denny Kleinschmidt, and Kelley McCone." Then he grabbed Sam's cloth travel bag and began marching up the stairs. Sam followed, grinning over his shoulder at us, but banged into Neal when he came to an abrupt halt halfway up. Neal turned, pointed at Denny, and said, "Half an hour."

Sam looked from his brother to Denny, one eyebrow cocked.

Denny said, "I'm supposed to give you a tour of the mansion in half an hour."

"A *contractor's* tour," Neal corrected. "Denny's our general contractor—"

"I'll look forward to it," Sam said.

I said, "If you don't mind, I'd like to tag along."

Neither Sam nor Denny looked displeased, but Angela frowned. "Sharon's Patsy's sister, up for the weekend," she told Sam. "She hasn't seen the entire place yet, but I really don't think this is the time—"

"Neal's already told me she's a private detective, Angela." Sam's wry inflection reminded me of what Angela had said about the two of them being friendly adversaries.

Angela flushed and glared at Neal. Obviously they harbored different versions of what the official story should be.

I said to Sam, "I'd also like to talk to you about the anonymous letter you received."

"Sure; it's in my suitcase. I'll bring it down later."

Sam motioned for Neal to continue, and they went upstairs. Patsy and Evans looked at one another, shaking their heads. I left my young charges in the custody of their mother and went outside to take a look at the orchard.

When I approached the pear trees, I could see that they were very old—gnarled and twisted. Many of their trunks had rotted away so they were mere shells, exposing hollow insides. But even these retained a tenuous hold on life; their upper branches were hazed with green. I stopped in the shade of the first row and looked back at the mansion, then moved along until I was on a direct line with the upstairs window where I assumed Eddie Huey had been working the day he saw the alleged ghost. It would have been easy for a person standing here to know when he was being observed.

The way I reconstructed what had happened, the "ghost" had gained access to the island from a boat that he had beached somewhere along the shore on the far side of the island. He'd donned his rags and tied his hangman's noose in the protection of the trees, then stood at the edge of them, waiting to be noticed. And once he had been, and had made his threatening gestures, he'd slipped away in the same fashion as he'd come.

I turned and began walking down one of the rows, under the canopy of branches, avoiding last season's rotting windfalls. The orchard stretched as far as I could see on either side of me. Ahead was the steep wall of the earthen embankment that doubtless encircled all of the island. It was quiet in the orchard, otherworldly, as if I'd stepped away from the mansion in time as well as in distance. Now and then a bird called and received an answer; a squirrel chittered somewhere over my head.

When I reached the embankment, I scaled it and stood on top, looking down on a narrow tule marsh that bordered the slough for a long way in either direction. This would make a poor landing place: It would be difficult to row through the reeds, and an outboard's propeller could easily become entangled. I couldn't see how far this marsh extended, or what the rest of the shoreline was like. Perhaps after Denny's tour I'd take one of the outboards belonging to the boatel and travel around the island looking for a place someone could have beached a boat.

Thinking of the tour, I looked at my watch and saw I'd been gone nearly half an hour. As I made my way back through the trees, I studied them more closely, imagining how the doll had looked when Jessamyn had found it hanging there. The shapes of the old trunks interested me, and I began to wish I'd brought my camera along. As an amateur photographer, I'm always looking for subjects that might be effective in black-and-white. But photography is something I work at sporadically: For months I lug the camera everywhere and look at everything as if through the lens; then I'll leave the camera to gather dust on the shelf for a year, promising myself that I'll take those rolls of film to the lab and develop them, but never quite getting there. Now I began to regret being in a fallow stage—and to suspect I was entering a time when the Nikkormat would be a constant companion once more.

There was so much here in the orchard that would translate well on film. That tree, for instance: nearly split, the fragments of the right side raised toward the sky like grasping fingers. Or this one, fallen into decay, but still putting forth tall, strong shoots. And the one to my right, with that whitish glare coming through the gaping hole—

A glare? There was no sunlight here, nothing that would produce that effect. And that wasn't the way the sun shone anyway, not with that whiteness. That wasn't light, it was . . . plastic.

I moved forward, my palms pricking, and reached inside the hole.

The object I'd glimpsed was plastic, all right, and it pulled out easily. What I was holding was one of those carrier bags the supermarkets have started offering along with the more traditional paper ones. It was grimy and must have been out here at least through last night's rain, probably longer. On one side it was imprinted with the name ALBERTSON'S, one of the big food chains.

I reached inside and felt cloth. Pulled it out and shook it. A man's shirt—blue, with holes and tears in the body, and both sleeves missing. Next was a pair of pants—tattered, with rips at the knees. And curled in the bottom of the bag was a heavy piece of rope, almost new. A rope that was tied in a hangman's noose.

Holding it made my spine tingle with excitement, but then I had to laugh at the absurdity of finding a clue in a hollow tree. Alf Zeisler's ghost was mighty careless with his possessions, I thought. But then, ghosts weren't supposed to *have* possessions. Nor were ordinary people supposed to go about in rags, toting nooses—which was precisely why these things had been stashed here.

But why leave them where they might be discovered? I wondered. Why not uncoil the rope so it would look perfectly innocent? Why not stuff the rags in the bag, weight it, and sink it in the slough?

Why not—unless they were intended to be used again.

My first impulse was to take the bag back to the mansion. Here it is, I could say, Exhibit A. Someone really *is* trying to frighten you people. But then I thought, No, I'll leave it here. Leave it here and see what he does next.

As I replaced the noose and rags in the bag, and the bag in the hollow of the tree, I glanced around to see if anyone was observing me. And then I laughed again. It was too quiet in the orchard for someone to have crept up on me. It was as quiet as the grave itself.

When I got back to the mansion, the only person in the reception area was Sam Oliver. He sat on the stairs, elbows on his knees, hands dangling. When he saw me he raised his left wrist, pointed at his watch, and said, "Half an hour."

I smiled and went to sit next to him. "You've got to realize you're on Delta time now."

"And that is . . . ?"

"From my brief experience, I'd say nearly always late."

"Can't say as I mind. My brother seems to think this visit is some sort of Michigan Inquisition, but to me it's a vacation."

"You're from Detroit, right?"

"Birmingham, about twenty miles north of the city."

"That's a pretty posh area, I've heard."

"Oh, sure. Our high school once got written up in a national magazine as a playground for rich kids. One of the photos showed a parking lot full of sports cars. We had three country clubs when I was growing up, more now. At five o'clock the bus stops are jammed with black cleaning ladies going home to East Detroit. There are more stockbrokerage offices than hardware stores. One of the brokerages has an electric sign like the ones that show time and temperature, only it gives the Dow-Jones instead."

"Oh." I couldn't tell if he was putting me on or not.

Sam gave a short, barking laugh. It reminded me of my neighbor's fox terrier. "Sorry—it's a question I get asked a lot, and every now and then I feel prompted to say something outrageous."

"That happens to me, too, when people ask what it's like to be a private detective. All that stuff's not true, then?"

"Actually it is true, but let me fill you in on my ritzy upbringing. Neal and I didn't have sports cars; we took the bus to school. It cost fifteen cents, and that had to come out of our allowances. Summers I caddied at one of those country clubs I mentioned, and during college I was a lifeguard. Neal—well, he washed out on the golf course, so he ended up walking neighbors' dogs for his summer job. My mother did all her own housecleaning, and none of us had an account with any of the stockbrokerages."

"But I thought your family had big bucks."

"We do. But my dad worked long and hard for them, and both he and my mother had this theory about waste being a bad thing. I'm afraid it rubbed off on me. About Neal I'm not too sure, and that's why I'm here."

There were a lot of other questions I wanted to ask him, but just then Denny came rushing through the front door, Neal behind him. I raised my arm, pointed to my watch, and said, "Half an hour."

Denny rolled his eyes and giggled—a laugh that was surprisingly high-pitched for such a big man. Sam gave another of his fox-terrier barks. Neal pursed his lips, trying to figure out what was funny.

Denny spotted his confusion and took advantage of it. "Look, Neal," he said, "there's a lot you have to do before dinner. Why don't you let me take Sam and Sharon around, and when we get back—"

"A lot to do?"

"The dinner, Neal. You don't want to entrust it all to Evans, do you?"

"Why not?"

"Think of the dinner. It's going to be special, for Sam's first night on the island."

Neal looked torn, but after a few seconds of considering, he agreed that Evans probably could use some supervision and hurried off toward the kitchen muttering something about even *Australian* lobster tail being expensive these days.

I said, "What on earth is Evans going to do when he arrives to supervise?"

"Put him to work and let him think he's in charge. It's a plan we got up together." To Sam, Denny added apologetically, "Neal's a good man, but sometimes he gets overexcited and makes things more difficult than they should be. But I guess you know that."

"Yeah, I do. You handled him well." Sam was looking toward the archway through which Neal had made his exit. "How long has he been this nervous?"

"Well, he's *always* been nervous, but he's worse since you called to say you were coming out."

"Damn! I really didn't intend to upset him."

"It's not only you. What with the cockroaches, and the workers quitting, and that damned doll—"

"What doll? What are you talking about?"

"Neal didn't tell you?"

"Tell me *what*?"

"No wonder he's nervous. He's hiding a whole bunch of things from you. I think you'd better ask him."

"Why don't you just tell me?"

"No, Neal should. You ask him."

For a moment I thought Sam was going to pressure Denny, but then he nodded. "Okay, I will. And now why don't we get on with this tour."

We started in the basement, where I noticed that the pails and dishpans had been taken away and the leak in the overhead piping skillfully—though temporarily—patched with heavy plumber's tape. Denny led us around, talking about structural soundness and the foundations and the viability of the existing wiring. He was less sanguine about the plumbing, but still managed to sound upbeat. Sam listened intently, asking occasional technical questions and talking about replacement costs. I had to hand it to him—the "rich asshole" was no slouch when it came to understanding the various facets of construction.

After a trip through the servants' quarters (Andrew was still sulking in bed and Patsy was playing hearts with the girls in the sitting room), the wine cellar (surprisingly well stocked), and the barroom (the backbar mirror was irreplaceable, Denny said, but there were alternatives to completely faithful restoration), we stopped in at Angela's office. The business manager was at her desk, riffling through a big stack of computer printout—displayed especially for Sam's benefit, I decided—and gave him a curt, professional smile. To Denny she offered the kind of condescending look she might to a butler. Me she just ignored. This last was not lost on Sam, who winked at me. Angela caught it—as she was obviously intended to— and stiffened.

As we went upstairs Sam said, more to himself than for Denny's or my benefit, "The woman will never unbend, not for an instant."

Denny said, "What makes her like that, do you think?"

"Angela's a very conflicted woman; with her everything's love–hate."

We were back in the reception area now. Denny stopped and looked at Sam. "How do you mean, love–hate?"

"She's got a lot of opposing sides to her personality, like we all do, but she can't seem to reconcile them." When Denny still looked puzzled, Sam added, "Let me give you an example. When we were in grad school at Michigan, I was attracted to Angela and wanted to date her. She would study with me or go out with me in a group, but that was it. The reason she gave was that she was Chinese and I was Caucasian, and the two don't mix."

I said, "That's not such an unusual attitude."

"Not unless, on the other hand, the person hates being Chinese."

"She does?"

"Part of her does, because she feels her ethnicity has kept her out of the mainstream of American business life. That, plus being a woman, she says, keeps her from having any real power or influence. There's probably a good bit of truth in that, but instead of turning her energies to trying to change things, she expends them on anger at her own kind—which doesn't do anyone any good."

What Sam had just said struck me as a possible explanation of Angela's treatment of me. She wasn't reacting to me personally, or me as a private detective, but as a female—one of the gender which, by her membership in it, had denied her access to success and power.

Sam went on, "It's the same with other things in her background. She was on a full scholarship at U of M, as she had been at Berkeley when she was an undergrad. Her folks were pretty poor, they ran a restaurant in Sacramento, and she's always had to pull her own weight. On one hand she was proud of having earned full financial support, but on the other, she was humiliated because she couldn't pay her own way.

"It's the same with the Delta. She used to talk about how much she hated it. She'd say how backward it was, how badly the Chinese had been treated. But at the same time she was so drawn to it that she'd spend all her summers here with her grandfather. I knew when Neal bought this place and needed a business manager that Angela would grab the chance. But she's also told me she resents being stuck here, rather than working for some Fortune 500 company in New York or L.A."

Sam paused, staring back down the stairway to the lower level, in much the same troubled way he'd stared after Neal earlier. "Love–hate. Always love–hate. I'm afraid for her, that someday all that self-loathing will win out and destroy her."

We were silent for a moment, and during it I found myself liking Sam Oliver a lot. Then I cautioned myself that this—and his earlier candor about his upbringing—could merely be a slick act he was putting on to gain our confidence. I said, "Hey, Denny, let's get on with this."

The tour of the first floor was perfunctory; it had been spruced and spiffed so much that even the unrestored dining room looked presentable. Sam made a number of complimentary remarks on the decor, and—proud big sister that I am—I hastened to point out that it was all Patsy's doing.

The library door was still locked, and when Sam asked why, Denny told him somewhat curtly that Neal would show him the room later. We were also denied entrance to the kitchen because of the dinner preparations—Evans was to explain the future plans for the restaurant personally—and soon we were on our way to the second story. There Denny explained the cost involved in having finished off the bedrooms and bathrooms Sam and I were occupying, and gave an estimate of what the total for the rest of the floor would be. Sam listened and took a few desultory notes, but otherwise seemed to be lost in thought, his new worry about Angela merging with his previous concern for his brother.

The third floor was the most interesting of all—at least for me. I've always loved musty attics, probably because when I was growing up the one in my parents' house was usually full of McCone kids and their friends trying to escape the presence of other siblings and *their* friends. As a result, I've come to adulthood attic-deprived, and whenever I venture into one I make the most of it.

And this floor was truly wonderful: It had steeply slanting ceilings and rough plank floors; cobweb-draped eyehole windows that admitted very little light; exposed beams and dark corners. It smelled of dry rot, dust, and—I fancifully thought—long-lost hopes and dreams. I stood in the hallway as Denny took Sam through the rabbit warren of rooms, breathing deeply. Then the dust got to me, I sneezed on the lost hopes and dreams, and I followed the two men, listening to talk of beefing up the existing wiring, installing a separate breaker box for this floor, running copper pipe, and complying with minimal building codes.

There must have been fifteen little rooms up there, partitioned off, but not finished. Some would be combined into suites, Denny said, some would remain as singles, and others would be turned into bathrooms. It was too bad, Sam commented, that the original owners had broken up the space like this. Yeah, Denny replied, but given the quality of the construction, what walls he didn't want to use would be easy to rip out.

"I love tearing things apart, don't you?" Sam said.

Denny gave his high-pitched giggle. "Oh, man, I sure do! Get my hands on that old sledgehammer and swing away . . . good for the old aggressions.''

I wandered down the hall toward a door at the far end.

"Do you ever pretend it's people you know that you're slugging away at?'' Sam asked.

"Sure. Once I even pictured your brother instead of a wall he was making me move for the third time. Real satisfying.''

I kept going through the door and found what—for me—was paradise. The room was heaped with junk: boxes, trunks, piles of discarded clothing and velvet draperies and moth-eaten carpets. There was even a baby carriage leaning to one side on broken springs.

Sam was saying, "Don't feel bad about smashing Neal in effigy. You should have seen what I imagined I did to my ex-wife the time I moved a wall in my condo. She must have been in psychic pain for weeks!''

They laughed together—conspiratorially, like boys in the locker room—and Denny said, "Ex-wives! I've always wished voodoo dolls really worked. Man, would that ever—''

I called out, "What's all this stuff in here?''

Denny said, "Huh? Where are you?''

"Down here at the end of the hall.''

They came to the door and looked inside. "Oh," Denny said, "this is the junk room.''

"Your junk? The group's, I mean.''

"No, stuff that was left here in the mansion when we took possession. There was an awful lot here. The good furniture we sold to an antique dealer, anything else usable went to the flea market. Between the two we made damn near two thousand bucks. Everything else we just stuck in here until we can get a dumpster hauled over on the ferry.''

"You mind if I go through it while I'm here?''

"Why should anybody mind? But why do you *want* to?''

I didn't want to go into my attic fetish, or the fact that the McCone family had hardly ever had any junk, because one person's discardables were another's treasure. We'd had to fight hard for our trash.

"I just like junk," I finally said.

Sam and Denny exchanged a look of camaraderie. There's nothing like a good venting of hostility toward former spouses to cement a friendship—between males or females.

"Well, I *do*," I said.

"If we were male chauvinists," Sam said, "one of us would probably shake his head and sigh, 'Women!' But since we're not . . ."

"You'd better not be," I said companionably, turning away from the junk for now and joining them in the hallway. "Because if you were, Angela and I would eat you alive. Not to mention Kelley; I think she's a budding Bella Abzug."

Denny said, "Good she is, too. It'll help to balance things out in that family. I think Andrew's going to be a Republican—Reagan style."

We all laughed, enjoying our newly found fellowship, and then went downstairs—Sam to confer with Angela about the books, Denny to take a nap before the much-heralded dinner, and me to borrow an outboard and tour the perimeters of the island.

9

I hadn't piloted an outboard since my Uncle Ed sold his when I was around seventeen. But after a few instructions from Max Shorkey and a preliminary turn around the site of the future marina, it all came back to me. Before I cast off, I asked Max how it had gone with Neal and the drying underwear. He grinned piratically and said that Neal had gotten "tight-assed" about it still being there, but that the brother had laughed and been a "real regular guy." He also added that he was sorry he'd called Sam an asshole.

It was coming up on four o'clock, and the sunshiny brightness of the earlier part of the day had faded. The sky overhead was once again a flat gray, and clouds piled on the eastern horizon. I told myself that I'd go as far as I could by four-thirty, then turn back. No sense in an inexperienced boatperson like myself getting caught out on the water in the dark—or in an unexpected storm.

I had complete confidence in the boat, though; both it and its twenty-horsepower Evinrude outboard seemed well maintained, and it had a life preserver and extra gas tank lodged under the stern seat, and an oar for emergencies. I steered it past the ferry landing, waving at Max, who was finally taking in the offending laundry, then putt-putted along on the edge of the tule marsh that bordered the orchard. There were no other boats in sight.

I studied the shoreline intently, looking for a break in the marsh or an indication that a boat had been driven in among the reeds. Everything looked as it must have when only Indians lived here centuries before. After going a ways, I spotted a couple of tumbledown board sheds, probably built to house orchard equipment.

They had steep, sloping roofs and empty holes where the doors should be, and doubtless contained nothing more than rusting hoes, broken ladders, and spiders. They did give me an index as to how far I'd come, though—well past the place in the orchard where I'd earlier scaled the levee.

I began to enjoy the feeling of slipping across the water, to feel secure in my little craft. The outboard engine burbled and chugged, and the boat handled easily. It wasn't too cold out here yet, and my sweater and jeans were adequate protection against the slightly rising wind. I began to wish I could stay in the boat, circle the island, and skip Sam's welcoming dinner, which had begun to sound more and more like an ordeal.

Before I'd left the mansion I'd run into Patsy on the stairs. She'd looked much less harried than earlier, and I'd been relieved—until I'd smelled her breath and realized she'd gotten into the wine again. She grabbed my arm and whispered confidentially, "It's going okay, isn't it?"

"Sam's visit? Well, he's only been here a couple of hours."

"But it's going to be okay, don't you think?"

"Probably. He seems nice enough, just concerned that Neal's gotten into something he can't handle."

"Well, if you say so, he must be okay. You've always been a good judge of character." She sighed with theatrical relief, then added, "What are you wearing to dinner?"

I motioned at what I had on.

"Oh, Sharon, no. We have to dress for dinner. So Sam'll realize we're, you know, civilized."

"Patsy, Sam is wearing jeans. If his are civilized, then so are ours."

"You don't understand. Sam leads a very sophisticated life. He'll expect certain things from us."

I smiled faintly. If beating down a wall in his condo while pretending it was his ex-wife was evidence of Sam's sophisticated existence . . . but then what did I know of such life-styles? I said, "Okay, what should I wear?"

"What did you bring?"

I made a fluttering motion with my hands, outlining my casual garb.

"Oh." She was silent for a moment, then her eyes narrowed and she leaned forward, peering at my face. "Green," she said. "A sort of ice green."

"What?"

"My ice-green dress. You can borrow it. It's always looked like shit on me, but on you it should be perfect."

"What's this dress like?" I asked suspiciously.

"Floor length. Off one shoulder. Stuff that looks like silk, but if you slop wine on it, you can toss it in the washer. There are sandals that go with it. And the necklace. I mustn't forget the necklace."

"Patsy, I don't know—"

"You'll look terrific, I promise. I'll leave the stuff in your room." She started upstairs, staggered slightly, and turned, clutching the banister. "Remember—cocktails at seven. Don't be late."

I scowled censoriously after her. My little sister, drunk and dictatorial in the middle of the afternoon.

Then I smiled. This, from someone who had guzzled down a bottle and a half of white zinfandel in the middle of the afternoon just last week!

But an ice-green, off-the-shoulder dress? Matching sandals? And this necklace—it was probably godawful. Me, dressing for dinner. Good Lord. . . .

Now I steered the boat farther from shore. The tules were thicker here, and there was no end to them in sight. Maybe the "ghost" had anchored a ways out and swum in. Glancing at my watch, I saw it was four-fifteen. I would probably have time to reach the point where Hermit's Slough merged with the north fork of the Mokelume before I had to turn around. The juncture would be easy to spot, Max had told me; there was a collapsed bridge sticking out of the water that had once carried a tramway for hauling the pears to a rail spur. It was now just a group of wooden pilings and twisted track on the island side, he'd said, but impossible to miss from the water.

His directions turned out to be accurate; after about fifteen minutes I spotted the remains of the bridge, up ahead and to my left. The pilings were darkened with age and canted sharply against one another; the narrow track had been twisted upward, and it looked like the talons of an inverted claw raised against the sky. Scrub pine had begun to encroach on the ruins, their boughs draping over them as if it were some bizarre arbor. I raised my eyes from it and looked at the horizon.

The clouds were really massing there now—a shifting finger painting in greens and purples and black. I sniffed the air and caught the scent of ozone. Rain coming, and coming fast. Time to turn back to the boathouse. I'd explore the rest of the shoreline tomorrow.

But before I was halfway back the rain came. One minute the high-piled clouds looked miles away, the next they were tumbling and blowing across the sky, growing blacker and more gravid. The storm didn't begin with tentative sprinkles; it splashed, splattered, pelted. I hunched over on the seat, wiping water from my face and trying to steer. The boat, which had handled so easily before, slipped sideways with the wind and the now-choppy current. I grasped the tiller with both hands, afraid I'd end up in the marsh. The rain quickly soaked through my jeans and sweater. My hair hung heavy against my back, trailing sodden almost to my waist. Water sluiced down over my forehead and obscured my vision. I swiped at it and took a firmer hold on the tiller.

Darkness descended quickly and I lost my bearings. My tennis shoes were soaked with water that had collected in the bottom of the boat, and I began to wonder if it would fill up so much I'd need to bail. Bail with *what*? The only vessel aboard was a full reserve gas tank. The wind suddenly changed direction, whirling the way dust devils do on the plains. The little boat shuddered and tipped.

Then suddenly, I saw lights. The red one at the island end of the ferry landing, and the yellow ones around Max's shack. They were quite a distance away, and it would take a long time to reach them because of the crosscurrent I was battling, but at least I knew where to steer. I pulled out the throttle and held the boat to a more or less steady course.

When I got closer I could make out the hulk of the ferry in its accustomed berth. Getting around it and landing at the boathouse would be tricky in this turbulence, and I didn't want to take the chance of wrecking the outboard. Better to head for the ferry slip itself, drag the boat up on shore, and get Max to take me back to the island. He'd be annoyed at me for getting caught out in the storm, and Stephanie would be furious at the potential danger to what she probably considered one of "her" boats. But at this point, their criticism would roll off me as the rainwater was rolling down my face.

As I neared the ferry landing, I cut the throttle and moved to the side, ready to jump and guide the boat. I misjudged, though, and it hit the side of the barge with a crash and a clang. I grabbed up the oar from the bottom and pushed clear. Then, after tilting the outboard out of the water so the prop wouldn't hit bottom, I poled toward the ramp. The bow of the boat scraped jarringly on the cement, and then it rested.

I dropped the oar back into the boat and jumped out, splashing up to the bow and grasping it with both hands. Planting my feet solidly, I leaned down and pulled with the weight of my entire body until the boat was far enough on shore that I felt sure it was secure. Then I straightened, pressing my hands to the small of my back as pain shot through it. The rain continued to pour down, and loose mud and gravel washed along the ramp and onto my sodden tennis shoes.

Goddamn it, I thought, if I've wrenched my back there's no way I'm going to sit up for that dinner. They can just bring me a tray in my room. And there's no way I'm getting dolled up in something off the shoulder after this soaking. My sweater and cords will have to do.

When the pain subsided some, I went around the ferry toward the amber lights near Max's shack. A few yards from the door, I banged into something, barking my shins. The sawhorse—the fool had left it out. I glared at it, then gave in to a childish impulse and pushed it over on its side. Feeling measurably better, I went up to the door of the shack and pounded on it.

There was no answer. I moved closer, under the overhang of the corrugated roof. I didn't quite fit, and a torrent of water fell right on my head. I yelled for Max and pounded again. When he still didn't answer, I pushed the door open and stepped inside.

The room wasn't more than twelve by twelve feet. There was no insulation, and wind whistled through cracks in the wallboard. A folded roll-away cot stood in one corner; the only light came from an old floor lamp, which was missing its shade; a six-pack of beer and some sandwich fixings—bread, mayonnaise, and that pressed-chopped-regurgitated stuff that comes in three-ounce plastic packets—sat on a rickety wooden table. Max wasn't there.

I stood inside the dooway, wiping rain from my face and staring around the room. The only chair was the folding one he'd been sitting on outside. The only reading material was a tattered copy of the *National Enquirer*. A shabby assortment of jeans and shirts and jackets hung on pegs on the wall. There was no window, no door leading to a bathroom, no running water, no heat.

I moved farther into the room, grabbing my hair and wringing it out. The water splatted on the floorboards. Immediately I felt ashamed of violating Max's living space like that. It wasn't much, but it was his, while he was waiting for his wife to come to her senses and let him come home. And then I felt even more ashamed of my sister and her friends for permitting an employee to live in such squalor when there were so many vacant rooms in the mansion. Why couldn't Max—

There was a noise outside. A dragging and a grunting.

Max?

I went to the door and looked out. Silence now. No one in sight.

But something was going on out there. And where was Max, anyway? From the looks of things, he'd been about to fix his evening meal, such as it was.

Normally I would have called out for him, but instinct made me keep quiet. I slipped through the door, keeping in the shadow of the roof, close to the shack's wall, almost oblivious now to the rain that splattered down on my head. Visibility wasn't good, but I thought I saw a shape over to the left side of the ferry, where the ramp sloped down to the slough. It was hunched over, straining at something that lay on the ground.

I sidled farther along the wall of the shack and peered through the sheeting rain. Saw a man—tall, with longish hair hanging damply from under a slouch hat.

"Hey!" I yelled.

Stupid move. He let go of what he'd been trying to drag and bolted up onto the ferry.

I started after him, then whirled, my brain registering what I'd seen on the ground. Ran down there. Squatted beside the still form. Touched his warm, wet face.

Max Shorkey.

He lay on his back, his good eye blank and slitted, rain washing over his face. The water that sluiced down the concrete from the back of his head was dark stained.

"Max?" I said. "Max, can you hear me?"

Even as I spoke I knew he couldn't. I fumbled with wet, clumsy fingers at the side of his neck where his artery should be throbbing. There was no detectable pulse.

Still, maybe something could be done for him. I reached across his body and pulled the walkie-talkie from his belt. I'd call the island, get help. Maybe an emergency medical team . . .

But I knew it was no use. I've seen too many victims not to recognize the flaccid and plastic look of recent death. Even if I were wrong, even if his body held some faint spark of life, it would have gone out by the time help came.

I rocked back on my heels, nauseated, heart pounding, peering at the ferry where the man I'd surprised had disappeared. Nothing human moved, and all I could hear was the gusting of the wind and the splashing of the rain. I looked down at the walkie-talkie, located the right button, and started to press it.

There was a sudden sound—movement over on the other side of the ferry where I'd beached the outboard. Scraping. Splashing. Somebody was trying to get away in the little boat.

I dropped the two-way radio, got up in a crouch, and ran toward the barge. Rounded its stern, pain bursting in my back where I'd wrenched it before.

My feet skidded on the gravel as I came out on the other side. A tall figure loomed in my path—waiting for me. I dodged to one side, whirled and began running up the ramp. Hands grabbed at my knees, pulled me off balance. And then I was falling face first toward the wet cement. . . .

10

God, I felt awful! My head ached, and everything was swirling around and tipping back and forth. Pretty soon I was going to have to throw up.

How the hell had I gotten this drunk?

Muscles were cramped, too. Must have fallen asleep on the floor because my back hurt and something was digging into my ribs. And it was wet there. I seemed to be lying in a puddle.

I opened my eyes, but saw only blackness. I tried to sit up, but my elbow was wedged under me. When I collapsed I got a faceful of water. I flailed around. Splashed. And pushed myself up against a wall.

The swirling and tipping went on. It was as if the wall itself was moving. Rain was falling, and I was soaked to the skin. Had I passed out outside?

I still couldn't see anything. I placed my hands in the water on either side of my drawn-up knees and felt metal, with joinings and ridges in it. Submerged several inches. When I ran my hands up the wall I was leaning against, I found it was curving, and only about two feet high.

A boat?

But I'd beached the boat. Pulled it up on the ramp and gone to look for Max—

And then I remembered the rest of it: Max's body. The tall man. Turning to run up the ramp. Being tackled. I must have fallen and cracked my head on the cement.

But how did I get *here*?

I pushed myself up on my knees and looked around. Saw water, choppy and running fast—the boat was adrift on a wide waterway. It tipped and swirled as if it were being sucked down a drain.

A drain!

My heart pounding, I dropped to all fours and splashed frantically through the rising water in the boat's bottom, feeling for the drain hole. My fingers grew chilled, in danger of going numb. I slipped and fell to one elbow. A panicky sob escaped my lips; I bit the lower one—hard.

Then I crouched there, clinging to the middle seat, and breathed deeply for a few seconds. When I had myself under control, I placed my hands in the water toward the stern and held them still and felt for a current.

It was easy to find—the water was entering swiftly. The hole was just in front of the rear seat. The plug was floating free, but attached by a sturdy chain to the ring around the hole. I fumbled with it and got it into position, then forced it back in, leaning on it with all my weight. When it was secure, I put my hand next to it and felt to see if any more water was seeping through. No motion.

Shakily I got up onto the rear seat, hanging on to both gunwales, afraid now that the roiling water would capsize the skiff. As I looked around again I thought I saw trees, far away across the water on either side of me. The boat was heavily burdened now, but there was no possibility of bailing. Nothing to bail with—I'd noticed that before. I felt over the side to see how much water the skiff was drawing. Too much, but I might be able to make it back to the landing all right.

If I could figure out where the landing was. And if the boat didn't capsize.

The night around me was terribly black. I couldn't make out any lights, however faint. And there were no landmarks to help me set a course. Nothing but the faint tree line in the distance.

I reached for the outboard, pulled the starter.

But it wouldn't start. It sputtered and coughed. Out of gas.

I felt under the seat for the extra gas can. But it wasn't there. Nor was the life preserver I'd seen earlier. I was adrift in a half-filled boat on some unknown waterway, without even a life jacket. Without . . .

Frantically I felt around on the bottom of the skiff. The oar was still there. I grabbed it up and tested the depth of the turbulent water. The oar didn't touch bottom. No possibility of poling, then, and no rowing with only one oar. I pulled it in and dropped it. It fell into the water in the bottom of the boat with a faint splash.

The wind was kicking up fiercely now, and the boat spun and rocked. I closed my eyes and hunched over, fighting a wave of nausea. When it had passed I stared at the far-off trees, straining to see anything that would tell me where I was.

The waterway seemed narrower now, and the current moved more swiftly. There were irregularly shaped objects sticking up above its surface. The skiff bumped jarringly against one, and I saw it was a tangle of debris and tree branches that had lodged on a sandbar or snagged on underwater vegetation. The boat strained against it for a moment, then broke free, tipping alarmingly. I threw my weight the opposite way to keep it upright.

I got up and moved to the bow. The skiff continued to rock dangerously as I reached down for the oar and looked around for another clump of debris to catch hold of. When the boat came abreast of one, I pushed the oar at it. But the current here was strong, and it swept the skiff on by. The oar caught on a forked tree branch and was wrenched from my hand.

I cried out in frustration, went down on my knees as the skiff swung around, traveling backward now. It bashed into a piling that stuck up out of the water, and I was flung against the side. When I righted myself and looked around, I saw more pilings and a twisted, clawlike shape faintly outlined against the horizon.

The collapsed railroad trestle!

The skiff slammed into another piling and I almost went over the side. I clung to one of the gunwales, looking for the shore. About fifteen feet away, and the current was running fast. Could I swim it . . . ?

The boat peeled away from the piling, slewed around in a complete circle, and bashed into another one. And suddenly I was in the water.

It was icy cold. I gasped in shock and took in a mouthful as my head went under. I kicked out for the bottom with my feet, but felt nothing. The current was dragging furiously at me.

My head bobbed to the surface; I swiped water from my face, looking around in a near panic. I couldn't see the boat, but straight in my path was a wicked-looking protrusion of railroad track. I kicked wildly and began swimming in a choppy Australian crawl, missing the twisted metal by inches.

I kept moving, but I was being swept sideways, along the shore rather than toward it. The water was numbing, and my tennis shoes and clothing were dragging me down. I took in mouthfuls of water; my lungs felt as if they might explode. The blood pounded in my head, and one leg began to cramp.

I thought: *I'm going to die.*

And then the current gushed violently, dividing two ways around a tangle of branches and slamming my upper body into it. With what little strength I had left, I flung my arms around them and hung tight. Panted and hugged them like a child hugs its mother after a nightmare. Stopped kicking and let my legs drag.

And touched bottom.

No touch of land had ever been so welcome. Even so, I didn't relinquish my hold on the branches for a long time. When I felt strong enough, I slogged slowly to shore, steadying myself on the exposed pilings. Splinters pricked at my hands, but they were so numbed that I barely felt them. My foot caught on a submerged piece of track and I turned my ankle. I wrenched my foot free, kept going.

Finally I reached the bank and crawled up it on hands and knees, batting aside the boughs of the scrub fir trees that grew there. At the top of the levee I collapsed and rolled over onto my back, unheedful of the mud and the rain that splashed down on me. I'd rest for a minute or two and then strike out across the island for the mansion. . . .

After a moment I began to think back—to the ferry landing, to Max's body and the tall man. It was clear now what had happened. I'd fallen on the cement, knocked myself unconscious. And then the man had put my unconscious body in the skiff and pulled its plug. He'd removed the extra gas can and the life preserver, and set the boat adrift, leaving me to drown. And if I'd regained consciousness only minutes later, he would have succeeded.

Had I been missed at the mansion yet? I wondered. What time was it, anyway? I raised my wrist and looked at the luminous dial of my watch, but it had stopped at five thirty-nine.

Well, it had to be much later than that now. After seven, the cocktail hour, when they'd have realized I was missing. Had they known something was wrong, or just assumed I was off conducting my investigation? They'd have to have known, because my car was still on the island. And if they'd tried to raise Max on the walkie-talkie, to see if he'd seen me or taken me ashore on foot, they'd have realized something had happened to us both and come looking.

But how would they know where to look? For that matter, how was I going to find the mansion? The island was thirty-five acres, most of it covered in orchard or dense vegetation. I wasn't sure which direction to go, wasn't capable of traveling miles. I was weak, cold. I could fall in the dark and break a leg. At the very least, I would contract pneumonia—

Stop it! I thought. *What's the matter with you? You're not going to give up now.*

I closed my eyes, ignoring the cramping and spasming of my muscles, and tried to visualize a map of the island. The ferry landing was here. There was the orchard where the doll had been hung. Here were the sheds I'd seen earlier from the skiff. Here were more pear trees. And here was the railroad bridge.

Okay, I thought, stick the mansion about *here*, and if you get up and walk on that angle, sooner or later you'll see lights.

I sat up and breathed deeply for a time. Then I got up and went to find those lights.

But it was rough traveling. Through gnarled trees that took on menacing shapes in the darkness. Over terrain that never once seemed level. Through underbrush that pulled and scratched and tore at my clothing. Through puddles and mud and lashing rain. And it grew colder, all the time colder. I stuck my hands in my armpits and mumbled inane encouragements to myself, the best of which was the promise of a triple bourbon. And I looked for the lights. I kept looking.

When I saw them they were not as I'd envisioned. For one thing, they moved—in a jerky, bobbing pattern, through the trees ahead of me. And besides the lights there were voices. They were familiar and frantic. And they were calling my name.

I tried to answer, but it came out a croak. I started to run forward, but my legs gave out and I stumbled. As I fell to my knees, I knew I was going to lose consciousness again. I only hoped they'd find me before it was too late.

11

It was Evans, they told me later, who had practically fallen over my crumpled body in the dark orchard. That was close to nine o'clock, and they'd been searching for me since seven-forty-five. As I'd imagined, a worried Patsy had tried to raise Max on the walkie-talkie when I didn't show up for cocktails, but had gotten no response. Stephanie had volunteered to take one of the outboards over to check on him, but when she'd gone to the boathouse, she'd found them both missing. And then Denny had remembered I'd been planning to go for a ride. He and Stephanie had rowed over to Max's shack in the third, motorless, skiff and found the place closed up and deserted. But Max's truck was still there, and that, plus the fact both boats were missing, made them think I'd stayed out too long and Max had gone looking for me. When they'd rowed back and reported this to the others at the mansion, they'd decided to help by mounting their own land search.

Of course, I wasn't in any condition to take in these details at first. They'd carried me back to the mansion—I'd only been half a mile from it when they found me—stripped off my wet clothes and wrapped me in blankets on one of the living room couches. I'd come to when Patsy sloshed some brandy into my mouth, getting most of it on a cut on my chin, where I'd fallen on the concrete ramp. I'd flailed around in a panic, screaming for them to call the sheriff. Patsy had pushed me down and told Evans she felt a doctor was more in order. He went to make the call, and she was still holding me immobile when he came back and said the phone line was down.

At that point I came fully awake. They were all hovering over me.

Patsy's face was the first I saw: ashen, eyes scared, lips compressed. Evans was looking over her shoulder, trying to remain calm, but not succeeding too well. Denny and Sam were doing better; Stephanie was putting on a show of competence and herding the kids from the room; Angela was impassive as ever. Neal was acting totally in character—wringing his pale, plump hands and rolling his eyes and exclaiming things that nobody paid any attention to.

Seeing all of them, I suddenly felt quite lucid. I pushed Patsy away and raised myself on one elbow—not an easy thing to do, cocooned as I was—and said, "What—the phone's dead?"

Evans nodded.

"Then somebody'll have to take a boat over to shore and get the sheriff."

"The . . ." Patsy glanced at Evans. It was clear they both thought I was hallucinating.

"The sheriff," I said more distinctly. "I assume you're under the jurisdiction of the county here."

Denny said, "Uh, yeah."

"Good. Get hold of the nearest substation."

Sam said, "Why?"

"Because Max Shorkey has been murdered."

They were all silent now. From their assorted expressions, I could practically hear their thoughts humming:

> *Poor thing, she's out of her head.* (Patsy)
> *We'd better get the doctor quick.* (Evans)
> *Uh-oh.* (Denny)
> *Maybe it really happened.* (Sam)
> *Oh God, oh God!* (Neal)
> *Stupid attention-grabbing bitch.* (Angela)
> *What did I miss?* (Stephanie, who had
>   just come back into the room)

Finally Sam said, "How do you know?"

"I saw his body, down at the ferry landing. He was lying on the ramp, and some man—I think he's the one who's been trying to frighten everyone off the island—was trying to move him. When he saw me he ran, and when I chased him he knocked me unconscious.

He stuffed me in the skiff, took out the life preserver, gas tank, and drainage plug, and set me adrift to drown."

It didn't sound like the hysterical ramblings of a feverish woman, but still they all looked dubious.

Denny said uncomfortably, "Look, Sharon, I don't want to blow this . . . idea you have all to hell, but when Steff and I were over at the landing at about seven-thirty, there wasn't a body on the ramp. No one there at all."

I paused. "Then the man got rid of it after he turned me loose in the boat." I wriggled my hand out of my mummy's wrappings and motioned for Patsy to give me the brandy glass. She did, and I sipped, remembering my promises to myself about a triple bourbon. Promises that had seemed so farfetched at the time. . . .

Sam was frowning now. I sensed he was the only person who even half believed me. "How did he get rid of the body?" he asked.

"Where do you think the other outboard went?"

His face was very still for a moment and then he nodded. To Denny, he said, "Better go for the sheriff."

Neal pushed forward. "Wait a minute, Sam, who's in charge here? This is my place, it's up to me to get the sheriff." He paused, breathing fast. "*If* we get the sheriff," he added.

Sam said, "Sharon's obviously seen something that should be checked out by the authorities."

"She's hysterical—"

"Does she look hysterical?"

"And besides, I should say who goes for who. *I* should give the orders. *I* should get the sheriff, not Denny, he's only the contractor here."

When he spoke Sam's voice was weary. "The ferry's over at the other side of the landing. Can you row a boat, Neal?"

"No, but—"

"Denny can. And I think he'd better get started right away."

"Right!" Denny looked glad to be leaving.

Before he got his windbreaker on, though, Angela cocked her head and said, "What's that?"

We all looked at her.

"I hear a horn. Over at the ferry landing."

Neal said, "*I* don't hear anything."

Patsy stood up. "I do."

Now I heard it, too. A car or truck horn, beeping insistently. After about ten seconds it stopped, and soon the ferry's engine turned over and began rumbling.

Patsy and Sam ran to the front windows. The others looked at me. Angela said, "I thought Max was dead, Sharon."

"He is."

"Then who's that bringing the ferry over?" Her finely penciled eyebrows arched triumphantly and her lips drew back in an unpleasant smile.

Right at that moment I hated her. Hated her because I knew she was a person who would take advantage of anyone else's weakness or infirmity to prove herself right. And then I realized that I might be physically infirm, but I was still mentally sound. I *had* found Max's body on the ramp, and it couldn't be him bringing the ferry over.

I said, "I don't know, but somebody ought to go see."

The operator of the ferry, surprisingly, turned out to be Tin Choy Won, Angela's grandfather. He wore a heavy yellow rain slicker and matching hat, but was still drenched and coughing raspily when he came into the reception area and dripped water and tracked mud onto the blue Chinese rug. Denny, who had gone outside to meet him, entered, too, doing similar damage.

Neal rushed forward first, crying, "The drop cloth! Patsy, for God's sake, what happened to that drop cloth?"

Then Angela hurried over and pushed Neal aside. "Grandfather!" she exclaimed, and broke off into Chinese. She put her arms around the frail man's shoulders and tried to remove his raincoat.

Tin Choy Won pushed her arms away and spoke rapidly to her. She shook her head, grabbing at the slicker. After a moment, he allowed her to strip it off and hand it to Denny. They held a brief conversation, and then she turned to the rest of us and said, "My grandfather has come to see me on a matter of some urgency. You must excuse us."

As they turned toward the stairway to the lower level where her office and living quarters were, I said, "Wait a minute."

They both looked back through the archway—she impatiently, he with curiosity. When he recognized me, his face creased in a slight, ironic smile.

I said, "Mr. Won, when you came over to the island just now, you had to pilot the ferry yourself."

"Yes."

"Max Shorkey wasn't there?"

"No. I beeped my horn, but no one answered. So I came anyway." I must have frowned, because he added, "Operating a Delta ferry is not such a difficult thing, Miss McCone. Most of us who were raised here can do so."

"I see."

"If that's all for now, perhaps you'll excuse us, Sharon?" Angela's voice was cold, with a nervous edge.

I watched them disappear around the turn in the stairs, then raised my eyes and caught Sam's gaze. He cocked an eyebrow at me and shook his head. *What do you want me to do now?* his expression seemed to say.

Before I could speak, Stephanie's husky voice came from somewhere behind me. "What's that all about, do you suppose? Grandpa's never come calling on Ms. Moneybags before."

"It's probably a family problem," Patsy said, her voice raw with a combination of jumpiness and exhaustion. "And I don't think it's any of our business. Right now Sharon's health is more important. We need a doctor—and I guess we'd better contact the sheriff."

Quickly Denny said, "I'm on my way. Now that the ferry's on this side, it'll be much faster." He went out the door, and before he closed it I could hear that the rain had slackened to a light patter.

Neal was still inspecting the mud stains on the blue carpet. "Oh God, I hope it's not ruined. The dinner's ruined. Everything *else* is going to be ruined. Oh God!"

Sam glanced that way, his mouth pulling down. For a moment I thought he was going to lash out at his brother. But instead he rubbed his mustache and took a deep breath. Then he went and put his arm around Neal's shoulders.

"It's not so bad, guy," he said. "Nothing's ruined."

"Everything is." Neal's voice was bleak.

"No way. We've been through lots worse than this."

"Have we?"

"Sure. Remember when Mom and Dad died? We got through that—together."

"But then I—"

"Sssh." Sam sounded curiously like a father comforting a small boy.

"But Sam . . . the dinner's wrecked."

"I doubt it. We still have all that food." Sam looked at Evans.

Evans—who had been hugging Patsy—let go of her and stood up briskly. "It's not wrecked, Neal. What you and I should do is start putting it together. We should be able to eat in half an hour."

Neal's round face looked faintly hopeful. Evans smiled encouragingly at him and motioned him toward the kitchen. Sam heaved a sigh and headed straight to the bar cart.

I relaxed some, lying back in my cocoon. Every muscle in my body pained, often with sudden, sharp spasms. My head and chin ached fiercely. I still felt somewhat out of touch with my surroundings, and things kept slipping in and out of focus. In spite of the fire on the hearth, the room was very cold. I sneezed.

Patsy leaned over me and peered at my face, the way she did at her kids when they exhibited symptoms. Unnecessarily she said, "Stay there."

I lay still, ignoring the now-vague presences of Sam and Stephanie, who were doing things at the bar cart. When Patsy returned some minutes later, she had four large white caplets in her hand. "Take these."

"What are they? I don't need sleeping pills. I'm exhausted already, and I have to be able to talk to the sheriff—"

"They're vitamin Cs. Thousand milligrams each. They'll hold you until Denny can come back with the doctor."

"I don't want a doctor. I want the sheriff."

"You'll get both. Take these."

"Since when did you get to be the boss in our family?"

"*Take* them."

I hate being told what to do. Just hate it. I have lost a couple of good jobs because I simply don't take orders well.

Grumpily I said, "I can't take them without something to wash them down."

"I'll get you some water."

"Brandy," I said, and settled back to wait for the sheriff.

* * *

The deputy's name was Benjamin Ma. He was Chinese, with thick black hair that flopped over his forehead and a round, youthful face. The closest I could judge his age was between twenty-five and forty; because of his air of assurance and general unflappability, I assumed he stood on the fortyish end of the scale.

When he came into the mansion, Ma was wearing a slicker and hat similar to Tin Choy Won's, except they were navy blue. He wiped his booted feet carefully on the drop cloth Patsy had dug out to placate Neal, and then handed his outer garments to Stephanie, as if she were a maid. She took them, wrinkled her nose at Ma's retreating back, and went off toward the kitchen muttering unintelligible—and probably derogatory—things.

As he crossed the living room to where I lay on the couch, I thought that Ma's heavy work boots, woolen shirt, and Levi's made him look out of place in these elegant surroundings. But then I realized Ma was better suited to the Delta than the mansion and its decor. His manner of dressing showed a keen awareness of the elements and their unpredictability; his firm tread and the confident way he handled his body showed he was fully capable of dealing with those dangers. All in all, his presence made the room seem silly and effete.

He waved away the off-white chair Patsy was offering, selected a dark-blue footstool instead, and drew it up next to my couch. "Okay, Ms. McCone," he said, "Mr. Kleinschmidt has briefed me on what you told him and the other people. And on the fact that you're a private detective from San Francisco. You got me called out of my house and dragged into this storm when I was off-duty. So this had better be good."

I dislike smart-mouth cops who get their backs up strictly because I'm a private investigator. The attitude—when I'm being fair and telling them what I know—indicates they're insecure and probably not very good at their jobs. But I sensed Ma's attitude had more to do with the fact he'd been called away from his own fireside than with my status as a private eye. So I said—groggily, because of exhaustion and three brandies—"I appreciate your coming here, Deputy Ma. And what I have to tell you *will* be good—if you bear with me. I'm tired, and hurting a good bit, and a little punchy. But if you let me tell it slowly, it'll make sense."

He nodded.

I told him. Ma nodded several times, asked occasional pertinent questions, but otherwise didn't interrupt.

When I had finished, I was aware of a shocked silence from the others in the room; now they were taking me seriously. Ma didn't speak either, looking thoughtful for a long moment. "You're right, Ms. McCone. It *is* good. And I thank you for being straight with me. I'll take a look around the ferry landing and the shack. Check Shorkey's pickup. There's a possibility his body was taken away in that, rather than set adrift, as you theorize. If so, we might be able to find it. But if it was set adrift in that boat, I'm afraid we don't stand much of a chance in this weather."

"But when you came in, I could hear that the rain had stopped."

"For now, yes. But the water's still turbulent, and that boat will have drifted a long way. The body may not turn up for a long time." Ma looked at Denny. "You said that Shorkey was living in that shack?"

"Yeah, but he's got a wife in Walnut Grove."

"We'll talk with her, then. And find out if there was anyone who had a grudge against him."

I said, "But I told you it was probably related to the difficulties they've been having here on the island—"

"Probably. You're only assuming that."

He was right. Max's killer had been a tall man, but that didn't mean he was the one who had been playing ghost on the island. I'd made the assumption because I liked it; it was tidier that way.

Patsy said, "Deputy Ma, what if Sharon *is* right, and the killer is someone with a grudge against us?"

"We'll explore that angle, too."

"But, I mean, how safe are we here?"

Ma paused, his face etched with lines of concern. I saw that my earlier estimation of the forties end of the scale was correct—maybe even generous.

"I can't offer you any protection," he said gently, "if that's what you're getting at. We're a small substation with a lot of territory to cover and, frankly, with the problems this storm is causing, we have our hands full."

Patsy made a small noise of dismay.

Ma smiled reassuringly. "I wouldn't worry, for tonight anyway. This house looks pretty secure, and you should be fine if you take simple precautions. By tomorrow we may know more about what happened, and even if we don't, the weather will most likely deter any further attempts at harassing you for a few days."

I said, "A few days?"

"I'm afraid this is only the first in a chain of storms."

A couple of the others groaned. Denny said, "Jee-sus Christ, we'll never get those boat slips built if it doesn't stop raining."

Stephanie said bitterly, "Who cares? The way things are going, we won't have any boats left to put in them."

I ignored the comment, mainly because I felt bad at having lost the skiff, and thanked Deputy Ma for coming.

He stood, looking around for his slicker, and Stephanie went off to fetch it. Denny put his windbreaker back on and said, "How can we get in touch with you, since the phone line's down?"

"Service should probably be restored by tomorrow morning. I hear it was a minor problem, and Pacific Bell's already gotten onto it. I'll be calling you anyway, to let you know what progress I'm making, and if there's further interruption in phone service, I'll come out again." Then Ma turned to me and smiled. "You'd better get some rest, Ms. McCone."

Denny accompanied the deputy to the ferry and then returned some fifteen minutes later with the doctor—a wispy, querulous man who complained to Patsy about being called out so late in such weather. Then he crabbed at me about allowing myself to have gotten into such a condition; took my temperature and poked me in the rear with an antibiotic shot; left some pills; pocketed Patsy's overly generous cash payment; and bitched at Denny as they went out the door about the choppiness of the ferry ride. I suspected Denny hoped the return ride would be even more choppy, to compensate for the abuse we three had taken.

Then Evans carried me upstairs to my room, ignoring my protests that I could walk. I was too doped up and tired to regret missing the dinner that was belatedly being served in the dining room. After Patsy had tucked me away, all three kids had to come in and kiss me and assure themselves that their Aunt Sharon wasn't dead after all. I could have sworn—but maybe it was only the effect of the shot—that

Andrew looked somewhat annoyed that I had stolen his place in the invalid's limelight. Then, finally and mercifully, they all left me alone.

I went to sleep quickly, and for a long time it was a soft sleep—dreamless, feather cushioned, floating. The kind that happens too few times, and usually doesn't last long enough. This one didn't, either. I began to dream.

The dreams were full of ugly forms and shapes: pear trees that reached for me with angry, deformed limbs; the twisted ruins of the old tramway; Max's sodden body. Waves lapped at my feet, then washed up to engulf me. Heavy clouds pursued me and pelted me with rain. I jerked awake, dozed off, woke again and again. I heard a voice—mine? someone else's?—muttering fitfully. At first I couldn't make out the words, and when I finally did, they echoed over and over in my mind:

The eye of the storm. You're right in the eye of the storm.

12

Sunday morning felt cold and damp. I huddled beneath the quilts for a long time, shifting this way and that on the soft mattress, testing the aches and pains in my muscles and joints. No matter what I did, I hurt. I kept swallowing, hoping the scratchiness at the back of my throat would go away. It didn't—but it didn't get any worse, either. Finally I got out of bed and wrapped myself in the heavy woolen bathrobe that someone had laid out for me on the window seat. Then I drew the curtains and looked out.

A thick tule fog enveloped the island. To us native Californians, the term "tule fog" is as natural as "pea-souper" is to Londoners; but to strangers who encounter it for the first time, both the name and the phenomenon seem foreign. "Tule" is, of course, for the reeds that grow in the marshes and lowlands where such fogs originate. The fog itself is dense, motionless, and very, very white. If you are driving through one, your headlights meet a wall—pristine and soft-looking as tissue paper, but completely impenetrable.

Tule fogs can be scary, especially when you're driving and visibility is confined to roughly a foot beyond your front bumper. On the other hand, they can be cozy and comforting if you're at home curled up with a good book in front of the fire. It all depends on your mood and circumstances. To me, this one was just plain depressing.

Since I'd awoken I'd tried to concentrate strictly on my physical problems. Now the events of the day before seeped into my consciousness, and I knew I'd soon have to deal with them. I was saved from immediate contemplation by a knock at the door, but— since I also didn't want to deal with people right then—I rushed into the bathroom, turned the shower on full force, and yelled, "Who is it?"

The door opened and Patsy's voice called, "It's me. I've brought coffee, and I want to take your breakfast order."

Breakfast. My stomach lurched. "I don't think I can eat."

"What are you doing out of bed, anyway?"

I dropped the robe and nightgown on the floor and stepped into the shower, making a lot of splashing noises and wincing when the spray hit the cut on my chin.

"Sharon?"

"I've got to wash the mud and crap out of my hair."

"When do you want breakfast?"

Jesus, she was turning out like Evans, always thinking about food!

"Sharon!"

"Never."

"You have to eat."

Now she sounded like our mother. "I want to sleep some more. I'll have lunch."

"It's already twelve-thirty."

"So I'll have dinner!"

There was a silence. Even over the sound of the shower I could tell it was a *hurt* silence. Then: "I'll be back around three. Enjoy the coffee." The door to the room shut—none too gently.

I picked up the shampoo bottle, poured some into my hands, and lathered. My fingers snarled in the knots in my hair. I pulled at them viciously, gritting my teeth. Then just as I was about to rip myself bald, I stopped, smiling wryly. Families. Goddamn families. Sometimes I wish we could just have been hatched from eggs.

Max Shorkey was dead, probably lying at the bottom of the slough. A killer was at large, possibly right here on the island. I had barely escaped dying, and wasn't too sure I wouldn't develop pneumonia. Andrew's arm was broken. Stephanie's precious boats were lost. Neal was heartbroken over his failing business venture. God knew what private hells the remainder of the group were suffering. But my little sister could still get pissed off because I'd refused breakfast and hadn't gotten out of the shower to talk to her.

Families.

I rinsed my hair, applied a whole lot of conditioner, and managed to untangle most of the knots. Then I spent a good hour in bed, sipping Evans's rich, dark coffee (Patsy had generously provided a small pot of it) and thinking over the events of the day before and planning a strategy for proceeding with my investigation. From the looks of the fog, I wouldn't be able to get off the island, but then, I didn't see any need to. I was convinced there was more I could learn from the people here in the mansion, and they were as confined by the elements as I was.

Unlike the morning before, the mansion hummed with life. I heard children's running footsteps and emphatic—often quarrelsome—pronunciations. Voices came from the living room below me; the adults' were muted but recognizable by their pitch and speed of delivery. A television set mumbled and was eventually replaced by the more harmonious strains of classical music. Water ran, pipes banged, and doors slammed.

All the sounds were normal and comforting—what you would expect on a Sunday. I had to remind myself that this was no ordinary Sunday, that a man had been killed, that I myself had almost died. I thought of how defenseless we all were should the killer return, and then I thought of my gun, locked in the glove compartment of my MG. Perhaps I should get it; it would be better if I were armed. . . .

But that wouldn't work. Normally when I carried the .38, I kept it in the side pocket of my shoulder bag, but I couldn't drag my purse everywhere I went in the mansion. And to go about with a gun tucked into the waistband of my jeans would set the adults on edge and panic the children. I couldn't leave it unattended in my room, either; one of the kids might find it. No, better to leave it where it was. The situation wasn't all that critical—at least not in broad daylight.

When I'd drained the coffee pot, I decided it was time I joined the mainstream of life on Appleby Island.

When I went downstairs, I followed the strains of classical music into the living room. The first person I saw was Sam, slumped in a chair, legs thrust out in front of him, arms folded. His eyes were closed, and he was either asleep or immersed in the recording. Denny lay stretched on one of the couches, his huge chest rising and falling in a regular rhythm; the comics section of the San Francisco Sunday paper was draped over his face, and the rest of it lay rumpled on the rug beside him. I went over and picked up the front section, glanced at the headlines, and when I didn't find anything particularly interesting, dropped it back on the floor. The paper felt damp; someone had probably driven into Walnut Grove for it, and it had soaked up a good measure of fog on the way back.

Neither man so much as twitched to acknowledge my presence, but when I looked up I saw that the library door stood open for the first time since I'd been there. I went over and looked in at a room full of old-fashioned leather furniture and a massive mahogany desk. Built-in bookshelves lined the walls, and on them were hundreds of handsomely bound volumes. Below the shelves were drawers and cupboards decorated with the same kind of elaborate carving as the door. In the gray light that entered through shabby sheer curtains on a pair of French doors, I saw that the wallpaper was faded, the leather of the sofa and chairs cracked and worn. The desk was layered with dust.

I stepped inside and looked around more closely, sniffing the room's musty air and feeling its dampness. It didn't seem as if it had been open for long—

"Sharon!" a voice exclaimed.

I looked toward the sofa that faced away from me in front of the fireplace. A head had risen over the back of it.

"Hi, Neal," I said.

He was frowning and staring fuzzily at me. His expression, coupled with the sleeping beauties in the living room, made me think of one of those English men's clubs you see in films, where all the members are sacked out after lunch in their leather chairs, snoring, brandies by their elbows. After a moment Neal said, "Are you supposed to be up?"

"Why not?"

"You're sick." Then he seemed to consider the various connotations of the word and added, "I mean, you've been through, um, an ordeal and you probably should rest—"

"Neal, don't mother me."

"Oh." Abruptly he sank down and disappeared from my view. I went around the couch and looked at him. He wore a wrinkled Black Watch–plaid bathrobe over equally wrinkled cords, and a pair of slipper socks. A red turtleneck peeked over the vee of the robe.

I sat down at the opposite end of the couch, avoiding a place where the leather was split in a big gash. Neal looked a little pouty, so I said, "I appreciate your concern, but I'm getting all the mothering I can take from my sister."

"Well, I just don't want you getting a chill and catching pneumonia—"

"I'm fine. Really." To emphasize it, I held out my arms, which were encased in my fisherman's sweater, then pointed at my fleece-lined moccasins.

Neal nodded, then leaned his head against the back of the sofa and stared into the empty fireplace.

I said, "Why don't you build a fire?"

"It's too much trouble. Besides, this fireplace and the one in back of it in the living room draw off the same chimney; it hasn't been swept, and two fires at once might be dangerous."

"You really ought to have it swept."

"I know, but Angela says we can't afford to."

I was beginning to wonder at the types of expenditures being made for this project. They had money for a computer and redecorating the public areas; Evans had all his elaborate kitchen equipment on order; a fleet of canoes that wouldn't have been necessary until the boating season had already been lost; Patsy had ordered still more decorating supplies on Friday. But the chimney hadn't been swept, and those pipes in the basement leaked; and as I remembered from Denny's tour, the wiring wasn't in such great shape either.

How much control did Neal have over Angela, who wrote the checks that went to pay for such extravagances instead of necessities? Or over the people who ordered them—Denny, Evans, Stephanie . . . even my sister? I would have liked to ask him, but I sensed it was a subject that might either send him into one of his dithers or make him unapproachable. The best thing would be to feel out the situation by asking questions of the others. Then, if something really seemed amiss, I would talk with Neal directly.

At the moment, though, I was also curious about the library. I said, "Neal, why wasn't this room restored along with the others? It's wonderful."

He brightened. "Isn't it? I think it's what really sold me on the place. The books . . . there are collectors and dealers who would give their eyeteeth to get in here. And they tried, too. But it was written into the owner's will that the books were to be sold along with the house. My luck.''

"The owner—that was Stuart Appleby? The one who killed himself?''

Neal tensed and looked away. "Yes," he said, "he shot himself in this room. The realtor told me he didn't have long to live anyway—cancer. There's a bloodstain where it soaked into the floorboards under that rug in front of the fireplace. And there was a bullet hole in the wall where he missed with the first shot. I had Denny patch it, and it's hardly noticeable. I don't care what went on here, though; the room is wonderful in spite of it.'' But he sounded troubled, and his eyes seemed drawn to the orange shag rug that didn't fit with the room and was probably somebody's castoff.

I didn't believe that he didn't care. While Neal might genuinely love the library, I sensed that part of its attraction for him was a morbid preoccupation with Stuart Appleby's suicide. Perhaps that was the reason he kept it off-limits to the others, so he could lock himself in here and brood. And given the precarious emotional state he seemed to be in, that could be dangerous. It made me decidedly uneasy, but I didn't know what I could do about it.

I said, "What kind of books are they?''

"All kinds. Mainly literature, the classics. There's a good deal of Western Americana, maritime history, and a lot of stuff on horticulture. The drawers and cupboards are full of old games and toys and stuff.''

The classics didn't interest me much, but the contents of the drawers and cupboards sounded fascinating. "Would you mind if I snooped through them some time?''

He jerked his head toward me, and I was immediately taken aback. The expression there was alarmed—no, threatened. He said, "Why? You don't think anything in this room has to do with what happened to Max and . . . everything else, do you?''

"No, I just like the room, and old things interest me. There's another on the third floor—Denny calls it the junk room—that I'd like to explore, too.''

For a moment he studied my face, as if trying to gauge my truthfulness. Then he blinked and said, "Of course. You're free to look at anything, as far as I'm concerned." He stood, drawing his robe more tightly around him, and started abruptly for the door.

Halfway there, however, he turned. His face had become pinched and mottled, features turning down in an inverted *V*. "Did Denny tell you you couldn't look in the junk room?"

"No."

"Has anybody tried to dictate what you can and can't do?"

"Of course not."

"What about Evans?"

"I've hardly had any dealings with him at all. Why?"

"I'll tell you why: This is *my* house. I—and only I—have the right to say who does what. I've put up with Evans's superior airs plenty of times, but no more. If he wants to continue his game, he'd better toe the line."

"What game?"

Neal paused distractedly; my question had broken his train of thought—or more accurately, his ranting. "The cooking game, what else?" he said after a few seconds. "Now you listen to this: If anybody gives you any shit about what you're looking at or where you go, just send them to me. I'll set them straight."

I didn't know what to say, so I merely nodded. After he left, I leaned back against the sofa's armrest, letting out my breath in a big sigh. Was Neal being paranoid, or did he have justification for feeling his authority was being undermined? And even with some justification, wasn't he overreacting? Denny was capable and seemed to run the physical plant, but he didn't go around giving orders. And Evans was so involved with the food that he barely noticed what was going on outside the kitchen. Besides, Evans had been Neal's good friend for years; they'd planned the boatel together. Why was Neal now saying Evans had better "toe the line" or else?

Or else *what?*

I wasn't certain. There was one thing I'd just learned, though, because I'd seen it in Neal's eyes as he'd spoken: Beneath that self-effacing, hand-wringing exterior, he had a very nasty streak.

The record that had been playing on the living room stereo had ended when I went back in there, and a series of grunts, snores, and wheezes from Denny replaced the music. As I moved past Sam's chair, he opened his eyes and said, "Huh?"

"Just me."

"Should you be out of bed?"

It was a question I was sure I would hear a lot—and rapidly get sick of. "Yes," I said shortly.

"Good." He closed his eyes again.

I wanted to talk to him about a number of things, but now was clearly not a good time. "You want the record turned over?"

"Please. It'll drown out the unharmonious symphony." He waved his hand toward Denny.

"Where's Angela?"

"Her office."

"Is her grandfather still here?"

"Yes. They aren't getting along, and when I went down there right after lunch, I heard distinct throwing-things sounds."

"She's throwing things at *Mr. Won?*"

"No, at her office wall. He's in bed with a temperature. But things must be pretty grim down there; Stephanie went to see if there was anything she could do to help a little while ago, and when she came up she was white-faced and headed straight for the door. All she could say was 'Fuck this scene. I need to take a walk.'"

I smiled, liking Stephanie's bluntness, then changed the record and went downstairs to the office. The door was closed, and I didn't hear any noises indicating breakage. I knocked, and Angela called out for me to come in. As usual, she looked composed and busily efficient, but there was a line between her eyebrows that I hadn't noticed before. Probably etched there by her acid temper, I thought uncharitably.

She had been writing something on a legal pad, and when she saw who was at the door, she pressed so hard that the pencil tip broke. She looked at it in disgust and tossed it on the desk. "What are you doing here?" she demanded.

"What I've been hired for—investigating."

"Hired? There's no money in the budget for the likes of you."

The likes of you. A quaint term. I hate it. The last time I heard it applied to me was when I was in high school and my boyfriend's mother told me she didn't think "the likes of you" was good enough for her son. He eventually knuckled under to her social aspirations and married a debutante who later became an alcoholic and set fire to the house three times. I suppose I should be able to take some consolation from that outcome, but the memory still rankles.

I dismissed it and stayed cool. "The reason I'm here, Angela, is to ask if you've had a chance to check on that other offer to buy the island."

"Offer . . . ? Oh, that. I called the realtor yesterday. There definitely was an offer, but it was a blind one, through an attorney in Antioch. I tried to call him, but he wasn't available, and won't be until Monday."

"Could the realtor tell you anything else about it?"

"Just that it was low. The Appleby estate turned it down the first time, and then the person raised it a couple of thousand, but it still wasn't nearly enough."

I thought of the rare books in the library and Neal's comment about collectors and dealers being eager to get their hands on them. That might be what the offer had been about, but I had no way of checking on it until tomorrow.

Angela, however, was not done with the question of my hiring. She said, "Just how *are* you being paid for this . . . snooping you're doing? As I said, there's no money in the budget—"

"My sister is paying me." She wasn't, really, since I wouldn't take her money, but that wasn't any of Angela's business.

"But those funds are committed—"

I waited for her to continue, my protective instincts surging, but she'd obviously realized her mistake. I said, "What is Patsy's money committed for?"

Silence.

"Does she know about this?"

"She . . . it's nothing definite. We'll only touch her money if the project gets in serious trouble."

"It's in trouble now."

Angela glared at me.

"Look around you: You've got a computer, some velvet sofas, a sixteen-burner stove on order, Chinese carpets, and a bunch of busted-up canoes. And in the meantime, you've also got puddles on the floor from leaking pipes, chimneys that haven't been swept, and there isn't a circuit breaker in the house. You say you plan to open for the boating season—but where's the marina?"

"The weather—"

"Have you seen any construction plans for it?"

"No, but—"

"What about work crews? Who's going to build it?"

"They quit. You know that."

"Why haven't more people been hired?"

Angela picked up the pencil and grasped it at either end, her fingertips—their nails an odd and unpleasant purple—white against it.

"And another thing—that computer," I added. "You told me Neal wanted it because he was a 'technology freak.' I've never met anyone less likely to be. If anything, he's a throwback to another century."

The pencil snapped and she looked down at it, then hurled the pieces across the room. "Shit! Do you realize how hard it is to coordinate a project like this? Especially when you're dealing with financial idiots? I *needed* that computer to make the job manageable!"

"Why put it off on Neal, then?"

"Because—just like you—nobody around here understands how badly I needed it. I've tried to make it seem Neal told me to buy it, so I could get them off my back. They're all resentful because there isn't enough money for the things *they* think are important."

"Like upgrading the wiring and plumbing, or fixing the roof?"

"*All right!*" She stood up, arms crossed, grasping her elbows protectively. "I've had enough of your abuse. You don't have any conception of what I'm up against, so why don't you—"

There was a tinkling sound, like that of a brass dinner bell, coming faint but clear from the hall. Angela bowed her head and said, "Oh, shit!"

"What's that?"

"My honorable grandfather." She spoke the words in a bitter parody that sounded straight out of a Charlie Chan movie.

"Neal said he was sick in bed."

"Yes. The damned fool came out in the storm in his old truck. Had a flat tire on the way and changed it himself in the rain. He even refused to see the doctor when he came to check you out—Grandfather has a horror of doctors—and now he's sick. I've got him tucked away in the room between mine and the ones where Patsy and Evans live, and all day I've been running in and out giving him aspirin and soup—"

"Why'd he come out here?"

"He came out because he was being Chinese."

"What?"

"He was being Chinese. Being overprotective. He has to act as representative of the great Won family and save his granddaughter."

"From what?"

She was so caught up in her anger that for a few seconds she stared blankly at me.

"From what?" I repeated. "The storm?"

"Of course the storm! What else?" She flung out a hand, and I sensed she was close to losing control, perhaps even throwing something as she'd done earlier. I also sensed she wasn't telling me the whole truth.

The bell tinkled again, more insistently. Angela slammed her fist down on the desk, so hard it must have really hurt. "God*damn* it, why does this have to happen to me now!"

I said, "Do you want some pills for him?"

"What?"

"I have some pills the doctor left for me. I don't need them."

She started rubbing her hand where she'd hit it. "You don't?"

"No. I'm feeling better." It was true; the scratchiness in my throat was gone.

Of course Angela couldn't accept a favor without getting in a dig at me. "Pretty tough, aren't you?"

I was tired of sparring with her. I stood up and said, "I'll get the pills. Maybe they'll keep your grandfather from acting so . . . Chinese."

13

I delivered the pills to Angela and then went down the hall to Patsy's living quarters. Andrew was the only one there, but that was all right with me; he was the person I wanted to talk to. He was ensconced in his bed again. A big sketch pad lay across his lap, and he was drawing weird, pterodactyllike creatures in lurid shades of felt-tip pen. They reminded me of the illustrations on the covers of the comic books he seemed to favor, and for an eleven-year-old, the drawing technique wasn't half bad.

I said, "It's a good thing you didn't break your right arm, isn't it?"

He looked up in surpise. "Mom said you were going to stay in bed all day."

I sat down on the bed. "Goes to show mothers don't know everything."

"They sure don't!"

"How come you're in bed?"

He shrugged.

"Well, it's not such a bad place to be. There are times when I spend whole days in bed, even when I'm not sick."

"Oh yeah? Doing what?"

"Reading. Watching TV. Sleeping." It was a slightly edited child's version of those pleasant, lazy days.

"Huh." Andrew seemed to consider it intriguing.

"I never thought of drawing in bed, though," I added. "Of course I'm not very good at it. Neither is your mother. Where do you suppose you got your talent?"

"From my father."

Andrew had never known his father, who'd left Patsy when she was six months pregnant. "Who told you that?"

"Nobody. I just know." He outlined one creature's wings in fuschia, then began filling them in with pea green.

"What has Patsy told you about him?"

"Just that he was a nice man and she loved him. But she loved Tom and Jeremy, too. Then they went away, and now she loves Evans. And she wants us to act like he's our father."

I was beginning to sense the root of Andrew's recent hostility. "How do you feel about that?"

"Like shit." He glanced up to see if he'd shocked me, then looked faintly disappointed.

"Don't you like Evans?"

"He's okay."

"But he's not your father."

"No. I'm too old to get another father."

"Maybe he could be your friend."

"Nah, *he's* too old for that. Besides, he's the reason we're living in this fucking place." Again he cast a sly glance at me from under half-lowered eyelids.

I kept my expression neutral. "You don't like it here on the island?"

"Hate it."

"Why?"

"It's cold and damp all the time, and there aren't any stores to go to or things to do, and I don't have any friends. And those other people are fuckin' *weird*, man."

"You mean Neal and—"

Andrew made a gagging sound.

"Don't you go to school?"

"Sure, got to take the goddamn bus and come right home on it in the afternoon. How am I supposed to make friends when I have to come straight home?"

"I don't know. It must be rough."

He eyed me for a moment, his face serious. "You're supposed to tell me I'm lucky to be here and all that crap."

"Why should I? I'm not sure that's true."

"Now I suppose you're gonna give me some advice." He pronounced the last word as if it were an epithet.

"No, I'm not. I don't have any. About all I can tell you is to hang in there."

He seemed to like that. "Look," he said after a few seconds, "you asked me a question yesterday, and I was pissed at everybody, so I wouldn't answer you. But if you want, you can ask me again."

"You mean about what happened right before you broke your arm?"

"Yeah."

"What happened right before you broke your arm?"

That actually got a smile out of him. "It was like this. I was asleep, and there was this tapping at the window. Woke me up. I went over there, and all I could see was this hand, waving like it wanted me to come outside. So I put on some pants and my parka and went. And this person was moving away through the yard where the clotheslines are. I followed it, and it went through the hedge to the garden and then up onto the terrace. It was going away toward the side of the house when I slipped on the steps."

"You say 'this person.' Was it a man or a woman?"

"A man, I guess. Big."

"Big how—tall or heavy?"

"Well . . . tall."

"What about his hair?"

"Long for a man's. At least, it stuck out from under his hat."

"What kind of hat?"

"Like a rain hat, pulled low on his face."

"What else was he wearing?"

"Raggedy clothes. Sort of like . . . well, one year I dressed up as a tramp for Halloween. That kind of stuff."

"What color were the clothes?"

"Black pants. And I think a raincoat. Lighter—tan, maybe."

It didn't sound like the clothing I'd found stuffed in the tree in the orchard, although I remembered the man at the ferry landing last night had been wearing that type of hat. Maybe Crazy Alf's ghost had an entire wardrobe stashed away someplace.

Andrew was watching my face again. He'd dropped his tough-guy act, and his expression was anxious. "It was that hermit, wasn't it?"

"The hermit's dead."

"His ghost, I mean."

"There aren't such things."

"How do you know?"

"You'll have to trust me on that one, Andrew. I just know."

"Then it's a real person."

"Yes."

"And he came after me."

He had, and I didn't like that one bit. A man who tried to intimidate adults, even a man who might have killed an adult, was one thing. But someone who preyed on children . . .

I didn't want my own anxiety to communicate itself to Andrew, but before I could cover it, he said, "You're scared."

"A little."

"So am I."

"It's okay to be scared. In fact, it's smart. If you are, you'll stay alert and nothing like what happened yesterday morning will happen again. If you see this person again, you should call one of us adults right away."

"Okay."

"And in the meantime," I added, "I'll try to catch him."

That seemed to reassure him, because he resumed drawing. I must have sounded a lot more confident than I felt. Andrew's description of the man—like the one given me secondhand by Tin Choy Won—wasn't really much to go on. It lacked the kind of substance I needed. Then as I watched Andrew's hand trace the shape of an odd, grotesque tree, I had an idea.

"Listen," I said, "do you think you could draw the man you saw?"

He looked faintly surprised, but said, "Sure."

"Do a bunch of drawings of him, everything you can remember."

"You mean like those people the cops use to make drawings when somebody describes a suspect?"

"Exactly."

"All *right!*" He ripped the pterodactyl page from the pad and dropped it on the floor. "I'll get started."

I stood up. "Thanks. I'll come back for them in a little while."

Before I could get to the door, though, he said, "Aunt Sharon?"
"Yes?"

"I don't hate Evans or Mom, you know. I'm just . . . well, I kind of miss how things used to be when we lived on the farm."

"I know. And Andrew, why don't you drop the 'aunt'? You're old enough to just call me Sharon."

He smiled with shy pleasure and bent his head over the sketch pad.

On the way upstairs, I experienced a faint but gnawing hunger pang, so I headed for the kitchen. Just like the first time I'd gone there, I found Stephanie seated at the table, smoking and drinking coffee. The want ads of the Sunday paper were spread out in front of her.

"Well, well," she said, "the prodigal arises from her bed of pain."

I wasn't sure what to make of the comment, so I merely nodded and went to look in the refrigerator. Some meat was marinating in a big pan, there were plenty of fresh vegetables, and several expensive-looking bottles of wine were chilling on the lower shelf, but I couldn't find anything to have for a snack. As I shut the door, I reflected on another area where expenditures here on the island seemed out of whack: food.

Stephanie was watching me, smiling wryly. "Pretty dismal, huh?"
"Yes. I'm starved, and there's nothing to nosh on."
"Try the pantry. There're crackers, I think."

I went through the door she indicated to an old-fashioned butler's pantry. On the shelf right in front of me was a box of Triscuits. I grabbed a handful, stuffed two in my mouth, then shrugged and appropriated the entire box. When I went back into the kitchen, Stephanie had folded up the paper and was pouring me a cup of coffee. I guessed that meant she wasn't too mad at me for losing the skiff.

All the same, I said, "I want to apologize—"
"It's not your fault."
"About the boat, I mean."

"Not your fault. Max shouldn't have let you take it out with a storm brewing. But neither of you could have known he was going to get killed and you were almost going to get drowned. So forget it."

Her voice was gruffer than usual, as if it had cost her a lot to admit no one was to blame. I suspected Stephanie loved boats the way cat owners love their pets—and that she was mourning their loss in much the same way I would mourn the loss of Watney.

I sat down, munching on Triscuits. "I heard you had a run-in with Angela earlier."

"Angela . . . oh yeah."

"What did she do?"

Stephanie shrugged. "She was just being a bitch, as usual."

"But you were trying to help."

"So? Ms. Moneybags doesn't give a damn—about her grand-father, or my feelings. Or any of us. I'd rather not talk about it, if you don't mind."

"Sure. Actually, I've got a couple of questions. How many people have access to the boathouse?"

"All of us. Max did, too."

"Is it usually locked?"

"Yes."

"And everyone has a key?"

"Well, no. Denny and I do. Max did. But there are extra keys to everything on a hook in the pantry. Anybody could have taken one."

"I see. What can you tell me about Max?"

"He's from Walnut Grove, lived there all his life. Married—has a couple of grown kids, I think."

"Who hired him?"

"Wasn't really a question of hiring. Max had always run and maintained the ferry for Stuart Appleby. Of course during the last years when Stuart was living here all alone, he didn't need Max full-time. But he kept him on half-salary and called him when he wanted to go to shore. When Neal bought the place, he decided it was better to keep Max on because he knew how to repair the barge. And since old Stuart had left him a little money in his will, Max was willing to work cheap. Then his wife threw him out and he was glad to have the shack to stay in."

That was the thing that had bothered me the night before—Max living in the shack when there was room for him in the mansion. "How come he stayed there? It's awfully primitive."

Stephanie shrugged and reached for a cigarette. Her slender fingers—attractively shaped but scarred in places, probably as a consequence of a lifetime of working with boats—fumbled with her Bic lighter. She waited until she had the cigarette going before she spoke. "He wanted to be there. He didn't like the mansion, and when we offered him a room, he said he wouldn't stay here."

"Why not?"

"Superstitious, I guess. He had a thing about Stuart Appleby's suicide. Besides, he kept saying that any day his wife was going to let him come home."

"How long had he been in the shack?"

"A couple of months. He moved there right about the time I came to the island."

"Mrs. Shorkey must be a grudge-holder."

"Wouldn't surprise me."

I sipped coffee, thinking about Benjamin Ma's comment that Max's murder might be unrelated to the things I'd come here to investigate. What if his wife *was* a grudger? Had nursed that grudge and come to the ferry landing . . . ? No, I was sure I'd seen a man. Well, what if she had a boyfriend, then? I said, "Stephanie, why did Max's wife throw him out?"

"Don't know."

"Who would?"

"Maybe Denny. They used to play cards and drink together a couple of times a week."

I set down my coffee cup. At least I knew where to find Denny— under the comics section on the living room couch.

When I went into the living room Sam's chair was vacant, and the only sounds were Denny's snores and wheezes. For a moment I contemplated letting him sleep, but then I decided my questions were more important than his beauty rest. Besides, he'd been out cold for well over an hour. I put my hand on his arm, which dangled loosely toward the floor, and shook it gently.

"Huh? Unh? Marianne?" he said.

"It's Sharon."

He raised his head and the comics slipped off his face. His eyes were unfocused and his face was screwed up like a squally baby's. "Oh Jesus," he said, "I thought you were my ex-wife."

"No, it's just me." When Denny swung his feet to the floor, I sat down beside him.

"I should of known better," he said, rubbing his eyes like a little boy. "If it was Marianne, she'd've kicked me awake."

"Violent, huh?"

"Sort of. What time is it?"

"Quarter after three."

"Jesus, I was really sacked out."

"You awake enough to answer some questions?"

"Sure. How come you're—"

"Because I feel perfectly okay. Right now I'm trying to get some background on Max Shorkey. I understand he was separated from his wife. Do you know why?"

"The usual. She'd caught him with some other woman and threw him out. Right after that she took up with one of his friends."

"Max seemed to think she was going to let him come home soon, though."

"He liked to think that. It was the only way he could stand living in that shack."

"But you don't believe it?"

"No. At first Max would talk about the guy and what a wimp and a loser he was. But later he admitted that he owns a restaurant over on the Porkpie Tract and has lots of dough. And he's also what you ladies call a hunk."

"Do you know his name?"

"No, but the restaurant is called the Water Witch."

I made a mental note to report that to Benjamin Ma when I next spoke with him. While it might be a lead in Max's murder, I wasn't too happy to hear it; I like neat packages with all the ends tied up, and if Max's killer was one of the members of a love triangle, it weakened the theory I was trying to build.

I said, "Stephanie tells me you used to play cards and drink with Max."

"Yeah, he was an interesting guy. For somebody from a small town who didn't have much education, he knew a lot."

"Like what?"

"Boats. Natural history. He'd traveled a fair amount when he was in the service. We got on—better than I get on with Neal or Evans."

"You don't care for them?"

"Oh, Evans is okay, but his thing with your sister is new, and they're all wrapped up in each other. Besides, he's always talking food, and I'm always talking diet." He gestured ruefully at his paunch. "You can see I'm more talk than action."

I smiled. "And Neal?"

"Neal's a jerk. He tries to buy your friendship. He's been trying to buy mine for five years, ever since he bought a three-unit building in San Francisco and hired me to renovate it. Trouble is, he doesn't really know what friendship's about. To me, for instance, it's a contract—you meet the other person fifty-fifty. Not all the time, of course. Some years, you'll put in eighty percent, the other person twenty. And vice versa. But over the life of the friendship, it kind of averages out."

I liked the concept, sensed in fact that it had been operating— unnamed and unanalyzed—in my own life. I said, "Neal doesn't uphold that contract?"

"Hell, no. Doesn't even know it exists. He either uses you or lavishes money and stuff on you. Like the food and wine here—he pays for all that, and he carries most of our other expenses as well. But the money and stuff are really just his way of getting a hold on you, so he can use you even more."

"But knowing all that, you still came up here to work for him."

"Sure. I needed a job, and I go where the work is. And Neal's only buying my time and my talent, anyway. Nobody can buy another person, and the sad thing is, he'll never realize that."

What he said fit with the other things I'd heard about Neal—and with the evidence of his nasty streak I'd witnessed earlier. But there didn't seem much point in discussing him any more now. I said, "Is there anything else you can tell me about Max?"

"You mean something that would give you an idea why he got killed?"

"Yes."

Denny thought, but after a minute he said, "No. Max was a good guy. I'm sorry he's dead: But I didn't know him, not really. What we talked about—except for the thing with his wife—was pretty general."

I thanked him and asked him when dinner was. Cocktails, he told me, were always served in the living room at seven. If that was the case, I thought, I'd better fortify myself with more Triscuits. But as I was crossing the reception area, I ran into Sam—the next person I'd intended to talk with.

14

am was dressed to go out, in a sweater, down vest, and heavy boots. He saw me and said, "Oh, I'm glad I ran into you. I got out that letter for you to look at."

"You mean the anonymous one?"

He nodded and took a folded piece of paper from his vest pocket. It was of a cheap quality, and I could see the rough edge on it where it had been torn off a pad. I unfolded it and read the typed message.

> You would be wise to look into the finances at your brother Neal's house on Appleby Island. The investment is not good and will fail if you do not do something soon.
>
> A Concerned Friend

The first thing that struck me was that the sender was not used to writing business letters; the sentence structure and phraseology were stiff, as if he or she were not very well educated. The typing, while neat, was uneven, and there were a number of careful erasures. I guessed the machine was some sort of manual, probably a portable, and that its keys had not been cleaned nor its ribbon changed in some time.

I said, "When did you receive this?"

"Two weeks ago last Thursday."

"And where was it postmarked?"

"I don't know. It came to my office while I was out of town, and the secretary opened it and threw the envelope away."

"Isn't it standard procedure to save envelopes when there's no inside address?"

"Yes, but she was a temporary, filling in for my regular secretary, who was out sick. She didn't have very good office skills, and by the time I noticed the envelope was missing, the trash had been incinerated."

I turned the letter over. There was nothing on the back, and no markings on the paper to show its manufacture. Naturally it had been through too many hands for the sender's fingerprints to have remained unobliterated. I doubted a police lab could have found anything more useful than I could at a cursory glance.

Still, I asked, "Can I keep this?"

"Sure." Sam started for the door.

"Where are you going?"

"Just out for a walk. In spite of the size of this place, I feel claustrophobic."

"Where're Evans and Patsy and the girls?"

"They went into Rio Vista to do some shopping. I think your sister thought of it as a way to keep the kids from killing each other."

I'd planned to talk with Patsy and Evans next, and now I was at loose ends. "Would you mind if I went for a walk with you?"

Sam hesitated. "I guess if you bundle up you'll be all right."

"Great. I'll be right back." I went upstairs to my room and traded my moccasins for lined boots, then pulled my blue wool jacket on over the bulky sweater. When I zipped it and pulled the hood up, I looked like a little kid in a snowsuit.

I found Sam waiting for me on the front lawn, and we set off through the fog toward the levee above the boathouse.

He said, "Did looking at the letter help you any?"

"Not much. It's so simple sounding that I can't imagine the writer knowing enough to recognize a risky financial situation. In fact, I'm surprised you took it seriously."

"I didn't, really. But where Neal's concerned, I feel obliged to check everything out."

I remembered the scene in the reception area the night before when Neal had almost broken down and Sam had comforted him. "You're very protective of him."

"Yes." Sam motioned at the levee, cocking one eyebrow in inquiry. "You feel up to climbing?"

"Sure. Actually I don't feel bad at all."

"Well, just don't overdo it."

"I won't."

When we reached the top, though, I was breathing fairly hard. Sam was tactful enough not to mention it, or maybe he was too impressed by the fog to notice. He thrust his hands into the pockets of his vest and said, "It's like standing on a peak between two valleys of snow."

It was an apt description. On either side of the levee, the fog lay white and heavy, obscuring the ground and the waters of the slough. The flat roofline of the boathouse and some of the taller trees poked through it, their outlines blurred and ghostly.

"Does it get like this often up here?" he asked.

"This time of year, I suppose it does."

"I'm used to the kind of fog you have in San Francisco, where it moves and swirls. That's eerie, but this is even stranger."

"Strange, but beautiful."

"An acquired taste, I guess."

I began walking along the levee, realizing I had automatically turned away from the ferry landing. Max had been killed on the other side, but I didn't want to go even that close to the scene of his death. Sam followed behind me, his boots scrunching on the hard-packed earth. After a while I said, "Are you much older than Neal, Sam?"

"Two years younger, actually. Why?"

"I just wondered. In most ways you seem younger—the way you look and dress. But in the way you relate to him, I'd have guessed you were the big brother."

"That's because it's a role I've always assumed."

"Why?"

"Neal's always needed protecting, and it's fallen to me. He wasn't very strong as a kid, and the others in school would try to beat up on him. So I'd step in and show them they couldn't do that to my brother." He laughed wryly. "In grade school, they called me 'Mighty Mouse' because I was always taking on the big guys."

"Did you win?"

"Sometimes. But more often not. When I think back on it, I realize they probably picked on him all the more, just to get to see 'the mouse' go into action."

"I wish I'd had somebody bigger to defend me."

"Was it just you and Patsy in your family?"

"Lord, no! There are five of us; I have two older brothers and another younger sister."

"Well, why didn't your brothers fight your battles?"

"Those guys? Are you kidding? They loved tormenting me. You know what they did once? They rolled me up in a rug. There was this rug that had just come back from the cleaners, and they grabbed me and stuffed me in there. I was screaming my lungs out, and my father came in, furious—it had cost a lot to clean, and for all he knew I was getting bubble gum on it. And do you know what my brothers told him?"

"I can't imagine."

"They said—with perfectly straight faces, so he believed them— 'Sharon rolled herself up in there, and now she's trying to blame us.'"

"What did he do?"

"Unrolled the rug and started giving me hell. I ran outside and hid in our tree house. After a while my brothers felt so sorry for me they admitted what they'd done."

Sam chuckled. "Still, it sounds like you had a good childhood."

"Better than I deserved, probably. Trouble was, I never realized it at the time." I paused. "I guess Neal didn't have a very happy childhood."

"No."

"Or adulthood."

"Not that either." Sam's voice was weary now.

I turned and began walking backwards, looking at him. He kept his head bowed, avoiding my eyes. "What's wrong?" I asked.

"Nothing."

"You want to talk about it?"

He shrugged, then put his hands on my shoulders and turned me around. "You make me nervous walking like that. You'll trip if you're not careful."

I kept going, waiting.

After a moment he said, "Okay—I'm worried about Neal. He's still not very strong, and I still feel obliged to fight his battles."

"Not emotionally strong, you mean."

"Yes."

"Do you know about his fixation on the library?"

"You mean keeping it locked and off-limits to everybody else? Yes, we've discussed it. I convinced him he was causing resentment among the others, and he's promised to keep it open from now on."

"Did he tell you he was doing it because of the valuable books?"

"Yes. Isn't that true?"

"Not entirely, I don't think." I told him what I'd surmised earlier when I'd talked with Neal. When I was done he was silent for quite a while. Then he said abruptly, "Let's find someplace to sit down."

I stopped and looked around until I saw a spot on the slough side of the levee where there was a pocket in the fog. A fallen tree lay there amid a cluster of scrub pine. I motioned at it, and we scrambled down and sat on the trunk.

"I didn't intend to upset you," I said.

"You couldn't know it would."

"But I thought you should be aware."

"I appreciate it." He laced his fingers together, arms dangling between his knees. After a moment he turned his hands over and looked at his palms. It reminded me of an old game we used to play— "This is the church, this is the steeple, open the door, and see all the people."

Eventually he said, "Neal's trouble didn't stop in grade school. When he got too big to pick on, the other kids just ignored him. He had very few friends, and no luck with the girls. It wasn't all meanness on the other kids' part, though. Neal didn't try to make friends; he'd developed a very tough protective shell, and had gotten good at sneering."

"Evans was his friend, wasn't he?"

"One of the few."

I wanted to ask about Evans—this potential brother-in-law whom I barely knew—but I sensed it was important for Sam to talk about Neal.

He went on, "Neal's grades were good in high school, and he got into Harvard. For a couple of years he seemed okay. Harvard is full of misfits; genius or creativity often skews the personality. Neal made a place for himself there. But then I arrived on campus—the little brother who was so normal and outgoing—and his friends liked and accepted me. Neal turned on his sneer, taking their welcoming me as a rejection of him, and they began avoiding him. His grades slipped, and eventually he was kicked out."

After a moment he added, "Sometimes I'm ashamed of being so ordinary and well adjusted."

"That's just because we grew up in an era when it was fashionable to be a little mad."

"Maybe. You ever feel that way?"

"Lord, yes. I was a cheerleader and a member of the honor society. My brothers were always getting into trouble and fighting with the cops. My sister Charlene had to get married at sixteen. Patsy ran away from home. And there I was, the good kid on the block. Sometimes I thought my parents didn't love me as much as the rest of them because I never gave them any heartaches."

Sam nodded.

"Did you finish at Harvard?"

"With honors. Neal went to live in a furnished room in Boston, using his inheritance from our grandmother. That was his final fall from grace as far as our parents were concerned. They drew up a will—"

"Patsy told me about that. I take it they died at around the same time."

"Yes."

"How did they die?"

He hesitated, opening his hands into the "see all the people" position. "They killed themselves," he said softly. "A suicide pact. My father was fatally ill, and my mother didn't want to go on without him. His pill overdose worked right away; it took her five more days to die, in a coma the whole time. Neal and I were shattered by the tragedy; it seemed a betrayal. And then he found out about the will." He drew his palms together once more; I could see his arms tremble with tension.

"How did he react?" I asked.

"He had a breakdown. He felt his failures had somehow contributed to their decision to kill themselves. I wasn't in such great shape myself, but I was able to help him through. I got him into a psychiatric clinic near Ann Arbor, so I could visit frequently. When I did, we talked a lot. We even attended a series of seminars on dealing with grief." He laughed—short and bitter. "Seminars on dealing with grief, for God's sake. Do you *hear* how inane that sounds?"

"Not so inane," I said distractedly, because the word *grief* had struck an odd chord in me.

Wasn't that a good part of what I'd been going through all these months? I thought. Wasn't it tied up with all this inertia and inability to cope and low-grade depression? Grief—for all the pain and death and misery I'd seen in my work. Grief—for all the bad things that had finally built up to a near-saturation point. And grief, too, for a relationship that I had cherished, but knew was dying. Maybe I'd better sign up for one of those seminars. . . .

"Sharon?" Sam was peering anxiously at me. "Are you feeling okay?"

"I'm fine. I think I understand now why you were so upset about Neal's preoccupation with that room. What are you going to do about it?"

He shook his head. "Don't know. Maybe now that he's leaving it open and the others can go in, too, it'll lose some of its magnetism." But he didn't sound too sanguine about that. He stood and held out his hand. "We'd better get back to the house. I've been informed that the special dinner that didn't come off last night is being restaged this evening. That means cocktails at seven—and don't be late."

I took the proffered hand and let him pull me to my feet, then looked at my watch. "It's only five."

"I think you need some rest, my friend. You're looking a little pale."

"You're not so perky yourself."

"I know."

We climbed the levee, walked along it in silence, and scrambled down the other side. As we started across the fog-shrouded lawn, I had to acknowledge that Sam was right. I felt exhausted, my throat was scratchy again, and I had the beginnings of a headache.

"Sam," I said, "what are you wearing to dinner?"

"Last night I was told coat and tie would be in order. Tonight I'm holding out for jeans."

"Me too."

He grinned and held out his arm. I ducked under it and slipped mine around his waist, and we supported each other across the lawn. In spite of the fact I found Sam a very attractive man—and sensed he reciprocated the feeling—there was nothing sexual about it. He was simply a newfound friend, and that pleased me very much.

I left Sam in the living room and went to the butler's pantry, where I remembered seeing a phone extension. As Benjamin Ma had predicted, the line had been restored to service, so I put in a call to him at the sheriff's substation. The deputy was out, I was told, but would return in a couple of hours. I left a message for him to call me, then went upstairs to take a nap.

When the alarm went off at quarter to seven, I felt much better; my scratchy throat and headache were gone. My muscles and joints still ached some, but apparently I was going to escape coming down with a bad cold. As I lay there waiting for my postnap grogginess to pass, I reflected that maybe Patsy was right about the magical powers of vitamin C. Normally I distrust anything that even faintly smacks of health faddism—including wheat germ, tofu, and Jane Fonda Workout tapes—but I suspected this latest development might make me a believer in megadoses of Cs.

After five minutes I got out of bed and looked into the closet where someone—most likely Patsy—had hung my clothes. Her ice-green dress was also there, but I shoved it aside and selected a pair of newish jeans and a dusty-rose corduroy shirt. Then I brushed my hair vigorously, applied some makeup over the cut on my chin, and went next door to Sam's room. He answered my knock immediately, attired in a ski sweater and cords.

"I thought I'd escort you downstairs," I said.

"Why, thank you, ma'am."

He extended his arm and I put my hand on it formally, and we swept down the staircase with great hauteur, as if we were the king and queen arriving at the palace reception. Unfortunately, the only person in the living room who noticed our clowning was Andrew, who sneered even more haughtily at us. The others—who had also opted for informal dress—hovered around the bar cart. Sam and I joined the queue, got our drinks, and had just sat down by the fireplace with Neal when Kelley came up and said I 'was wanted on the phone.

Neal said, "Use the extension in the library, if you like."

It surprised but pleased me. Maybe, as Sam had hoped, his brother was letting go of his obsessive hold on the room. I thanked him and, carrying my drink, went in there and sat down at the desk. When I pulled the old-fashioned black phone toward me, it made double tracks in the dust.

It was Benjamin Ma, returning my call. "Yes, Ms. McCone," he said, "what can I do for you?"

"I was checking to see what you'd turned up on Max Shorkey."

There was a pause; I suspected Ma was belatedly remembering his promise to call with a report. "You must have a strong constitution, young woman. The way you looked last night, I didn't expect you to be up and around."

"It's all due to vitamin C."

"Ah, yes." There was a sound of paper rustling. "Well, Ms. McCone, I'm afraid I don't have much to report. We checked the ferry landing and the shack carefully, both last night and again this morning. There was no evidence of the foul play you reported. Mr. Shorkey's truck was parked next to the shack where he apparently always leaves it, and it hadn't been driven—couldn't have been, because it has a badly corroded battery."

"So that means Max's body *was* set adrift."

"Possibly."

"And I don't suppose it will turn up for some time."

"It's doubtful. As I said last night, there's a new storm front on the way that will complicate our job of recovering it."

"Did you talk with Max's wife?"

"Yes. She hadn't heard from him in a week."

"There's something I found out about her that you should know. She's taken up with a new man—"

"Cal Williams, owner of the Water Witch. I've talked with him. Both he and Mrs. Shorkey were at the restaurant in full sight of the staff and customers during the critical time last night."

"*Both* of them?"

"Yes, she's hostess in the dining room there."

"I see." I wasn't displeased. It meant that I could still operate on the theory that Max's murder was tied to the incidents here on the island. I said, "Well, thank you for returning my call. I guess that's about it."

Ma's voice changed now, became more personal and concerned. "You folks all right out there?"

"We're fine."

"No prowlers or further suspicious incidents?"

"Nothing."

"Good. But I think you should be aware that the weather report doesn't look promising."

"How bad is it?"

"Inconclusive, right now. But from my experience, I'd say you should be prepared in case there's a bad storm."

"I'll warn the others."

"Do that. And call any time you need us."

I hung up and leaned back in the cracked leather chair, sipping my drink. In the other room the cocktail party was definitely under way.

I remained sitting, thinking of Max and why he'd been killed. The obvious conclusion was because of something he'd seen. But how much could he have seen in the dark, in a driving rainstorm? From all indications, he'd been inside his windowless shack preparing his supper shortly before he'd died. Had he heard something outside, gone to investigate it? Or had someone lured him into the open with the intention of killing him? And if so, why?

Something he *knew* that was dangerous to his killer?

Maybe. But there was no way of knowing—yet.

A roar of laughter from the other room interrupted my thoughts. They were certainly having a good time, I reflected, considering the tragedy that had happened at the ferry landing only twenty-four hours before. A couple of them had expressed regret about Max's death, but no one seemed very upset. Perhaps that was because he wasn't really one of them, but it still seemed callous. It was almost as if he had never existed. Maybe for them, he hadn't.

I kept sitting there, reluctant to go out and make polite chitchat. The truth was, the Appleby Island crowd—with the possible exception of Sam—had begun to get on my nerves. The more I thought about them, the more I wondered about their pasts, their motives for being here. And now it occurred to me that it might be a good idea to run a background check on each resident. I picked up the receiver and made a call to Greg Marcus at his home in San Francisco.

He sounded surprised to hear from me, but not displeased. After we talked for a few minutes, I explained what I wanted.

"Up to your old tricks, Ms. McCone?"

I noted that he didn't call me by the loathsome nickname— "Papoose"—that he'd coined for me years before. Perhaps, like me, Greg was mellowing. "You mean taking a busman's holiday? Yes, but don't tell Hank."

"I won't. How many people do you want me to check out?"

"Six," I said, including Sam, but omitting my sister and the kids.

"Jesus, you don't ask much of an old beau, do you?"

"I'll buy you dinner when I get back."

"You're on. Give me their names." I gave them; when I'd finished, he asked, "All of these people Californians?"

"Sam Oliver's from Michigan, and Stephanie Jorgenson recently moved here from the Seattle area."

"Well, I'll see what I can do. I can get a reply from CJIS by tomorrow afternoon, as well as CJIC. But I'm not sure about NCIC; the FBI hasn't been too cooperative with us lately." CJIS was the state Criminal Justice Information System; CJIC was the information center for various California counties.

"I'll appreciate anything you can come up with."

"I'll do what I can. Where can I call you?"

"I think it's better if I call you at the Hall tomorrow afternoon. I don't know how many extensions there are here, and I don't want a phone call to attract an eavesdropper."

He hesitated. "You going to be okay there?"

Greg had always exhibited a paternalistic side that drove me crazy, but I recognized the question as motivated by genuine concern and didn't resent it. "Yes, don't worry. I'll talk to you tomorrow."

I hung up and kept sitting at the desk, wishing for a further excuse to prolong joining the party. But I couldn't think of one and, besides, my drink was almost gone. Finally I sighed, got up, and went back to the living room.

15

The rest of the cocktail hour and the dinner weren't nearly as dreadful as I'd thought they would be. I got another drink and sipped it, allowing the talk and laughter to eddy around me, smiling when it seemed called for. When dinner was served, the appetizer—scampi in a garlic sauce—more than made up for the company. Neal was subdued and kept his commentary on the various wines to a minimum. Evans's veal piccata received lavish praise, and the dessert turned out to be strawberries in Grand Marnier, a favorite of mine.

The dessert, however, reinforced my feelings about the monetary extravagance here on the island; the berries had to have been flown in from a warmer clime.

After dinner, we were all standing around the bar cart when Patsy came up to me and suggested I join her and Evans downstairs in their quarters for a "Get to know one another" session. While I did want to become better acquainted with her new love—for various reasons—I begged off. I wasn't feeling bad, but the thought of any more social chatter threatened to revive my afternoon's headache. I said, "I think I'd better go to bed. Would you let me have a few more of those vitamin Cs?"

She hurried off to get them, and I poured a generous dollop of brandy. Neal was standing next to me. I turned to him and said, "Is it okay if I borrow something to read from the library?"

He hesitated, and then his face brightened. "I have just the thing for you. In fact, I just finished reading it." He went off to the library and returned with an old leather-bound tome that looked like it had been handcrafted on a small press; its title was *An Intimate History of the Sacramento Delta.* "It has an entire chapter on the Applebys," he said, "their history up to the turn of the century."

The subject appealed to me; if I was going to spend much more time here, I might as well make a study of the place and the people who had settled it. I took the book and the vitamins upstairs, along with the brandy, and when I was comfortably tucked in bed, I began reading the chapter entitled "The Applebys of Appleby Island." Unfortunately I'd only gotten as far as the subheading "The Hermit War" when the alcohol, my still-weak state, and exhaustion overtook me. I laid the book on the nightstand, switched out the light, and was asleep almost immediately.

The first noise I was aware of was a scurrying. I moaned and kicked at the heavy quilts. Rats, I thought. We had a rat problem in the city and I often heard them skittering around in the attic above my bed.

The sounds came closer and stopped. There was a sliding noise to my left. And then the scurrying went away, and the door to the room shut softly.

I sat up groggily and reached to my right for the bedside lamp, but it wasn't there. Then I came fully awake and realized I wasn't in my own bedroom, but in the guest room at Appleby Island. I reached to the table on the left, and my hand bumped something and sent it to the floor. Glass shattered. I fumbled some more, got the light on, and looked down. What had broken was the brandy snifter I'd brought up here after dinner. But something else was gone from the table: the book I'd been reading before I'd gotten so sleepy.

I jumped out of bed—and stepped right on a fragment of broken glass. Stifling a cry, I hobbled to the door and looked out. The corridor was dark and deserted. I limped back to the bed again and sat, drawing my foot up across the opposite knee and looking at the cut. It was superficial, deep enough to bleed some, but not bad enough to require stitches. I hopped to the bathroom, found a Band-Aid in my travel kit, and doctored my foot. Then, scowling, I went back and picked up the fragments of the snifter.

The bedside clock showed two-thirty. Someone had wanted that book badly enough to sneak into my room to steal it at an ungodly hour. Who? Neal, because he was fixated on the library and its books? Hardly; he'd loaned it to me. Had anyone else displayed an interest in it? I couldn't remember, which probably meant no. Besides, *why* would anyone want it?

I thought back to what I'd read before I'd gone to sleep. Chapter: "The Applebys of Appleby Island." Subheadings: "Beginnings," "An Empire in Pears," "The Hermit War." . . .

I got up, pulled on the heavy robe that had been left in the room the night before, and went out into the corridor. There was no sound save for a faint series of snores coming from Sam's room. Downstairs in the reception area a small lamp had been left on. It cast enough light that I could start across the living room to the library without turning anything else on.

Through the doorway I saw someone shining a flashlight on the rows of books.

I moved as quietly as I could, trying to make out the figure behind the flashlight's beam. And then I banged into something. There was a cacophony of tinkling glass, and the light in the library went out.

The goddamned bar cart! I shoved it away from me and rushed around it toward the doorway. Before I could get to the library the French doors behind the desk crashed open, and a figure ran out through them. I ran over there, dodging around the heavy furniture, but by the time I got to the door and looked out, whoever had been there was gone.

I stepped outside and moved along the path that led around the house to the terrace, the flagstones cold under my bare feet. No one was in sight. I scanned the lawn, looking for a fleeing figure, but saw no one. How on earth had the intruder vanished that quickly?

After peering around through the darkness for a couple of minutes more, I retraced my steps and went back into the library, shutting and securing the doors. When I turned on the light, everything looked the same as it had when I'd been talking on the phone earlier in the evening. I waited for a moment, expecting that the others had been roused by the commotion and would come running to see what had happened, but the mansion seemed to be slumbering as deeply as before. The sturdy construction of these old buildings had both its advantages and disadvantages, I reflected.

I went out into the living room and turned on all the lights, still listening. There was a faint thumping noise, and I stiffened. It thumped again, and I decided it must be a tree branch hitting the house, but I still felt uneasy. I thought, as I had that morning, of the .38 locked in the glove box of my car.

Leaving the lights on, I went through the reception area and out the front door to where the MG was parked on the circular driveway, and got the gun. Holding the gun ready, I went upstairs and moved along the corridor, listening at the rooms where Neal, Stephanie, Denny, and Sam slept. No lights showed, and I could hear that Sam was still snoring; Denny's wheezes were clearly audible, too. Stephanie's door was ajar, and when I looked in I could make out her sleeping form in a bed under the window. Neal's door was shut; I touched the knob gingerly and found it wouldn't turn. I wondered if he had always locked himself in at night, or if this was a practice he'd developed since the trouble had started.

When I went down to the basement, the only sound I heard was a steady dripping. Water splatted onto the floor beneath the leaky pipes, and I made a mental note to tell Denny his patch job wasn't working. The door to my sister's quarters stood open, and I entered, checking Andrew's and the girls' rooms to make sure they were safely abed. I didn't intrude on Patsy and Evans's privacy, but before I left I heard my sister mumble fitfully in her sleep.

Down the corridor in the opposite direction, the door to the room Tin Choy Won occupied was locked, as were those to Angela's bedroom and her office. I chalked that up to the business manager's jealous guarding of her privacy, coupled with what I read as an extremely healthy dislike of her fellow residents.

Relieved that the intruder had apparently only entered my room and the library, I started back upstairs. But then a flaw in my logic struck me, and I stopped a few steps from the top, clutching the gun harder. All along I'd been consciously operating on the assumption that the person who had been playing these dangerous pranks, the person who had killed Max, was an outsider. But my actions spoke of a subconscious suspicion of the residents; otherwise I wouldn't have asked the types of questions I had, nor requested Greg Marcus run checks on them.

What if the person who had entered my room wasn't an intruder at all? I wondered now. He'd been familiar enough with the mansion to know where I was sleeping, to approach my bed and take the book from the nightstand in minimal light. And he'd known that I had the book in the first place. The person's quick disappearance also indicated an insider; he might know some way back into the house— an accessway that would permit him to reenter and slip back into his room unnoticed.

I went back to the library and looked at the shelves where the person had been shining the light on the books. In this section they were mainly on horticulture, but I didn't think he'd been after some light reading that would help his garden grow. If he was the same person who had removed *An Intimate History of the Sacramento Delta* from my room—and while I could concede there might be two people creeping around the mansion with books on their minds, I couldn't actually believe it possible—he'd probably been after information about the Applebys.

But why—especially in the middle of the night? An outsider could have looked it up in the public library; he didn't have to take a boat to the island and break into the mansion to find what he needed to know. And an insider could have examined the contents of the library at his leisure—

No, he couldn't have, I reminded myself. Until that afternoon Neal had kept the library locked. And he was probably still watching it carefully, too carefully for anyone to inventory its contents unobserved.

But why would anyone want the information, anyway? I considered the question for only a few seconds; the answer was obvious. Whoever had perpetrated the grim jokes had run out of ways to frighten people. He'd probably hoped to find fresh ideas in the history of the ill-fated family.

Or perhaps he wanted to keep the rest of us from learning any more about them than we already knew.

I still wasn't totally prepared to believe that one of my sister's friends—odd and ill-assorted as they were—was a murderer. And I wasn't about to voice such a suspicion until I had proof. I also wasn't going to be able to go back to sleep for some time.

I went out to the bar cart, poured a brandy, and carried it back to the library. After sitting down on the sofa, I stuffed the gun between the cushions within easy reach and tucked my now-icy feet up under me. As I sipped the drink, I smiled wryly. When I'd agreed to come up here and help Patsy, it had occurred to me that I might be able to relax while I was out of the city. Maybe cut down on the drinking. Now I was afraid that by the time I left I'd be a fit candidate for A.A.

From where I was sitting I could plainly see the orange shag rug that covered the stain from Stuart Appleby's blood. I jerked my eyes away from it, but they traveled involuntarily along the wall until they rested on a freshly patched place—the spot where the last of the Applebys had mistakenly placed the bullet he'd intended to put through his brain. I was beginning to understand why Neal— especially with his personal history—was fixated on this room. While it was gracefully proportioned and had a solid dignity, there were also reminders of the darker side of life, and a subtle atmosphere of wildness and despair.

I sipped the brandy and considered that for a moment.

All right, I told myself, there *are* feelings bottled up in old houses. In places where tragedy has occurred, a sensitive person is liable to pick up on those feelings and empathize with them. As we said in the sixties, you get "vibes." Neal had felt those vibes. Now I did, too. Suppose a third person had picked up on them and decided to play them for what they were worth? The strange appearance of the "hermit" in the pear orchard could have been designed to interest Neal in the history of the island, to drive him more frequently into the library, where he might discover more facts about the now-defunct clan. And given Neal's problems, an obsession with this particular room was the last thing he needed.

It was an intriguing thought.

Who would benefit if Neal broke down again? The obvious person was Sam. But what about the others involved in the project? For a while I considered each of them—including my own sister—but came up with nothing conclusive. Somehow I'd have to find out more about their financial and contractual arrangements.

My brandy snifter was empty. I set it down on the table and went to the bookshelves, starting at one end, reading each title, looking for anything that would give me a clue to what the person with the flashlight had been after. When I found nothing that made any sense, I started in on the drawers below the shelves.

I found a Parcheesi game, a set of Chinese checkers, and decks of cards so worn and brittle that they would probably crack if riffled.

There was a cribbage board made from an ivory tusk that would fetch a handsome price at an antiques store, and a carved chess set that any aficionado of the game would kill to own. There were poker chips, a bag of marbles, a bunch of mostly broken Pick-up Sticks, and a tangled-up Slinky. Trivial amusements to while away the days when the fog crept in or rain fell.

The cupboards below the drawers harbored an even odder assortment. A metal Tetley tea cannister was full of mismatched buttons. Old seventy-eight records in albums with brown paper holders— worn, chipped reminders of a gentler day when people danced to the music of Glenn Miller and Benny Goodman. A blue-and-red quilted sewing box stuffed with remnants—velvet, silk, dotted swiss, organdie. There was a toy dog—brown and white, with one blue eye and one yellow eye. A box full of bundles of bank statements and canceled checks. Decorative Christmas candles in the shape of fir trees and angels and Santas; the glitter on the wax trees had turned from silver to gunmetal gray. There were vases that had once held bouquets from the garden. A tarnished silver cigarette box and table lighter. A chipped Hummel figurine. A glass paperweight with a winter scene inside; when I shook it, it snowed, but the flakes were now brown with age.

My watch showed three-twenty when I opened the last cupboard and looked in at a stack of photograph albums and letter files. I pulled them out and hauled them to the sofa. Then I got another drink and sat down to go through everything.

At quarter to five I was halfway through the letters. I refreshed my drink and kept reading. Sometime after that it began to rain. The drops tapped against the French doors, soft as children's fingertips. My eyes felt dry and gritty; my head began to ache. I read on.

At a little before six-thirty, I set the last letter aside. Then I opened one of the albums again and looked at the long-dead people who stared solemnly into the camera, taking this business of being photographed seriously. I knew these people now, knew their story. It was a far greater tragedy than I'd imagined, beginning long before the night Crazy Alf Zeisler had been lynched, and continuing— because someone had chosen to capitalize on it—to the present day.

16

I t had happened this way:

Late in 1866 William Appleby arrived in the Delta, determined to establish an agricultural empire. He was from the South—Georgia— and had fought hard and well in the Civil War. With the onset of Reconstruction, he left the family home for good. (He could not stand, he wrote the wife he left behind, "to suffer the cruelties and indignities perpetrated by the hands of the victors.") There was much talk of the rich farmlands in California, and of how—now that the Gold Rush had slowed—the real fortunes there were to be made from the soil. Appleby knew land, had an uncanny talent for growing things. That he had to leave his wife and daughter in Georgia under the protection of the youngest of his four sons mattered not. (Upon his arrival in the Sacramento Delta he wrote them, "We will be united once again, in this most beautiful and prosperous land.")

Appleby quickly staked his claim on the island that was to bear his name ("A fair place between a strong river and a gentle slough, a place for us to grow"), and with the help of his sons Jed, Caleb, and Adam, he began planting the orchards that would later make him his fortune. A home was constructed, too ("A crude structure, but sturdy, and it will keep the winter rains from our heads"), and in 1867 he sent for his wife Eleanor, daughter Louise, and son Matthew. But the journey west was a rigorous one, and Eleanor's health had already been seriously weakened by the privations of war. Only William Appleby's children arrived in California. Packed in Eleanor's trunk, along with her carefully mended clothing and the family Bible, were William's letters. She had saved every one of them.

Stunned by a loss he now realized he should have guarded against, Appleby turned to the land for solace. He spent long hours in the orchards, aided by his sons, and ignored his only female child. (A cousin in Macon wrote, apparently responding to a letter from Appleby: "I know you are bereft, and you say your only consolation is in the soil and hard labor. But you would do well not to neglect Louise. She loved her mother very much, suffered with her during the War, and nursed her as she lay dying. Do not forsake her; she needs her father.")

But there were problems on the island that took Appleby's attention from the sixteen-year-old Louise. The hermit, Alf Zeisler, was becoming more and more bold. He uprooted the sapling pear trees, burned outbuildings, even resorted to such petty tactics as pulling drying laundry from the lines and dragging it through the mud. Appleby feared that one night the hermit might burn the roof over their heads. ("This blackguard who threatens your property," the cousin wrote, "why do you not just shoot him?") Appleby was a peaceable man, however, willing to allow the hermit his shack and garden plot ("How can you say he has a right because he was there first? Here in Georgia, we would never have allowed it to get so out of hand!"), but fear made him less and less tolerant.

During this campaign of terror, the responsibility for the household fell to Louise. ("You are working her too hard," an aunt in Savannah counseled. "She has written to me, and her letter was filled with loneliness and despair. If you are not willing to take a new wife as yet, pray encourage one of your boys to marry. It is not good for a young woman to bear such a heavy burden, nor to be so isolated from those of her own sex.") And indeed Appleby did worry about his daughter; in spite of her weariness from the constant cooking and washing and cleaning, he noted a wildness in her. She roamed the island, often late at night, and she seemed to be holding in check an anger that seethed just below the surface of her gentle facade. ("If you fear her temper so much that you liken its breaking loose to the 'raging of the waters during flood season,'" the Savannah aunt wrote, "you should send her to me, before a great harm is done.")

But William Appleby had conceived of a better plan: A distant relative had settled in San Francisco some years before, and from all appearances the man and his family were well to do. They had a home in a part of the city called Rincon Hill, and their letters spoke of many rooms and servants. He would send Louise to them, at least until this business with the hermit was resolved. ("Perhaps in such genteel and cultivated surroundings, she will become more calm," the aunt concurred, "or at least find herself a suitable husband.")

But to Appleby's astonishment, when he presented his plan, Louise refused to leave the island. (Long after the tragedy, the aunt wrote, "She sent a letter saying you were attempting to shunt her off to wealthy relations, but that she was determined not to go. I did not think it was devotion to you and the boys that prompted the decision, but hatred and a perverse desire to disobey your wishes at every turn.") After weeks of arguing with his daughter, Appleby grew impatient and ordered her to pack her trunk for the steamer ride to San Francisco. Louise raged at him, and he locked her in her room, but late that night she somehow got out and disappeared for three days. And when she finally returned—dirty, disheveled, and defiant—she announced that she had been with the hermit. Not only had she been with him then, but many times before. And she was carrying his child. ("I have had the news from both you and Louise," the aunt wrote later, "and my heart weeps for you. How dreadful to be estranged for life from your only daughter! And how much more dreadful for the unborn child. Whatever shall you do about it?")

On that terrible night the welfare of the unborn child was the last thing on William Appleby's mind. Matthew, his youngest son, was left to guard his sister; the others went with their father after the hermit. They tracked him across the island, through the orchards, and eventually into the tules at the water's edge. Trapped him there like they would a raccoon in a Georgia swamp. And then they dragged him back and hanged him—not from one of the sapling pear trees as legend had it, but from the big sycamore near the present house. (Appleby revealed these details to the cousin in Macon, who wrote back congratulating him on "making justice prevail after such a monstrous crime.")

Within twenty-four hours, Louise Appleby had been dispatched on the steamer to the wealthy relations in San Francisco. ("She is calm," the distant cousin wrote from Rincon Hill, "and does not seem to grieve for the hermit.") Appleby sent money which he could ill afford for her upkeep, but neither he nor any of his sons went to see her. ("We have received your generous bank draft, but assure you it is not necessary. Helping you in your time of need is recompense enough. But Louise asks occasionally of her brother Matthew. Would it not be possible for him to visit?") Apparently Matthew never did.

On April 23, 1870, the baby was born. A boy named James Alexander. William Appleby wanted nothing to do with the infant or his daughter. ("Of course we sympathize with how you feel. Louise and James may remain with us indefinitely.")

In the meantime, Appleby's pear empire was flourishing. With the profit from the other crops he'd put in to tide himself over until the pear trees matured, he began to buy additional land in the Delta. The three older boys married and moved to these fertile parcels, developing them according to their father's instructions. William also found a bride—the daughter of a wealthy Stockton rancher—and began to talk of building her a mansion, such as his prosperous neighbor, Louis Meyers of Grand Island, and others had recently begun. It was only talk, however, and the young bride died of influenza in 1874, leaving Appleby her considerable inheritance.

Then in August of 1875 news came from San Francisco: Louise and the baby James had disappeared. Evidently she had been slipping out nights to meet a Swedish merchant seaman with the Northern Pacific Line. On one of these she had packed her own and James's things, taken him, and left for good. ("We knew nothing of this alliance," the San Francisco cousin wrote somewhat defensively. "Most of our information comes from the servants. But Louise did leave a note, asking us not to search for her. What do you wish us to do?")

What Appleby wished them to do was absolutely nothing. He had washed his hands of his daughter years before, and now that she was gone, he would never be forced to confront the reality of an illegitimate grandson. Immediately he wrote into his will a provision prohibiting Louise or any of her descendants from inheriting, and gave instructions to his sons to do the same. ("You are correct. It is better we consider Louise dead and buried. Needless to say, you must be relieved to see the end of this unfortunate affair.")

Whether William Appleby was actually relieved was open to speculation. What he went on to accomplish was fact. He established one of the richest agricultural empires in the Delta. He built his mansion and, before it could be completed, he buried another young wife. Appleby did not live to enjoy his mansion, either; in September of 1886, shortly after its completion, his drowned corpse was found in the turgid waters of what was now called Hermit's Slough. There was much talk at the time of how he came to be there, but few conclusions. And more than one person suggested his death might be "God's retribution" or "Crazy Alf's curse." ("These rumors must be very painful to you," the San Francisco cousin wrote to Matthew, "as we know your father did what he must under the circumstances. Louise had been violated, and he was bound to avenge her.")

Matthew continued to live at the mansion after his father's death, and in a few years took a wife. While the orchards were fruitful for him, the marriage was not, and he produced only one child, Stuart, a change-of-life baby born to his much-younger wife in 1920. The other Appleby sons fared well in their agricultural enterprises, as did their offspring, until the collapse of the pear market in the 1920s. The families were plagued by various tragedies, however: Jed's sons were killed in one of the deadly peat fires that often flared up in the rich Delta lowlands; Caleb's boys became estranged and left California, never to be heard from again; Adam's only daughter died in childbirth, and his grandsons were killed in World War I.

Every time one of these tragedies struck the Appleby clan, obituaries in the Sacramento or Stockton papers would extol the once-great pear empire and then mention—in suitably hushed but dramatic tones—the "strange curse that many say has fallen upon the family." If William Appleby thought an end had been put to the affair of the hermit on the night Louise and the baby James disappeared, he had been very wrong.

Finally only Matthew's son Stuart was left at the mansion. In 1940 he had married a schoolteacher from Walnut Grove, but she and their twenty-five-year-old daughter were killed in an auto wreck on one of the levee roads during the disastrous rains and floods of 1972. And in late 1985, alone and fatally ill, Stuart ended his life with a bullet through the brain. He was the last of the Applebys.

17

sat in the library until close to seven, thinking over what I had read and listening to the mansion come alive around me. The morning before, these sounds had seemed cheerful and commonplace indicators of a household gearing up for another day. Now everything I heard was tainted with my own feelings of unease. Yesterday it had been "us" against "him"—the outsider. Now I was afraid Max Shorkey's murderer might dwell here with us.

Finally I got up and put the albums back where I'd found them. I debated taking the letter files upstairs to my room, but finally I tucked them into another cabinet, far back behind an assortment of objects. They'd probably attract less attenion there than they would if hidden in my closet, and it didn't really matter if the person who had been in here the night before found them and took them; I knew what they contained, and was not likely to forget it. Besides, I wasn't sure if the information about the Applebys' history was relevant in any meaningful way to what had been happening here. Wasn't sure if reading it had benefited me or not.

Next I had to decide what to do with my gun. By daylight, the impulse that had made me go out to the car and get it and then prowl the silent house seemed a melodramatic one, but I wasn't quite willing to relinquish the .38. I solved the dilemma for the moment by stuffing the gun in the deep pocket of the robe. It made the garment sag ridiculously on the right-hand side, but my appearance was the last thing I was worried about.

In the kitchen I found Evans whirling coffee beans around in an electric grinder. He wore a cheery grin, his usual ratty jeans, and another rugby shirt, also in bad repair. I thought of my sister's spiffy new wardrobe and wondered why she hadn't also bought her boyfriend some decent clothes. But from what I'd observed of Evans, he simply didn't care about clothes— didn't care about anything much except cooking and Patsy and the kids. And I had to admit I liked his priorities; they were refreshing to me, especially after the trivial people and values I often encountered in the city.

He said, "You're up early. Coffee'll be ready in a few minutes."

I sat down at the table and adjusted the robe so the weight of the gun wouldn't be too obvious. I felt light-headed and slightly out of touch with my surroundings, the way you are on too much brandy and not enough sleep. But I was certain I wouldn't be able to go back to bed now; my mind was too full of the saga of the Applebys and the things I planned to do today. Better to rely on coffee to get through the morning.

Evans poured water into the coffee maker, then moved about the kitchen efficiently, getting out eggs, bread, and bacon. He stirred up orange juice in a clear glass pitcher, opened a new carton of milk, set out plates and cutlery on the table for a buffet-style breakfast. All the time he whistled happily. I watched this man who one day might become my brother-in-law and again realized how little I knew of him.

By way of getting to know him better, I said, "I guess you'll be glad when you have a real restaurant kitchen to work in."

He responded with a big smile. "You'd better believe I'm looking forward to it. This one is difficult at best. And the new one's going to be the kitchen of my dreams. Neal gave me a free hand in planning it." As he worked Evans began to rattle on about the new sixteen-burner gas stove, two commercial ovens, a walk-in freezer, and a compact salad station.

I drank the cup of coffee he brought me, and nodded when he went to refill it. Evans lit a burner on the ancient gas stove with a wooden match and began to cook the bacon, sipping from his own coffee cup as he turned the strips. Now he was talking about his experiences in Paris and how working under a perfectionist *sous* chef was equivalent to being on a battlefield. ("Except they don't use bullets; they're more likely to poison you if you screw up.") From his chatter and all other appearances, Evans seemed a happy man—confident, uncomplicated, exhibiting a keen enjoyment of life.

So why did he make me so uncomfortable?

I thought of Neal's comment that Evans had better toe the line if he wanted to go on playing his game. Perhaps it was that game that put me on my guard, because I sensed it wasn't merely cooking, as Neal had claimed.

I watched Evans for a moment, trying to imagine him as a murderer. As the perpetrator of a series of deadly pranks. I tried to picture him employing subterfuge. Doing something underhanded. And then I dismissed the idea as ridiculous. It was difficult to imagine this cheerful, pleasant man concocting anything more complicated than a chocolate mousse tarte.

When he had finished with the bacon and paused in his monologue to poke through the refrigerator, I said, "Evans, who ordered your new kitchen equipment? I know you picked it out, but who wrote the actual purchase order?"

"Angela did, after we'd gone over what I wanted."

"And when it arrives, who will check the invoice?"

"Angela, again. Of course, she'll get my okay on it, to verify that the stuff is what I wanted and was received in good condition."

"What happens then?"

Evans looked mildly puzzled at the line of questioning, but he seemed more concerned with whatever was eluding him in the fridge. "Then she'll issue a check and pay for it."

"Who signs the check?"

"Both Neal and Angela. Neal goes over the invoices after the rest of us okay them, and if everything seems in order, he signs and then Angela sends the checks out."

It seemed a fairly standard business arrangement, with countersignatures and safeguards. Maybe, I thought, I just had a suspecting nature. Maybe I didn't know these people well enough to trust them, or to understand the dynamics within the group. But I *still* had the feeling that somewhere along the line Neal was being taken.

Evans was whistling again, breaking eggs into a pottery bowl. His fingers, unusually slender and tapered for such a big man's, pulled the shells apart with an easy grace I'd never mastered. I got up and refilled my coffee cup. He said, "Having trouble waking up?"

"Sort of."

"That's one problem I never have anymore—not with the monsters from below." He motioned at the kitchen floor with a wire whisk.

"The kids get up early, do they?"

"Yeah, even today, when they're not going to school."

"Why aren't they?"

"Patsy has to take Andrew in to the doctor's to have his cast checked. Kelley didn't want to ride the school bus alone. So Patsy decided to indulge the kid, for a change."

"Jessamyn's not in school?"

"No. She's a couple of months too young for kindergarten, and it was a hassle for us to get her to the nearest preschool. She'll start in the fall. It'll be a mixed blessing; the little motormouth will want to give us a minute-by-minute description of the events of her busy day." He smiled fondly, whipping at the eggs.

"You really care for the kids, don't you?"

"I love children, and I've always wanted a family. For a while I was afraid it was something that had passed me by. And then I found Patsy, and not only did I have somebody to love, but I also had a ready-made family on top of it." He spoke with such simple, controlled emotion that I felt myself warm to him.

Evans turned to the stove, setting an iron skillet on the lighted burner. "You hungry?"

"Not right now." My digestive system wasn't ready for breakfast—not when I'd been drinking brandy only an hour or so before. "I think I'll go upstairs and get dressed first." I went over and set the empty cup in the sink, holding the robe so the gun wouldn't make it sag in such a telltale way. It was an unnecessary precaution; Evans merely nodded, his back to me, absorbed in melting butter for the scrambled eggs.

Upstairs in my room, I locked the door—a precaution that had occurred to me since encountering those similarly locked doors last night—then carried the gun into the bathroom with me, hanging the robe on a hook and leaving the .38 in its pocket. I took a long shower, turning on the massage head so it pulsed, hoping the steady rhythm would dispel some of my grogginess. Often I do my best thinking in the shower, and this was no exception. By the time I'd gotten out and toweled off, I had a plan—at least for the morning.

The wardrobe I'd brought for what I'd expected to be a three- or four-day stay was rapidly becoming depleted. I always travel light, and my unexpected catastrophe in the boat had wiped out an entire change of clothing. For a moment I felt a stab of concern for my favorite green sweater, but then I brightened. It wasn't in the closet; maybe Patsy was planning to wash it and would return it to me, good as new—she'd always been good with clothes.

In the meantime, the jeans I'd had on the day before were perfectly presentable, and there was still the pink crocheted sweater my Aunt Margaret in Minnesota had sent me last year. This morning, the warm color helped, since I definitely looked pallid.

The gun still presented a problem. I finally stuffed it in the outer compartment of my purse and slung the bag over my shoulder. I didn't plan to go out immediately, but it wouldn't seem odd for me to be carrying the bag if I intended to leave eventually.

Downstairs in the reception area, I bumped into Denny, who was just coming in. I greeted him and asked, "Have you seen Angela?"

"Yeah, I just took her over on the ferry. She said her grandfather needed some stuff from his house in Locke."

"How is Mr. Won?" He was the reason I wanted to find Angela. If he was feeling up to it, I needed to ask him again about the hermit. When we'd last spoken, I'd sensed he was holding something back, and now that I knew the full story, I wanted him to confirm it. Also, I was curious about how many people in the Delta knew about Louise Appleby's illegitimate son and their eventual disappearance.

Denny looked troubled. "Not so good, Angela says. He really got a soaking in the rain, and at his age . . ."

"Should we get the doctor?"

"Angela tried, but he was out on an emergency. It might be just as well, because she says her grandfather hates doctors and would probably refuse to be examined. Anyway, she still has some of those pills you gave her."

"Let me know when she gets back, would you? And I'd like to go over to the other side of the ferry landing later, if you wouldn't mind."

"Sure. I've got nothing better to do."

"Why not?"

"I haven't been able to buy any of the supplies to do the work that's needed inside. The next project was supposed to be the boat slips, but I don't have any workers. Couldn't do anything in this rain, anyway."

"Is it coming down hard again?"

"Not yet."

"Benjamin Ma was worried that we might be in for a bad time."

"Well, he ought to know. He told me he's lived here his entire life. His family was among the original settlers at Walnut Grove, and later they moved to Locke."

"Can this house withstand a really bad storm?"

"Has for a hundred years—why not now?" Denny grinned reassuringly and went into the living room.

I stood there, undecided as to what to do next. The information he'd just passed along about Benjamin Ma was encouraging, though. If the deputy's family had been in the area that long, he would be plugged into the Delta's network of rumor and superstition about the Applebys, and—when the time came—that might make him receptive to what I'd found out. If I could ever make sense of it.

By now it was after eight-thirty. I went to the kitchen and forced down a respectable amount of breakfast. Patsy, Kelley, and Jessamyn were there with Evans, and we spent a while talking about various innocuous topics: the local school district, Evans and Patsy's first meeting, their plans to buy a new van. The conversation reassured me about them; they seemed to be a real family. The only member I worried about was Andrew.

When I asked about him, Patsy said, "He's in bed in a sulk again. I think it's your fault."

"What did I do?"

"You asked him to make some drawings, and you've never come to look at them."

"Oh, Lord, I'd totally forgotten! I'll go see him right away."

"Please," Patsy said. "It would do a great deal for my sanity."

On my way downstairs I ran into Angela and Denny. She was carrying a plastic grocery bag and looked harried and tired. "Angela," I said, "how's your grandfather?"

"Not very well."

"Should we try to call the doctor again?"

"I don't know. I'll see." She hurried downstairs before I could say anything else.

I turned to Denny. "Mr. Won must be really sick."

"I guess, from the way Angela's acting. She was down at the ferry landing leaning on her horn for about ten minutes before I came to get her. At least that's what she told me—all the way back here."

"Well, she's upset—"

"No, she's a bitch." Denny turned away from me and walked out of the house into the rain.

I found Andrew reading another comic book. It seemed to me he spent an abnormal amount of time in bed, and I wondered if it was habitual or had just started when he'd broken his arm. Either way, it wasn't healthy for an eleven-year-old to insulate himself from the world with pillows, sheets, and blankets. That was potentially dangerous escapist stuff, better left to adults.

When he saw me in the doorway, he sneered. "Oh, it's you."

"Are you mad at me?"

"Why should I be?"

"Because I didn't come back for the drawings."

He shrugged elaborately. "Hell, no. Mom said you weren't feeling good after dinner last night and besides, they're just a bunch of stupid sketches."

"I'm not going to make any excuses, Andrew. I felt bad, and I forgot. I'm sorry."

"Oh-that's-all-right." His words ran together, as if he'd spoken them often in his short life, and they gave me a sudden insight into what it would be like to be Andrew. He was the oldest of a single mother's brood: brother to the intellectually precocious Kelley and Jessamyn, the charmer. When Patsy didn't have a man around, Andrew was elevated to the position of man of the house, and probably a lot of responsibility for his sisters fell onto his bony shoulders. When Patsy did have a man, Andrew was demoted, and his mother's attention was drawn away from him and focused on her new love. And when that happened, the already introverted kid withdrew further, hiding his hurt behind a shield of bedclothes and comic books and, sometimes, hostility. It made me ache for him, but I knew my sympathy was the last thing he wanted.

I said, "It's not all right. I need those sketches. They're even more important now than they were when I asked you to make them."

"What do you mean—now?"

"This will have to be our secret. I can't tell anyone else."

"Well, *I* won't tell."

I was quite certain he wouldn't; young as he was, it felt good to have him as my ally. "All right—I saw the hermit last night. I mean, I saw the person who's pretending to be him."

"Where?"

"In the library." I told him what had happened, concluding, "So you see, the sketches are especially important now."

As I'd spoken, Andrew's thin face had flushed with excitement. Without a word, he got out of bed and removed the sketch pad from his bottom bureau drawer. I sat down on the bed and looked through it.

The sketches were remarkably good, the figures well drawn and close to lifelike. They resembled the man who had attacked me at the ferry landing: tall, in a baggy raincoat, shabby pants, and a slouch hat. The trouble was, they told me nothing new.

I didn't want to let Andrew see my disappointment, so I went back through the drawings, studying each intently. "I think I have an idea," I said.

He waited, tense and still flushed.

"I'll need more help from you, though. Will you do some more sketches? Start with when you saw him at your window."

"That was just a hand."

"That's okay. Start with it. Once you get it down on paper, you may be able to picture a face to go behind it."

"You mean like a face I've forgotten I've seen?"

"Yes."

"All *right!*" When I left him, Andrew was pulling his big container of felt-tip pens and another sketch pad out of the drawer.

I went down the hall to Angela's office and knocked on the closed door. Her "Come in" was snappish, and when she saw me she flashed a look of irritation.

"I won't take much of your time," I said. "I just need the name and phone number of the lawyer in Antioch—the one who handled the low offer on this place."

"Oh." She turned to her Rolodex, wrote something on a pad, and handed it to me.

I started for the door, but turned while I was still half a step inside the office. "Angela, have you tried to get the doctor for your grandfather again?"

"He'll be unavailable until two—but I assure you I'm capable of calling him myself when the time comes."

Weary of her unnecessary nastiness, I shrugged and went out, closing the door hard behind me. What had Sam said about her? Something to the effect she would never unbend. He was certainly right on that score.

Upstairs I used the phone in the library to call the lawyer—Edward Peeples. His secretary said he was in court and agreed to give me a three o'clock appointment. In a way I was relieved that my business couldn't be conducted by phone. I was dying to get off the island for a while. But right now, I decided, I had better get on with what I planned to do here. I went looking for Denny and finally found him in the boathouse.

The old corrugated-iron building was cavernous, a dark and drafty space echoing with the drumming of the rain. In spite of its great size and relatively few contents, it was disorderly: Partially coiled ropes were flung together in a pile near the door; life jackets, plastic floaters, extra gas cans, bundled-up tarps, and other nautical gear were stuffed haphazardly onto some makeshift shelves. A sturdy aluminum skiff similar to the ones that had been lost and a couple of bashed-up canoes—possibly those that might be salvaged—lay in the middle of the concrete floor. The floor itself was filthy with mud and cigarette butts. The chaos and dirt somehow fit my image of a place managed by Stephanie—although I didn't know why I had assumed she was slothful.

Denny sat on the floor at the far end of the building, his back to me, feet dangling into a boatwell. It was about six feet deep, with steps going down into it and a door on the slough side that could be cranked up to permit the boat to enter and leave. He heard my footsteps slapping on the concrete and turned his head. His sky-blue eyes were like lamps on which someone has turned down the dimmer switch. As I drew closer I saw he was smoking a joint and smelled its pungency.

He patted the floor next to him, and I sat, folding my legs Indian-style. When he offered me the joint, I shook my head. Denny shrugged philosophically and dragged on it. When he finally exhaled, he said, "That's the trouble with this place—nobody to get stoned with."

"Not even my sister? She's grown her own for years."

"Not anymore. Patsy's as straight as the president of the PTA."

"Why, do you suppose?"

"Evans —he's on the way up. Going to become Mr. Restaurateur. In a few years, he claims, Crazy Alf's will rival Chez Panisse— "

"What?"

"That restaurant in Berkeley—"

"No, what's he calling the one here?"

"Crazy Alf's, after the hermit."

Now that was interesting.

"You didn't know that?" he asked.

"No."

"Well, that's what it's gonna be. Seems kind of morbid to me. I mean, is he gonna dress the waiters in rags? Or maybe have little nooses as part of the centerpieces? I don't know . . ."

I didn't either, but the name seemed in bad taste to me, especially in light of what I'd read in the Appleby family letters. Of course, Evans wasn't aware of the contents of those, and the name *was* a part of the Delta folklore. . . .

The silence that fell between Denny and me was punctuated by the rain on the iron roof. It was steady, but not hard, and it didn't seem to have picked up much. Maybe Ma's prediction of a new front moving in was wrong.

Denny continued to smoke, his powerful, freckled hand cradling the joint as he might a baby bird. I'd noticed he had a gentle way of handling things—from his knife and fork at the dinner table to the hammer he habitually wore at his belt—that was at odds with his size. After a moment I realized I was staring and looked away into the gloom around us. Next to the shelves what was evidently an outboard motor stood on a wooden stand, a tarp thrown over it like a hood.

I said, "Denny, I thought you had to row the skiff over the other night when you went to check on Max."

"Yeah, I did."

"If that's a motor over there, why didn't you attach it?"

He glanced at the stand. "Oh, that wasn't here then. Steff found it yesterday, through an ad in the paper. She figured we needed at least one outboard, in case the ferry broke down."

I remembered her seated at the kitchen table, the want ads spread in front of her. "That was good thinking, especially with this storm front moving in." I paused, and after a moment asked him about the supplies he ordered and how they were paid for. What he told me was more or less what Evans had already explained.

He said, "You think somebody's screwing with the books?"

"I'm not sure."

Denny waited, then looked hurt because I didn't confide in him. He sucked on his joint and stared down into the empty boatwell. The few feet of water trapped there was an opaque yellowish-brown; the odor that rose from it was a stale mixture of oil and decaying plant life.

I said, "Did the Applebys keep a lot of boats?"

He shrugged.

"This is a pretty elaborate setup."

"I don't know anything about boats, lady."

It annoyed me that I'd alienated him. In his usual friendly state, Denny could be a fount of information. But something more than my abruptness had put him in this mood, driven him out here to smoke dope. Angela's earlier nastiness? Maybe if I stayed with him a while longer I'd break through this uncharacteristic reserve and he'd tell me. But I also had work to do. "You do know about operating the ferry, though."

"Ferry's simple. When I first got here, Max showed me what I needed to know, in case something happened to him. . . . Shit, it seems funny to think of him saying that, now."

"You don't think he meant anything serious by it, do you?"

"Nah, all Max was worried about was if we wanted to go someplace and he was out at a bar or spying on his wife."

"Spying?"

"Yeah, he did that, sometimes. He'd follow her and her boyfriend. Max was like that—he wanted to know what was going on. I bet he knew a lot more about all of us than we ever suspected."

"You think he spied on you people on the island?"

"Not really. He was just observant, that's all."

Now that Denny mentioned it, I realized Max had seemed more familiar with the people on the island than I would have expected of someone who didn't live there. He'd displayed a good grasp of the nuances of some of their characters, and he'd certainly had his own—probably informed—opinion of their business venture. Perhaps it had been his powers of observation that had been his undoing. Maybe, as I'd speculated earlier, he *had* seen or heard something that someone else hadn't wanted him to.

I said to Denny, "Will you take me over to the other side of the ferry landing now?"

At the suggestion, he seemed to snap out of his depression, as if it had been the enforced rainy-season inactivity that had been getting him down. "That's right," he said, "you mentioned you wanted to go." He stood, dusted his hands off, and reached out to pull me to my feet.

There was no opportunity for further conversation on the ferry ride, because the engine was acting up and Denny spent most of his time back there, babying it.

When Denny brought the ferry to a stop, he came forward and helped me unhook the heavy chain. "Now what?" he asked.

"I want to look around Max's shack. I won't be long."

"Take all the time you need. I'll try to see if I can't figure out what's going on with that engine. It's like the damned thing knows Steff was worried about it breaking down and is trying to prove her right."

I nodded and jumped down from the ferry and went up the concrete ramp toward the shack. The door was still unlocked, but someone—Ma or one of his men—had turned off the old floor lamp, and it was very dark inside. I felt along the wall until I came to the lamp and switched it on. The room looked the same as it had two nights before, even to the abandoned sandwich fixings on the table. I began moving through it, inventorying the contents. In the corner, wedged behind the folded roll-away cot, was a brown-and-white-checked carrying case that looked like it might contain a portable typewriter. I stared at it, trying to visualize the shack as it had appeared the last time I'd been there. I didn't remember seeing the case, but it was in an odd place, and most likely I'd missed it.

I went over there and knelt down, pulling the case toward me. It was heavy, and its handle bore the Smith-Corona trademark. When I opened it I saw a typewriter that was not dissimilar to the one that I—

and thousands of other students of my generation—had carted off to college. Its keys were dirty and the ribbon was worn. . . .

I rummaged in my bag and pulled out the anonymous note that Sam had received. Then I ripped a sheet from my notebook, rolled it into the platen, and duplicated the few lines. Because the quality of my own typing was about as bad as that of the sender, they matched almost perfectly.

Sinking into a sitting position on the floor, I looked from the sample to the letter and back again. I thought: Max—the sender of this note? Max—the person who was concerned enough to summon Neal's brother?

Several things fit: Max had considered the business venture risky; he was keenly aware of what went on at the mansion; he—like the sender of the note—didn't have much education. But would Max have cared enough to write to Sam? I wasn't sure; I hadn't known him well enough to make that judgment.

After a few minutes, I put both pieces of paper back into my purse, closed up the typewriter case, and moved it over by the door. Then I continued to prowl through the shack—which didn't take a great deal of effort, given its size. I inspected the pockets of the clothing that hung on the pegs, but came up empty-handed, save for a quarter and a matchbook from the Ryde Hotel. I felt inside the work boots and sneakers that were lined up near the door. I even riffled the pages of the *National Enquirer* that lay on the table next to the now-decaying food. Then I unhooked the fasteners on the cot and opened it.

Squashed flat on top of the rough gray blanket between the cot's two halves was a small cardboard box, the kind that letterhead stationery comes in. I let the cot sag open, grabbed the box, and took it to the table. It was full of stationery supplies: a tablet of the same kind of cheap paper Sam's letter had been typed on, two kinds of envelopes—plain and with transparent windows—and preprinted invoice forms.

I pulled the folding chair over to the table and sat down and went through the invoices. They were blank, of a standard type, and had been printed with a number of different names and post office box addresses: Ace Plumbing Supplies, Buy-Mor Paints, The Chef's Works, Melrose Market, Brandt's Contractor's Supply, Central Marine, The Galleria. The latter struck a familiar chord, and I realized it was the designers' showplace in the city where Patsy had shopped.

I sat there for a while, fingering the invoices and letting an idea form. Not much of an idea, but a connection between the skimming of funds that I suspected and the actual method by which it might have been done. There were plenty of details I couldn't yet fathom, mainly because I've never understood the principles of bookkeeping or accounting, but I wasn't worried about them now. With the proper help I could sort them out.

What I couldn't figure was—given his reputed lack of education— how Max had been able to accomplish such a thing. Or why his typewriter had also been the machine on which the letter to Sam had been written. If he were realizing a profit from the sloppy financial management at the island, why would he have gone out of his way to make Sam take a closer look at the operation?

After a while there was a tap on the door. Denny. I stuffed the invoices back in the box, tucked it under my arm, and picked up the typewriter on the way out. Denny glanced at it, but without a great deal of curiosity.

"Find what you wanted?" he asked.

"Hard to say, since I'm not sure exactly what I was looking for. Did you figure out what's wrong with the engine?"

"No. I don't know exactly what I'm looking for, either. Still sounds funny, but whatever's causing it is hard to spot."

We boarded the ferry and he started it up. Over its burble and growl, he yelled, "That noise—you hear it?"

I listened. It was a grinding sound, and it might have had something to do with the cable. But the ferry was so noisy anyway that it was difficult to pinpoint where a specific noise came from. Finally I shrugged at him, set the typewriter down next to the engine house, and walked forward to watch the mansion come into view.

It was raining harder now—big fat drops that landed on the hood of my jacket and rolled down and splashed onto my nose. The mansion's white facade blended into an increasingly thick mist. I was beginning to hate the rain, the damp, the fog. I only hoped it would let up for my trip to Antioch. Maybe the lawyer there would tell me something that would help me clear this mess up. Then I could turn the whole matter over to Benjamin Ma, get back in my car, and go home to San Francisco.

And then I thought: Go home to what?

Behind me, Denny said, "What the fuck!"

I turned. The grinding noise had increased measurably. "What's wrong?"

"Don't know."

The noise became even louder. Then there was a sound like metal shearing. The ferry lurched, kept going in a series of jerks, and then slewed sideways.

I stumbled and grabbed at the side railing. The box of invoices and envelopes slipped from under my arm. I whirled, reaching for it, and lost my footing completely. As I fell to the deck, the vessel shuddered and slewed again.

Before I could try to get up, Denny shouted, "Stay put!"

18

I did what Denny told me and stayed down on the deck. The shuddering and grinding stopped as he cut the engine. Suddenly all seemed quiet; the rushing of the water and patter of raindrops was muted in comparison with the commotion that had just gone on. The ferry strained sideways with the strong current and seemed to drift a little. Denny came out of the engine house, breathing hard.

I said, "What happened?"

He shook his head, wiping sweat off his forehead. It stained the curls that hung down on his brow a dark red. "Damned if I know. Scared the shit out of me, though. You all right?"

"I'm fine. Did it sound to you like something was wrong with the cable?"

"Maybe. I don't know enough about how it works to say. But I'm not gonna chance turning that engine on again."

I got to my feet and looked around. We were just about in the middle of the slough. "I guess we'll have to swim for it."

"No, we won't. At least you won't; you got enough of a soaking the other night. What I'll do is swim to the island and get the skiff, then come back for you."

"I'd sure appreciate that. At least you can use the new motor, rather than rowing."

"The hell I can. Steff bought it cheap; she's gonna have to tinker with it awhile to get it running."

"Are you sure you want to—"

"No, I don't *want* to. But I *will*." Denny went to the island end of the ferry, unhooked the chain, and after a moment's hesitation

157

lowered himself into the water. Then he yelled—a loud "Jesus Christ!"—and struck out on a thrashing crawl.

I watched him for a few seconds, then looked down at the deck. The invoices I'd dropped were plastered to its wet surface. I got down on my hands and knees and began to gather them up. The ink had run on most, but the names were still readable. The box lay over by the engine house, and what was left inside was still dry. I reassembled the whole thing, picked up the typewriter, and was waiting at the end of the barge when Denny returned in the skiff, oars splashing clumsily as he pulled hard against the current. It took our combined strength to bring the boat aside, and he barely managed to hold it there while I lowered the typewriter and myself aboard.

We were silent as he got the boat turned around and headed back. When we were more or less on course, he said, "Well, this really screws us, doesn't it? The ferry's busted, and all our cars and trucks are on the island. I suppose in an emergency Steff could get that outboard going and somebody could go over and use Max's truck—"

"Its battery's dead. Benjamin Ma told me that last night." I thought of Max's comment the night I'd arrived, about it being stupid for them to take their vehicles across to the island rather than leave them at the landing, near the road. The wisdom of that had been borne out now.

Denny said bitterly, "Great. Just great."

"Maybe you can get the ferry working again."

"Like I said, I don't know a damned thing about it. Max told me how to run it, not how to fix it."

"What about Stephanie? She knows boats."

"Boats, yes, but I don't think she understands this ferry any better than I do. But maybe she can help me. At the least, I want to get it out of the middle of the channel. If those storms they're predicting hit and it's still out there, we might lose it."

"You mean it could break loose from the cable?"

"Or sink."

I shook my head, thinking that the loss of the ferry would make that of the canoes and outboards seem minor. And then I realized that with the ferry out of commission, my plans for the afternoon were effectively canceled. There was no way of getting to my appointment in Antioch. I swore in exasperation.

Characteristically, Denny didn't ask for an explanation, just kept rowing.

When we got to the island, I was surprised nobody was there to greet us. It seemed to me they would have heard the commotion or seen the ferry was in distress and come running. But apparently the sound of the engine hadn't seemed strange at that distance, and the landing was hidden in trees, out of sight of all but the third-floor windows. We pulled the boat up on shore and trudged up the drive. When we reached its top I said, "I've got to get something," and veered off toward the car.

Denny called after me, "Well, I'm gonna get a hot shower and some dry clothes. Let me do the explaining about the ferry, will you?"

"Gladly."

I unlocked the MG's passenger-side door and slipped onto the seat before I took the .38 out of my bag. For years I'd kept one of the pair I owned in the glove box, which I'd had fitted with a special sturdy lock; its twin was at home in a concealed strongbox. I'd never had any problem with either gun falling into the wrong hands (mainly, I suspected, because the car looked too disreputable to contain anything of value, and the partially renovated house was too disorderly to tempt a thief). But now I wondered if I was doing the right thing in leaving the gun in the car unattended.

I sat there for a moment, contemplating the maps and flashlights and first-aid kit that were the other contents of the glove box. I thought of the person who had run from the library the night before. And then I pictured Jessamyn and Kelley and Andrew—their curious eyes spotting the gun in my room or in my purse, their eager hands reaching for it. No, it *was* better to leave it in a place that had thus far proved secure.

After I'd relocked the car, I picked up the typewriter and the box and went up the drive to the mansion. There was no one in the public area, and I hurried upstairs to my room without encountering a soul. The typewriter went into the wardrobe behind my suitcase, and after some thought I adopted Max's method of concealment and stuffed the box under the mattress. Then I dried my hair and freshened up, found the paper on which Angela had written the Antioch lawyer's number, and went down to the library to use the phone.

Edward Peeples had returned from court and, once I had explained about my lack of transportation, he agreed to answer my questions about the offer on the island by telephone. What he could tell me wasn't very helpful, though: He had been asked to make a blind offer by another attorney, Bob Barnes of Sacramento. Barnes, a casual acquaintance who owned a cottage near Peeples's on Snodgrass Slough, had a client who wished to remain anonymous. Peeples didn't know why there was a need for secrecy, but he gave me Barnes's office number and suggested I talk with him.

Barnes was out to lunch, but his secretary said he was due back in about fifteen minutes and would call me. I sat waiting at the library desk, drawing patterns in the dust with my fingertips. The rain was coming down harder now, and when I turned around to look out the French doors, I noticed a leak at the top of one of them. Fat droplets oozed through the crack from outside and dribbled down the beveled panes, leaving streaks like tears on a dirty face. I turned back to the desk and wrote "bucket" in the dust as a reminder. The phone rang, and I picked it up.

The connection was fuzzy, but Bob Barnes's voice boomed out through the static. It was Southern-accented, smooth and smarmy as one of those TV evangelists who have recently been plaguing the airwaves. I explained that Edward Peeples had referred me and asked about the blind offer on Appleby Island.

Barnes said, "And what exactly is your interest in Appleby Island, little lady?"

I resent being addressed by familiar, diminutive terms by men I don't even know, but I held my temper and said, "I'm a private investigator hired to look into some problems there."

A pause. "I see. And you're interested in what, again?"

"The offers you instructed Mr. Peeples to make on the property."

"Offers. Let me see . . . offers." Even given the poor quality of the connection I could tell he was deliberately making the words sound vague, stalling for time.

"Surely you remember them, Mr. Barnes. A low offer, which was turned down, and a slightly higher one, also rejected. You can't have that much legal business of that nature."

He laughed, the good-fellow-well-met kind of laugh. "You're right, little lady, I don't."

"What can you tell me about the client?"

"Not a thing."

"You're invoking attorney–client confidentiality?"

"If you want to talk fancy, yes."

"Even if your client may have been involved in a crime?"

Another pause. "What kind of crime?"

"There's been a murder here and the sheriff's department is investigating. I'm cooperating with them."

This time the silence stretched out a good fifteen seconds, and when Barnes spoke, his voice had lost all traces of good humor. "Then let the sheriff contact me."

"I'll tell him to. But will you answer one more question?"

"Maybe. Make it quick."

"Did your client have anything to do with the rare-book business?"

"Huh." From the tone of the monosyllable, I couldn't tell whether the question had surprised him because of its accuracy or because it was totally out in left field. Finally he said, "I don't think I care to answer that—or anything else," and hung up.

I replaced the receiver and drew a big question mark in the dust, then swiped it off with the palm of my hand. The two calls had given me no real information, and I was glad I hadn't been able to waste time making the long drive into Antioch. Besides being very poorly rewarded for my efforts, I also—judging from the sound of the rain and the wind that was beginning to gust down the chimney—would have had a rough time negotiating the roads on the way back.

The sound of the wind reminded me of the poor quality of the phone connection when Barnes had called. It would be a good idea to call Greg Marcus now for the results of the checks he was running, in case the line went dead again. I dialed his extension at the Hall of Justice in San Francisco; he picked it up on the first ring.

"Oh, good," he said. "I was hoping you'd call because I've got a meeting in half an hour, and I don't know how long I'll be. CJIC responded. CJIS hasn't yet, and NCIC was as I expected."

"Anything interesting?"

"Not really. Nothing on Sam Oliver, naturally, since he's from out of state. Also negative on the Jorgenson woman, Angela Won, and Neal Oliver. Denny Kleinschmidt was busted twice for possession of marijuana, but the charges were dropped for lack of evidence. There's a restraining order out prohibiting him contact with his ex-wife, Marianne Kleinschmidt. Evans Newhouse had three DUI arrests in Ukiah a few years ago; went to drunk-driving school and has been clean ever since."

"And that's it?"

"That's it. You owe me a dinner—how about at Stars?"

Stars was one of the expensive "in" places in the city. "Try the Gold Mirror," I said. It was a neighborhood Italian restaurant, and for my money beat out the trendy establishments in every way.

"You're on. Take care, huh?"

"Will do. And thanks."

I hung up, thinking that I would never have pegged Evans for a problem drinker. But then, it had been a few years ago, and people can change. The restraining order on Denny puzzled me; he'd described his *wife* as the violent one. I'd have to keep it in mind and try to work the conversation around to it the next time I talked to him privately.

After a moment I decided it would also be a good idea to check in at All Souls. I dialed the familiar number and asked Ted—who sounded faint and far away—for Hank. When my boss came on, the connection got even worse.

"Where are you?" he asked.

"Still up in the Delta."

"When are you coming back?"

"I don't know. There's a storm brewing—"

"There's a storm brewing here, too—inside." He proceeded to tell me about a trial date that had been moved up, a complaint from a client that my most recent report had been sketchy, and a new client who needed my services yesterday. Then he added, "Do you want your phone messages? Ted just handed them to me."

I didn't know what I'd be able to do about them, but I said, "Yes, please."

He read them to me. They all seemed to be from people who wanted something, even Don. His had a distinctly petulant tone: "Have you gone on vacation early, or what?"

Hank said, "Things aren't so good with you two, huh?"

"None of your business."

Unfazed, he went on, "Oh, I almost forgot. Your mother called."

"She called me at the office?"

"She couldn't get you at home and she was tired of talking to what she calls 'that ridiculous machine.' She told me she's been trying to get hold of Patsy in Ukiah and the phone's been disconnected. She's afraid something terrible's happened to her."

"Oh Lord! You didn't tell her where I'd gone?"

"I didn't tell her a thing, but she sounded pretty upset, so you'd better call her."

"Right. Is there anything else?"

There was a fuzzy sound that escalated into a crackle.

"Hank?"

". . . by Friday."

"What?"

". . . Superior Court . . . Judge . . ."

"*What?*"

The line hissed and went dead. I jiggled the button, but now there wasn't even static, just that nothingness that indicates total interruption of service.

"Well," I said, "at least I won't have to explain Patsy to our mother right now."

Then I became aware of voices in the living room—excited, angry. One was Denny's, another Stephanie's, and a third was Neal's. Occasionally Sam's calmer tones interrupted, but were drowned out in the general chaos. The primary words that came through to me were "ferry," "disaster," "take it easy," and "you asshole." I got up from the desk and went in there.

The four of them stood in the middle of the room between two groupings of furniture. Angela sprawled in a chair behind them, watching with an amused expression. Sam looked frustrated because no one would listen to him. Stephanie had gone white around the mouth. Neal's face was mottled and he waved his hands wildly as if trying to air-dry them. But Denny was the most agitated—face beet red, eyes bulging, breath coming hard. I listened to a few exchanges and understood why.

> Neal to Denny: "Yes, I called you an asshole! You're a goddamned *asshole* to take that ferry over when the cable was about to break."

Denny: "Jesus Christ, we don't even know if it *was* the
    cable!"

Stephanie to Denny: "That's the trouble! Like I told you the
    other day, you don't know a fucking thing about that
    ferry. You should have made Max teach me, but no, you
    knew it all!"

Denny: "Max didn't trust you—"

Stephanie: "Max was a stupid son of a bitch, and Neal's
    right—you *are* an asshole!"

Sam: "Listen, why don't we sit down and discuss this
    rationally—"

I said loudly, "Everybody shut up!"

They all turned, shock draining their faces of expression. Behind
them I could have sworn I saw Angela's mouth twitch as she
repressed a smile. There were footsteps in the reception area, and
then Patsy and Evans's worried faces appeared in the archway.

Neal said to me, "Where do you get off telling us to shut up?"

"Somebody had to. You sounded worse than the kids."

From a corner of the room, where I hadn't observed him, Andrew
said, "I beg your pardon!"

It broke the tension somewhat. Sam threw up his hands and
flopped into a chair. Denny and Stephanie smiled sheepishly at each
other. Only Neal remained rigid, hands fisted. I went over and guided
him toward the sofa. "Let's talk, okay?"

He sat, but his stiff posture didn't change. Patsy and Evans came
all the way into the room and took places on the opposite sofa. "What
happened?" she asked.

Denny said, "The ferry broke down. It's stuck out in midstream,
and I'm worried about getting it to the landing before the storm really
hits."

My sister's face sagged, and she glanced at Evans. He put his arm
around her shoulders, but I could read defeat in his expression, too.
They had placed all their hopes on this venture, and now were faced
with visions of failure and potential financial ruin. There was a long
silence, punctuated by a gust of wind and heavy rain.

Stephanie said, "I've been thinking—there has to be a hand
winch."

Denny said, "A what?"

"Some kind of backup system on the ferry, so if the engine fails you can crank it back to shore. All the little ferries in the Puget Sound area had them. I'll bet if we look—"

"Why the fuck didn't you say so before?"

"Didn't think of it right away."

I listened to them, wondering. What if the ferry's failure had been deliberately engineered at a strategic time when a storm was approaching and the residents would be trapped on the island, frightened enough to want to leave for good? Who would be the most likely parties to have arranged that? Stephanie, by her own admission, knew a lot about boats. Denny knew a fair amount about mechanical things, and I found his professed ignorance of the ferry's workings a little hard to swallow. I thought of them as I'd first seen them on Saturday morning, walking along the levee, appearing to be arguing. And I remembered the first words I'd heard Denny say, to Stephanie as I'd entered the kitchen a little while later: "It's dangerous, and I won't—"

What was dangerous? *What* wouldn't he do?

Denny said to Stephanie, "You think you can find that winch?"

"If there is one."

"Then what are we waiting for—?"

There was a knock at the front door. We all looked that way in surprise, and it was a moment before Sam stood and went to answer it.

The caller was Benjamin Ma, attired in his heavy slicker and boots. He wiped his feet on the tarp, pushed the hood of the slicker back, but waved Sam off when he tried to help him off with it. "Can't stay long," he said. "I just wanted to check on you folks and see if anyone wants a ride off the island."

Sam asked, "How did you get here? The ferry—"

"Sheriff's department launch. I saw the ferry. Sometimes the cable seizes up in this kind of weather. Too bad Max isn't here; he'd know what to do."

Somewhat regretfully I discarded my convenient theory of sabotage. I said, "Speaking of Max, have you found out anything else?"

Ma shook his head. "Like I told you, the body may not be found for some time. And frankly, we don't have the manpower to investigate; we've got our hands full with weather-related incidents."

Stephanie said, "I think *I* know what to do about the ferry. It has a backup mechanism, right?"

"Yes," Ma said. "If it's in good repair, you can probably crank it back to the landing before the storm gets really bad."

Stephanie flashed a triumphant glance at Denny. He said, "Let's go, then."

Ma held up his hand. "Wait. I want to talk to all of you. I'm concerned about you folks; we're in for a bad blow. If any of you want to evacuate, we'll be glad to take you right now in the launch."

The word *evacuate* echoed around the room. I think I even repeated it myself.

"How bad will it be?" I asked.

"Hard to say. Maybe as bad as two winters ago."

I remembered the newspaper and television coverage of the destruction. Apparently Patsy and Denny did, too, because they both said, "Oh no!"

I said, "What do you advise us to do?"

"That's up to you. I can't make up your minds for you."

"But you must be able to give us some insight that will help us to make the decision. None of us are Delta natives like you, or even very familiar with what it's like under the kind of conditions they're predicting."

"Okay," he said after a slight hesitation. "If you decide to stay here it'll be rough. But Appleby Island and this house have held firm for over a century. Those levees were built to last, and they've been well maintained. You may have to prepare your friends"—Ma looked around the room with the expression that I reserve for Yuppies invading my favorite neighborhood restaurant—"for some hardship."

Denny said, "We already are prepared. We're not as soft as you make us out to be."

His prickly response surprised me. But then, he'd been through a good bit of abuse over the matter of the ferry, and Ma's implication had probably rubbed an already raw spot.

Denny's reply seemed to call up a similar combativeness in Ma. He said snappishly, "Do you have emergency food supplies?"

Denny motioned at Evans.

Evans said, "Yes. Canned goods. Dried food. One of us is a

former farm owner, and she brought months' worth of food stores with her." He squeezed Patsy's shoulders and in spite of her earlier tension, she smiled at him.

Ma asked, "What about bottled water?"

Denny said, "The real estate agent who sold the place to Neal warned that the pump on the well could go out at any time. We couldn't afford to replace it immediately, so I made sure we stored a couple of weeks' worth of drinking water."

"You have an auxiliary generator here?"

"Yes." But Denny's tone was evasive. I suspected the generator was one of those things—like the pump—that should have been repaired or upgraded, but hadn't been.

Ma seemed to sense it, too, because he added, "What about candles? Flashlights? Batteries?"

"I've seen to that."

"Plenty of blankets? Heavy clothing? Wood and matches?"

"Check."

"Medical supplies? First-aid kits?"

"Yes," Patsy said.

"Transistor radios so you can keep tuned to the weather channel?"

"We've got them," Stephanie said.

"What about sandbags? Are there any on hand in case there's a break in the levee?"

"Denny and I had a load delivered. And we know how to reinforce if we have to."

Ma looked mildly surprised. "Then you should be all right. That is, if you're all good friends and able to pull together during the rough times."

There was a silence.

I said, "Deputy Ma, give us the other side of this—what about evacuation?"

When he looked at me, I saw understanding in his eyes; he'd also felt the emotional climate in the room. "If you evacuate, you should do so tonight. The launch is here. The island will survive, and if there's damage to the house or the outbuildings, well . . . they must be insured."

I looked around the room. Everyone was silent. Patsy and Evans exchanged glances. Angela frowned off into space. Denny looked quizzically at Stephanie. Sam watched Neal, and Neal sat rigid, his teeth clenched so hard his jaw bulged. When I looked over at Andrew, I saw he had withdrawn, white-faced, arms hugged tightly across his bony chest.

I waited, feeling the outsider, but no one else seemed to want to take charge. Finally I said, "Deputy Ma, I don't think this is a decision anyone's prepared to make right now."

"You don't have to. Obviously we'll be patrolling the waterways, and can arrange to stop back in a few hours. They're setting up shelters now—in Walnut Grove and Rio Vista. You'll be welcome there. But I must warn you: If you want to evacuate, do it when we come back. After that I can't promise anything." He turned and made for the door, was through it before Sam could open it for him.

The door slammed shut, and the silence in the room grew. The rain splattered against the French doors and windows, and the wind backed up in the chimney, sending out plumes of smoke.

Patsy let out her breath in a long sigh. "Well," she said. "Well, what does everyone think?"

Evans said, "We have to consider the kids' safety."

Neal said, "This is my island and I'm not going anyplace."

Sam said, "We could go to San Francisco, Neal, take a hotel room until this blows over."

"No."

Sam shrugged.

I settled back on the couch, waiting.

In a small voice Patsy said, "I keep thinking of Franks Tract."

I asked, "What's that?"

"It's open waterway now, but it used to be farmland. It was flooded back in the thirties when a levee broke, and it was too expensive to pump it out, so they just abandoned it. There's all sorts of farm equipment down there under the water. We took the boat across it once, and I felt like I was in a graveyard."

Her voice held a tremulous, melodramatic note that I didn't like one bit. I glanced at Andrew and saw he was listening intently, his arms hugged even tighter than before. "So?" I said.

"What if that happens here—with us on the island?"

"It's not likely." It wasn't exactly a lie; I didn't know what was possible and what was not.

"But what if it *does*?"

"If you're afraid of that, you should probably evacuate."

Denny stood up briskly. "Before we decide anything, I want to get that ferry to the landing. What say, Steff?"

"Sure. It's already getting dark, so the sooner the better."

As they went out, I looked at my watch. It was not yet three, but the light outside had the purply quality of dusk. I thought about evacuating, taking the sheriff's launch to a warm shelter full of fellow refugees. And I thought of staying here in this cold, drafty mansion with this group of strange and often unpleasant people. The one place offered safety and camaraderie; here the bickering had already started, and if it escalated it could become dangerous. To say nothing of the danger from the person who seemed to *want* everyone off the island. . . .

But there was really no choice for me. I'd come here to do a job, and I'd have to see it through. The only way I would leave Appleby Island was if all the others decided to do so.

Angela spoke for the first time since I'd been in the room, tentative words that were very unlike her. "My grandfather is very ill."

Sam said, "Then you should go, so he can get medical attention."

"You don't know those emergency shelters. I do. It's not going to be much better there. He could die in one of them, or during the ride on the launch."

"Then stay. There are enough of us that we can take turns nursing him."

"You're staying?"

"Yes."

"Why?"

Sam gestured at Neal.

"'Thy brother's keeper?'" Even in this grim situation Angela couldn't resist needling.

Neal started to rise, his face flushing in fury, but Angela stood and said, "I'll go check on Grandfather. I'll ask him if he wants to evacuate. If we go right away, perhaps I can get him to the hospital in Rio Vista."

Neal's mouth was working as she went out. He stared at the archway, then pounded his fists on his thighs.

Sam said, "Don't let her get to you, guy. I don't."

Neal didn't reply.

Evans said, "Patsy, what about the kids?"

My sister merely turned her head against the curve of his shoulder, as if she were too weary to consider the question. Evans looked undecided. Then Andrew came up behind them and leaned down, putting his head between theirs. "Mom? Evans? Don't worry about us."

Patsy rolled her head and looked up at her son. "Of course we'll worry. This is going to be a bad storm—"

"Tell her it's okay." Andrew appealed to Evans. "I can take care of those girls. We'll be all right, and that way you only have to worry about her."

Evans barely suppressed a smile. "You'll keep the girls in line, and I'll take care of your mom?"

"Sure. It's better than going off to one of those crummy shelters. Let's just stay . . . home."

"Thought you hated it here."

Andrew shrugged. "It sucks, but it's all the home we've got."

Evans nodded. "Okay, that's the way it'll be. And thanks." To the rest of us, he said, "Patsy and Andrew and I vote to stay."

Neal said, "I'm not leaving. And I don't think Denny or Stephanie will want to go, either."

"My flight's not until Sunday," Sam said.

I hesitated, wishing I were home. Wishing I'd never heard of Appleby Island or any of these people. And knowing I'd stay. Because I had to know the truth. I always had, for as long as I could remember.

I said, "I'll stay, too."

19 _____

Once the decision had been made to stay, the tension in the room eased somewhat. Patsy and Evans and Andrew went downstairs to explain the situation to the girls. I told Neal about the leak over the doors in the library and he wandered off to find a bucket. Sam decided to seek out Angela and see if there was something to be done for Tin Choy Won. That left me alone and feeling at loose ends.

Finally I went upstairs, intending to go to my room and reexamine the typewriter and blank invoices, but halfway down the hall I thought of the junk room on the third floor. Originally I'd asked Neal if I could poke through it because I was fascinated by such places; now, considering what I'd found in the library, I felt an obligation to do so. While I couldn't link the contents of the Appleby letters to the current events on the island in more than a superficial way, my subjective sense—honed fine by my years in the business—warned me there might be a deeper connection. There was no telling what further information the junk room might yield.

I retraced my steps and continued up the stairway and down the hall to the cluttered room. The only light, I found, came from a single bare bulb hanging down in its center, but it seemed adequate for my purposes.

I sat down on a rolled-up carpet next to some cardboard boxes and began going through them. They were jammed with frayed towels; sheer curtains that had shredded with age; once-fine linens that had been darned in many places; embroidered tablecloths that showed the ineradicable stains of many meals. Next to them were crates stenciled with the name APPLEBY ORCHARDS that contained heavier items: discolored fireplace andirons, rusted tools, cracked and chipped dishes, brass drapery hardware, mismatched china, and glass doorknobs. Much of this must have been placed here by the Applebys. The rest had been carted up when my sister and her friends took possession of the house.

An old baby carriage leaned drunkenly against the wall, its springs broken on one side. It contained a worn crocheted blanket in a faded shade of pink and some sort of fuzzy white stuffed animal—a lamb? Wedged into the corner behind the carriage was a toy box full of the discards of childhood: wooden alphabet blocks, dolls, a broken top, a red plastic hand organ with a threadbare plush monkey on top. I picked it up and turned the crank; the monkey moved up and down to the strains of "Pop Goes the Weasel."

I wasn't sure why at first, but the hand organ made me feel sad and weary. This toy had once been bright and brand new, had delighted a child, perhaps on a birthday. Now it was a castoff, fit only for the dump. And the child? I thought I knew; she had been Stuart Appleby's daughter, who had died in a car wreck in her twenties. I sighed and replaced the organ gently in the toy box.

It seemed to me that I'd spent most of the past decade poking through the detritus of other people's lives, examining the ruin they— and circumstances—had left behind. No wonder I felt low.

I sat down again on the other end of the carpet. It smelled strongly of mildew. Beside me was a great heap of clothing and linens, probably dumped there by Patsy and the others when the job of clearing out the mansion had become overwhelming and the impulse for neatness had deserted them. I pawed through it listlessly, feeling reluctant to handle the rumpled and dirty things, my spirits sinking further.

The pile consisted of more stained tablecloths, doilies, sheets and pillowcases, moldy-looking blankets, towels in hideous shades of salmon and maroon. There were dishcloths and dirty rag mopheads, work clothes and housedresses, worn braided throw rugs and scorched pot holders. There were—

Dishcloths.

I picked one up, held it to the light. Yellow. Like the one that the hanged doll's costume had been fashioned from.

Quickly I went through the rest of the pile, looking for a cloth that had been cut. And over to one side I found it—or at least, fragments of it. A few straight pins like those that had been used to hold the doll's costume in place were scattered on the floor.

I gathered up the pieces of cloth and stuck the pins through them, then stuffed them in my pants pocket. I regarded the clothes in the pile with renewed interest; there were enough for a variety of disguises. Then I went back to the toy box.

The first doll I dug out had blond hair and a baby face. Another, with a china head, would be worth a good deal to a collector. A rag doll was losing one leg, and a rubberized one had grown brittle with age. But at the bottom of the box was a doll with a darker complexion than the others, dressed in tattered buckskin. It was the squaw that went with the hanged brave.

I stood holding the doll, wondering why the one Jessamyn had found in the orchard had been deliberately dressed in the pieces of dishcloth. Then I remembered that the hermit, Alf Zeisler, had worn rags. The person who had dressed that doll was striving for verisimilitude.

The person who had dressed it. Someone who had access to the mansion—and to this room.

One of us.

It only confirmed what I'd already feared.

After a moment I sat down on the rug again, clutching the doll, and thought things through. Who had access to this room? Was it only the residents of the mansion? What about the workers? Possibly, since they'd been doing carpentry inside, but somehow I doubted they had anything to do with the hanged doll. There was Max Shorkey, of course, but I gathered he'd seldom come to the mansion. Right away I could eliminate Sam; he hadn't arrived until Saturday.

As an act of faith, I had to eliminate Patsy and the kids. Evans . . . I certainly hoped not, for my sister's sake. That left Neal, Denny, Stephanie, and Angela.

Angela . . .

I thought of the exorbitant expenditures for the wrong things. The invoices I'd found, the typewriter. And of how Angela might have been skimming funds. But I still didn't see where Max fit, not at all.

Dammit, what I needed was someone with financial expertise. Someone who could confirm that what I suspected about Angela might be possible. Anne-Marie could have helped me; besides a law degree, she had an MBA in accounting. But Anne-Marie was in the city, and the phone line was dead. I couldn't call her, so I'd have to—

Ask Sam. Could I trust him?

I continued to sit there clutching the doll. The rain splashed against the windows and the wind rattled them in their frames. Suddenly there was a rumble, and a far-off crash. The sky brightened, then faded. On top of everything else, we were having an electrical storm.

Sam. What did I know about Sam?

Very little, except for selected details that he had chosen to tell me. But when I'm unsure about a person, I tend to go with my gut-level instincts, and my instincts about Sam were very positive.

I got up and went downstairs to look for him, but when I got to the second floor, I decided to first go down and try to talk with Tin Choy Won. I'd formed a suspicion about the typewriter and invoices, as well as the anonymous letter, and I thought Mr. Won could confirm it.

When I looked into his room, however, I found him asleep. His breathing was ragged and irregular, and I started through the door, meaning to check his pulse and temperature. Perhaps Patsy should look in on him; she'd had a good bit of experience nursing her kids. If she said he should go to the hospital, someone could take the skiff and summon the sheriff's launch—

"What are you doing?" Angela's voice was hushed but angry.

I turned. She stood behind me, one foot thrust aggressively forward, tapping her toe. Her hands rested on her hips, elbows akimbo.

"I'm concerned about your grandfather, Angela. Have you been able to reach the doctor?"

Her rage was momentarily deflected as she looked over my shoulder into the shadowed room. "No, he never returned to his office, and now the phone's dead. Grandfather's pulse rate and temperature aren't good, but when I spoke with him earlier about going to the hospital, he refused. You know how old, superstitious people can be about hospitals."

"Maybe you should overrule his wishes."

She bit her lip. "I don't know."

"I'm sure we can get word to the sheriff's substation, ask they bring the launch back right away—"

"Look, he's my grandfather. Let me worry about him, will you?"

"You're playing with his health, maybe his life—"

"Deputy Ma said the launch would be back. I'll decide then. And don't try to go in there again without asking me first." She brushed past me and motioned rudely for me to leave.

I clamped my teeth together, resisting the impulse to call her a bitch. Then I went upstairs to talk to Sam.

I found him in his room, sprawled in a ruffly flowered armchair and reading a lurid-looking paperback western titled *Duel at Gold Buttes.* When he saw me standing in the doorway he tossed the book on the floor and motioned for me to come in. "What's that?" he asked, looking at the doll I was carrying.

I didn't want to muddy the issue I'd come to talk about, so I said, "Just something I found upstairs in the junk room. I'll tell you about it later, but right now I need to ask you what you think about the financial situation here."

"It's bad, no doubt about that. I've had some exploratory talks with Angela and Neal. Tomorrow—when I assume the storm will have passed and she'll have gotten medical attention for her grandfather—I intend to sit down with both of them and draw up an overall plan."

"What kind of plan?"

"For future spending. There are certain things that need to be taken care of right away. The auxiliary generator that Ma asked Denny about, for instance. It isn't worth shit. Other things, like decoration and buying boats and some of the kitchen equipment, will have to wait. They've got their priorities all screwed up, and they're going about this project wrong. Anyway, after we've formulated a new plan of attack, I'll consult with each of the other individuals about the areas they're in charge of and make sure they're aware of how it's got to be."

"So you're not going to advise Neal to pull out of the project?"

"He's in too deep—both financially and emotionally. I'm especially concerned about that emotional investment, so I'm not going to cut off his funds. But I'm not releasing any more of his money unless I know exactly what it's going for." He paused, seeming to listen to himself. "I know I sound hard-nosed and holier-than-thou. It's Neal's money and, in spite of my parents' will, he ought to have control over it. But I've told you about that hang-up I have about waste."

I went to sit on the edge of the bed, facing him. "I have a similar hang-up, but it has to do with human waste, people being misused."

"By 'people,' I take it you mean Neal."

"Yes."

"You think the others are using him badly?"

"Maybe not all of them, but . . . is it possible someone's been skimming funds here?"

He patted his mustache, eyes thoughtful, but not shocked. When he didn't speak, I went on to tell him about the invoices and typewriter I'd found in Max's shack.

When I'd finished, he said, "Let me get this straight. What you're saying is that someone has been typing up bogus invoices for amounts higher than what is actually owed, and getting Neal to sign checks to pay them."

"Right. The company names on the invoices all sound like suppliers they've been ordering from. Also, they're suppliers of goods, rather than services."

"Why is that significant?'

"A lot of people who provide services—chimney sweeps, for instance—demand payment at the time the work is done, rather than invoicing. It could account for the way necessary repairs have been neglected."

"It still doesn't make sense. The check would then go to the supplier and be credited to Neal's account. Reputable companies—and I know the ones they've been dealing with are solid—wouldn't give a kickback."

"What if the company names on the invoices are also bogus? Ones that are similar to the actual suppliers? Banks will open accounts in any business name with very little documentation. The checks could be deposited to the account, and then the amount owed to the real supplier could be drawn out and forwarded."

"That's possible."

"The invoices—the legitimate ones—come in and are okayed by the person responsible for the ordering. They're also okayed by Neal before he signs the checks. But suppose he's shown a fake invoice on which the person's initials or signature has been forged? Would he check on it? Ask the person who did the ordering the exact name of the supplier or the amount of the invoice?"

Sam pushed his glasses up and pinched the bridge of his nose. When he spoke his voice was weary. "Probably not. I notice we're both avoiding naming the person who would be responsible for this. It all points to Angela, doesn't it?"

"I'm afraid so."

"In a way it doesn't surprise me. Maybe deep down I've always suspected she could be unscrupulous, but I've tried not to acknowledge it. I certainly never would have recommended her for this job had I . . . well, no matter. What *does* surprise me is that you found those invoices and typewriter at Max's shack. And that the anonymous letter was written on that machine. Did Max— "

"No, I don't think so. Take the two things separately. I didn't see the typewriter when I went to the shack Saturday night. I may have missed it; God knows I was tired and wet and worried about getting back here. But in spite of that, I think I would have noticed it, because it was an item I wouldn't have expected Max to own."

"So?"

"It had to have been left there later, not only after my visit, but also after the sheriff's men had been through the shack. Benjamin Ma knew Max; he would have found it odd, too. A lot of people had the opportunity to put it there: I know for sure that my sister, Evans, Denny, Stephanie, Angela, and whoever went to pick up the Sunday paper have been off the island since Max died."

"Well, I'm the one who went to get the paper. I wanted to take a look at the countryside; unfortunately no one thought to tell me that the fog was so dense I wouldn't be able to see anything. I know when Denny, Stephanie, your sister, and Evans were gone, but what about Angela?"

"She went to Locke early this morning, to pick up some things from Tin Choy Won's house. I think one of them was the typewriter, another that box of invoices. When she returned, Denny had brought the ferry back to this side. There was plenty of time for her to leave the stuff in Max's shack before she beeped for him to come get her."

"Let me see the invoices, will you?"

I went to my room and got the box from under the mattress. I gave it to Sam, and he looked through its contents for several minutes.

Finally he asked, "Why do you think she was keeping this stuff at Mr. Won's?"

"She couldn't very well type up the bogus invoices here, could she?"

"No. But why bring them here now?"

"Her grandfather's very sick. If he dies, she might not be able to remove things from his home so easily. Perhaps she felt safer, given that you were looking into the financial situation, with them in a place not connected with her."

Sam sat up straighter. His eyes had grown hard with an emotion that was not quite anger—not yet. "That brings up one big hole in your theory: the anonymous letter. Angela wouldn't have written it."

"She didn't. I think Tin Choy Won did."

Again he looked thoughtful rather than surprised. I suspected that in his line of work Sam had seen as much of the darker side of his fellow man's behavior as I had. But while he wasn't easily shocked, he was capable of rage, and I saw it building now in his eyes and the set of his mouth. Crisply he asked, "Why?"

"Mr. Won seems to be a very moral person. I sensed that in the disapproving way he spoke of Angela when I visited him on Saturday. He probably had found the invoices, perhaps even saw Angela typing some up, and realized she was doing something illegal. I suspect he wrote that letter to you in an attempt to derail her activities before they got her in serious trouble."

Sam was silent. His eyes glittered behind the panes of his glasses. His anger was a tangible presence in the room now, and to a certain degree I could feel it infect me. I didn't especially care for his brother, but I sympathized with Neal's inner turmoil and desperately hungry needs. And I liked Angela far less than him; it seemed contemptible that she would take advantage of such a weak creature.

Sam said, "Well, there's only one thing to do, isn't there? We have to get to the bottom of this—now."

"I doubt we'll get anywhere by confronting Angela."

"No, she'd just deny everything. She's a *great* little denier."

"But if we can get proof . . . she may have kept dual records, you know. Two sets of books."

"That's possible. Knowing Angela, she'd want to know her

proceeds from the embezzlement down to the last penny. Hell, she's probably run projections on how she's doing."

"And she'd keep the records in the computer," I said. "It's by far the safest place. I doubt anyone on the island knows how to operate it." I paused, then smiled at him. "Except you."

He smiled, too; it wasn't a pleasant expression.

"Unfortunately Angela's almost always in her office," I went on. "She sleeps in the room next door, and now that Tin Choy Won's sick down there, she's constantly within earshot of him, in case he needs anything."

"There must be some way to get her away from there. I wouldn't need long."

"How about if you set something up with Neal? Have him demand a conference with her. He could say he wanted to go over the accounts before you meet with them."

"Good idea. I'll talk with him and then meet you downstairs in half an hour."

The computer's screen glowed eerily in the darkened office. I'd decided we shouldn't chance having an electric light shine under the closed door, so Sam had turned the machine on and was rummaging through a file of disks, holding each up to the screen's light to examine its label. The disks looked like smaller versions of the still-jacketed forty-five records of my teenage years, and on each one's label an identifying phrase was lightly written in what I recognized as Angela's angular, slanting hand.

I said, "Anything yet?"

"No. It's all very curious. The file names on these disks are idiosyncratic at best. I can't imagine what the hell she's using them for. I'll have to try . . . hello!"

"Is that it?"

"Possibly." He slipped a disk into the unit under the screen, then tapped on the keyboard next to it. I watched as green letters and numbers appeared against the darker background.

I don't feel comfortable with computers; they make me twitchy. For one thing, I don't believe that something as small as a silicon chip can be the life force behind what appears to be a semihuman entity. I prefer to think—as people used to about cameras—that some disembodied and probably malign spirit inhabits them. Sometimes this spirit is deceptively friendly and lets man use it to his benefit. But when its baser impulses move it, it can rise up and swallow man's accumulated store of knowledge. My technically oriented friends tell me this is a ridiculous attitude, and I suspect they're right. Underneath I guess it's merely my convenient excuse for not learning what might be a difficult new skill. I can't even type properly; Lord knows what havoc I might wreak with a computer!

Finally the screen showed what looked like a table of contents, a list of words or abbreviations, none of which appeared to be more than eight characters long. I read: std.ltr, xmas.cds, b.days—

"Shit!" Sam hit something on the keyboard and the listing disappeared. "It's personal stuff—her Christmas card list, for one." He removed the disk, filed it, and selected another. "That's what she's doing with the computer my brother paid for, for Chrissake! Granted, it's not the most costly on the market, but it set Neal back a couple of thousand anyway. And she didn't need it to begin with; anyone could have fucked up this project the way she has with the aid of a quill pen—"

"Calm," I said.

He grinned sheepishly, inserted the disk in the machine, and pressed two keys. The listing that appeared this time seemed more in line with what we were looking for.

"Recs," I said.

"Receivables, probably."

"Advs?"

"Probably money advanced to the principals. Angela's salary, for instance."

"Util. Utilities."

"Right. But this is odd."

"What?"

"The natural place for the payables file is on the disk with these others, but I don't see it."

"Maybe she labeled it differently."

"Maybe." He studied the screen intently. "I *do* see two files that puzzle me: 'reg.' and 'abacus.' "

"Abacus. That's the board with beads on it that the Chinese use in lieu of a cash register. Reg . . . oh!"

"You may have it!" Sam tapped a key and a line moved down the list and highlighted the letters *reg.* in a block.

"Register . . . regular . . . something like that," I said. "It could designate the real accounts payable. And abacus could be the accounting of what she's been embezzling. You know, the first time I came in here, she made a joke about an abacus. I thought it was an ethnic reference, but—"

"I think you're right. When we were in grad school, there was a Chinese restaurant we'd go to. The owner used an abacus, and Angela used to laugh about it and say the abacus was a device the Chinese used to cheat the Anglo customer. It all fits."

"Stupid of her to use something you could figure out."

"Well, she probably never thought anyone— much less me— would get into these files. I'm going to retrieve both and print them out. I need to go over them pretty carefully before we confront her."

"But you're as certain as I am about what she's been doing, aren't you?"

He looked up at me, his face sad and vulnerable in the green glow. His earlier anger had passed and had left only a tired resignation.

I put my hand on his shoulder and squeezed it. He pulled his lips back in a poor imitation of a smile and turned to the keyboard.

20

When Sam had printed out the contents of the two files, he took them upstairs to his room. The door to the room Tin Choy Won was occupying was shut, but not locked. I decided to look in on him.

As before, the old man lay quietly in the bed next to the only window. A night-light burned in a socket on the baseboard to his left. Its feeble rays highlighted the bed's four spindly posts and made them cast deformed shadows on the wall. Beyond the heavy woven curtains I could hear the wind gusting and shrubbery scraping the glass—a nerve-tingling sound not unlike tiny fingers scratching on a blackboard. The room was cold, and a draft tickled the curtains.

I went over and looked down at Mr. Won. He lay on his back, arms at his sides, covers pulled to his chin. His face was waxen and still, his body formally posed like one in a funeral parlor. But his chest moved fitfully up and down. Each breath was raspy and labored.

I put my hand to his forehead and felt the fever burning in his frail body. I wanted to take his pulse, but was afraid that unticking the covers might disturb his much-needed rest. The bottle of pills I'd given Angela stood on the nightstand. I picked it up and held it to the light; there were only two capsules left. When I set it down I felt the icy air coming from behind the curtains. A sick man should not be sleeping so close to that window, especially since the storm would only get worse.

I bent down and looked at the legs of the bed. Although it was old, it had been modified with casters. The floor was hardwood, and I thought that I could move the four-poster to a warmer corner of the room without waking Tin Choy Won. I went to the end closest to the window and gave it an experimental shove. It slid easily.

Before I moved the bed, I went around the room and found the warmest place, to the right of the door. Then I went back to the four-poster and pushed it slowly. Tin Choy Won groaned once in mild protest, then lapsed back into sleep.

After the bed was in place, I went to the closet, looking for an extra blanket. There was none, but a heavy popcorn-stitch bedspread, folded three times, provided the right thickness. I draped it over Mr. Won, then smoothed the sheets under his chin. One of his pillows—in a case with little red tulips all over it—had fallen to the floor as I'd moved the bed; I picked it up, but left it on the foot of the mattress rather than attempting to slide it back under his head. He seemed to be resting comfortably, and I didn't want to disturb him now.

For a moment I stood looking down at him, wondering what had brought him to the island on Saturday night. Then I thought of our conversation earlier that day, and of how I'd told him one of the reasons I'd come to the Delta was because my sister was worried about the arrival of Neal's brother, the financial expert. Mr. Won had probably come here to make sure Angela had family at her side if Sam uncovered the wrongdoing that even he, her uneducated grandfather, had already detected. Angela had said Tin Choy Won was being "Chinese" and "overprotective." What he had actually been doing was offering love and support. What he had gotten for his pains was probably pneumonia.

I watched the old man sleep a while longer, willing him to continue his labored breathing until we could get him medical attention. And pitying him because, once his health was restored, there would be even greater pain for him to face. I'd witnessed Sam Oliver's anger; I had no doubt that Tin Choy Won's granddaughter was going to be prosecuted for her embezzlement.

I was in the second-floor hallway on my way to my room when I heard hammering coming from its opposite end. I followed the noise to where Denny was nailing a big piece of plywood over a broken window in one of the unoccupied guest rooms.

"What happened?" I asked.

Denny swung the hammer, hitting the nail head with grace and accuracy. In spite of his controlled movements, I felt an anger coming from him that was confirmed when he spoke. "Fucking branch from that cypress tree outside whacked the glass. I've been telling Neal for weeks that we should get the trees trimmed back. But would he listen? No way. 'Angela says there isn't any money in the budget for that.'" His tone was a cruel parody of Neal's whining. "Well, fuck Angela, and fuck him, too. I'm sick and tired of not being listened to."

I couldn't think of anything to say, so I stood and watched him until the plywood was in place. When he turned, I asked, "Did you and Stephanie get the ferry back to the landing?"

"Yes. Like she said, there was a hand winch. She also pointed out that we ought to put the skiff back in the boathouse, so we wouldn't lose *that*, too. So we did, and then we came back here, and now I'm trying to keep this house from coming apart."

As if to emphasize Denny's fears, a gust of wind wailed outside and there was a groaning and tearing from somewhere high above. Something fell past the room's other, unbroken window, and smashed on the ground below.

"What was that?" I said.

Denny stood listening. The wind wailed again, but nothing else fell. "Slate," he said, "from the roof. Another thing I told them to take care of. But what do I know, huh?"

What could I say? I just patted him on the arm and went down the hall to my room. The corridor was icy cold, and as I passed the stairway to the third floor I could hear the wind whistling up there. A couple of the third-floor windows were already broken; I knew that from the tour Denny had given Sam and me. And, as evidenced by the falling slate, the mansard roof wasn't completely intact, either. Denny had his work cut out for him.

The first thing I saw when I went into my room was the doll I'd brought down from the junk room. It was lying on the window seat where I'd left it, and above it the panes of glass formed black mirrors, reflecting me as I stood in the doorway. Although it was only a little before five, it was full dark. I went over there and knelt on the seat, trying to see outside. When I cupped my hands around my eyes and leaned so my nose pressed against the glass, I could make out the shapes of the cypress and corner palm tree, swaying wildly against the sky. Light from the lower windows shone on part of the lawn, and already it was littered with branches and fronds. The cars and truck and van that stood in the driveway looked forlorn in the onslaught. I stared at my MG, wishing it were home in my garage, and that I were in front of my own fireplace, a glass of cheap red wine and a paperback in hand.

Another gust of wind, more violent than the earlier ones, rattled the panes in front of me. I recoiled from the cold, hugging myself and rubbing my arms for warmth. Then I went to the wardrobe and changed into a heavy turtleneck and my fisherman's sweater, took off my boots, and crawled into bed. I propped myself against the pillows, pulled the covers up over my shoulders, and began to think about what I'd discovered that day.

Sam's computer expertise, coupled with his personal knowledge of Angela, had helped me get to the bottom of one of the things going on here on the island. I should be pleased with that, but there was still so much more that didn't make sense. Angela's embezzlement seemed unrelated to the matter of the hanged doll and the "hermit," or the roaches. Why would she want to drive everyone away when she stood to profit by their continued spending? I also doubted it had anything to do with the loss of the canoes; she hadn't authorized the purchase of any more of them—which would have been the logical move had she cut them free. And Max's death? Well, I didn't like Angela, but I didn't see her as a murderer.

I'd had experience with embezzlers before. I've known plenty of white-collar criminals. They seldom kill, even when cornered. It's not that they're more moral than armed robbers or drug pushers; it has nothing to do with being a better class of criminal. But they *are* brighter and play the odds better. They know that respectable-looking people with MBAs rarely serve long sentences for their crimes. If they're at all clever, they get time off for good behavior. Later they write books and end up on TV talk shows.

All right, I thought, you're effectively eliminating Angela from involvement in anything other than embezzlement. But you are fairly certain now that these other things have been perpetrated by an insider. Think about the others.

Denny. He's got potential for violence. The order restraining him from having contact with his former wife proves that. He doesn't like

Neal much, is angry at him for not listening to his recommendations. But Denny needs this job; he wanted to get out of the city; he goes where the money is. And annoyance with an employer is pretty slim motivation for sabotaging his project, anyhow. Unless he's crazy. . . . No, he's peculiar, like everyone here, but not crazy.

Stephanie. Wish I knew more about her. She's cynical, seems mildly depressed a lot of the time. Came here to get away from Seattle, much like Denny. Knows boats, seems to love working with them. Would she destroy what she considered to be practically her own boats? Doubtful. But what was it Denny said to her when she was railing at him about the ferry? Something to the effect that Max didn't trust her. In what way? Because she's a woman, and to Max, women shouldn't be working around boats? Remember to ask Denny.

Neal. On the surface, sabotaging his own life's dream seems totally illogical. Insane. But think about him. *Does* he behave in a logical manner? *Is* he sane? No to the first question. And the other? I just don't know.

Evans. Now there's an odd one. So friendly and boyish. Patsy's got complete faith in him, but she's been fooled before. And Neal—his supposed friend—seems to feel Evans has treated him badly in the past, relishes making him "toe the line" now, if he wants to go on with his "game." The cooking game, as Neal said? No, now that I think of it, when Neal told me that it sounded as if he were covering, because he'd said too much already. Wish I knew what was going on there. . . .

Now here's the tough one: Patsy. My own sister. I should know her, but we've seen so little of each other in recent years, and I haven't lived with her since I left home to go to college. And she's changed drastically since her earth-mother days. Gotten brittle and nervous. Why? Evans, probably. Or this place—it would give anyone a case of nerves. But could it be something more?

I hugged the covers closer around me, feeling a flood of guilt at even briefly considering my little sister for the role of murderer. But at the same time memories came back from our childhood: her standoffishness, her single-mindedness, her concern with what *she* wanted—and never mind the rest of us. And there were also impressions from our adulthood: her fierce insistence on independence, at the expense of Ma and Pa's feelings. Her belief that her kids came first, even if it infringed on the rights of others. If Patsy saw a way to secure a future for herself and her kids, would she allow anyone to stop her?

I didn't know.

But I also didn't know how driving Neal off the island, driving everyone away, would benefit any of the people here. The intent was so obvious, the motive so obscure.

There was a tap at the door. I called out and Sam entered. He held the computer printout, and his eyes were even sadder than before. He said, "I've seen enough of this. You ready to go downstairs?"

I pushed the covers back and swung my feet to the floor, reaching for my boots. "I take it what I suspected is true."

"I've got enough evidence here for any court to convict her."

I slipped my feet into the boots and stood. Sam's arms hung limply at his sides. His face was etched with fine lines of weariness.

I said, "You don't have to confront her like this, Sam. Do it privately. Tell her you know what she's been doing and ask her to give back the money and just leave."

"I can't."

"Why not?"

"There's an implicit contract between friends. Denny was talking about it a couple of nights ago when he and I got into the brandy—"

"I know; we've discussed it, too."

"I'd never put a name to it, but I realized it's the basis on which I've always operated. Now Angela's violated that contract. I have no more obligation to her."

I didn't pursue it. I knew what it was like to have my faith in an individual irreparably breached, and I remembered I'd reacted in much the same way as Sam. Silently I followed him downstairs.

When we entered the library, Angela was leaning against the wall next to the French doors, her arms folded across her breasts, her lips pursed in annoyance. The jeans and black hip-length sweater she wore accentuated her height, and in the light from the lamps, her skin took on a cadaverous cast. Next to her, water still seeped through the crack at the top of the doors; someone had stuffed a towel on the floor at their bottom, but it was soaked and a puddle was forming on the hardwood. Outside the wind battered at the mansion; the cypress trees beyond the doors creaked under its force, and their branches scraped at the wall. Neal sat at the desk, sheets of printout spread in front of him. He was tracing a line under an item with his forefinger and frowning in concentration.

Angela noticed us, dismissed me with a contemptuous glance, and said to Sam, "Thank God you're here! I've been going over these accounts with him for more than an hour, and he still can't seem to understand the difference between a debit and a credit."

Neal didn't say anything, but the hand that had been doing the tracing flexed convulsively. I half expected him to flare up at her, but I guessed his subdued behavior was both because he had been acting the dunce to keep her there, and because he was finally realizing how bad the project's financial position was.

Sam didn't say anything either, just went over to the desk and looked down at the printout. Angela's eyes flicked from his face to the similar papers in his hand, and she bit her lip and became very still. I sat down in one of the big leather chairs, unwilling to participate, except as an observer. I may have been the one who had caught Angela out, but dealing with her now was Sam and Neal's prerogative.

After a moment Sam looked up at Angela and said, "Abacus." There was no mistaking the hardness of his tone, nor the anger he was struggling to contain. Neal heard it, and flinched. Angela stiffened.

"Abacus," Sam said again. "Why not plain accounts payable?"

"It's just a label, Sam," she said.

"Uh-huh. And 'reg' is just a label, too. Right?" He held up the sheets he carried so she could see what they were.

She bit her lip again, harder, and waited.

"Well, Angela, do you want to tell us about 'abacus' and 'reg'?"

"I wasn't aware you were in the habit of snooping through other people's private files."

"These are *not* private files. They're records pertaining to this business venture; receivables, advances, payables. Only there are two sets of payables. Care to explain why that is?"

She turned abruptly and looked out the doors beside her. The wind rattled their panes and even where I sat, halfway across the room, I could feel a frigid draft.

Neal said, "Sam, what are you talking about?"

"I'm talking about Angela maintaining two sets of books. They show the suppliers of the goods you've been purchasing. In some cases the names are the same, in others they're not so different that you'd notice if you weren't the person doing the actual ordering. The amounts paid out are much higher in one set of accounts—the ones she's been showing to you."

"But . . ." Neal swiveled and looked at Angela. She stood with her back rigid, staring out into the black nothingness beyond the door. "But I see the invoices themselves, and they've always been initialed by the person who placed the order."

"You see fake invoices, fake initials."

It took a few seconds for Neal to absorb what his brother was telling him. He looked down at the printout in front of him. "But what's this about an abacus?"

"See the code word at the top of the sheet? It's a not-so-funny private joke between Angela and herself. Too bad one of the few people who would understand it accessed these files."

Spots of color appeared on Neal's cheeks. His mouth worked, and he made a couple of unintelligible sounds. Then he pushed the desk chair back, stood up, and grabbed Angela by the upper arm. She tried to pull away, and he spun her around and slammed her up against the wall. At the impact, fear came into her eyes. Sam did nothing to stop his brother.

Neal's voice came out high-pitched and breathy. "Is he right, you bitch? Is he right about what you've been doing to me?"

Now Angela was the speechless one. She glanced frantically at Sam, but he just looked away.

"Answer me!" Neal shook her furiously. She pushed at him, but he hung on.

I was halfway out of my chair, about to intervene, when Angela broke his hold and shoved him so hard he fell backward against the desk. "Keep your filthy paws off me, you goddamned . . . eunuch!"

Neal struggled to steady himself, his mouth dropping open.

"That's right," Angela said. "Don't think I don't know about you. You're a weak, impotent, helpless little eunuch. You can't do *anything*!"

Sam moved then, around the desk, and took Neal's arm. He guided him to the chair and sat him down. Neal was wheezing; I was afraid he would have some kind of attack.

Sam turned to Angela and said, "We're not discussing anyone's sexuality here. What we're talking about is embezzlement."

The legal term, out in the open for the first time, seemed to quell Angela's rage. She put her fingers to her mouth and held them there. Behind Sam, Neal still breathed hard, but with more control.

After about thirty seconds she said, "Sam, I didn't mean—"

"Didn't mean what? To call my brother a eunuch? Or are you claiming you siphoned off those funds by mistake?"

"Sam—"

"I'm going to have you prosecuted for this. If the phone line wasn't out and the sheriff's men weren't busy with more vital concerns, I'd have your ass hauled off to jail tonight."

"Sam, no." She stepped toward him and put her hand out, but he knocked it away—hard. She backed up again, rubbing her knuckles. "Sam, you don't want to do this to me. We've been friends too long. I'll repay the money, every penny of it—"

"We were friends. *Were.*"

She turned her back and started for the door, but Sam was quicker, blocking her. He said, "Where do you think you're going?"

"Downstairs. My grandfather—"

"It won't do you any good to try to destroy those files. I have the printout, and I've also taken the disks."

For a moment I thought she was going to hurl herself at him and rake his face with those long purple nails. Then she shuddered and got herself under control. "My God," she said, her voice breaking falsely, "what do you think I am?"

"I know what you are. And it disgusts me."

She looked around desperately. Then she started for the French doors. I rose and went after her.

And then the lights dimmed. Flared up again, brighter than before. Flickered at that high intensity for a few seconds. And went out.

21

The silence in the room was as total as the darkness.

Then Sam said, "What the hell . . . ?" Neal groaned. And Angela bolted.

I could hear her fumbling at the doors. I followed the sound, bumped into her, and pinned her arms behind her back.

"Stop it, damn you!" she said. "I've got to get out of here! My grandfather's alone down there."

I held on to her. "The lack of light won't bother him. He was sleeping soundly when I looked in about an hour ago."

She struggled against me. "You looked in on him? I told you—"

"Shut up!" Sam said.

Neal groaned again.

I had to admire Angela's nerve. Even now—unmasked as an embezzler and rejected by her only friend here—she was still on the attack. At Sam's words, though, she quieted and stopped trying to pull away from me, but her stance told me she was only waiting for the opportunity to slip from my grasp. I pinned her arms harder, and had the petty satisfaction of hearing her grunt in pain.

Sam said, "Neal, where're the flashlights?"

"I don't know. There're some candles in one of the drawers, though. Under the maritime history collection."

"Where's that?"

"Second section of shelves from the door."

"Okay, I'll get them." Sam began to move slowly. I heard him bump into something—probably the chair I'd been sitting in earlier—

and then a drawer slid open and he said, "Here they are. Anybody got a match?"

Silence.

"Shit."

Neal said, "There might be some in the desk." Another drawer slid open, and his fingers made scrabbling sounds inside it.

Angela stood so still I was scarcely aware of her breathing. Sam moved across the room again, toward the desk. The blackness was total; I couldn't detect any outlines, shapes, or shadows. And the lack of them told me how truly black it was outside—all over the island, maybe all over the Delta. I shivered, and felt a similar tremor in Angela's body.

"I've got some matches," Neal said.

"Give them to me." I heard Sam set the candle on the desk, and in a moment light flickered, then caught and flared more steadily. Sam positioned a thick red candle in an ashtray in the center of the blotter. Immediately I caught the faint scent of bayberry, like a memory of Christmas past.

As the flame burned higher, I looked around. We made a strange tableau. Angela stood with her head bent; some of her hair had pulled loose from its high-piled arrangement, and the strands straggled down the nape of her neck, making her look deceptively vulnerable. Neal had slumped back into the desk chair. Sam leaned stiff-armed on the desk.

After a few seconds Angela raised her head and said, "Sharon, do you mind?"

I glanced at Sam.

He shrugged. "Let her go. She's not leaving the island in this storm."

I relinquished my hold. She moved away, toward the chair I'd formerly occupied, rubbing her upper arms and scowling.

Since the lights had gone out, the mansion had been abnormally quiet. Now I began to hear sporadic sounds: running footsteps, a child's wail, adults banging into things and cursing. The library door opened, and Denny stood there, a flashlight in either hand.

"Hi, guys," he said.

Sam smiled grimly and went to get one of the lights. "I'm glad you knew where these were kept."

"The hell I did! I got lucky when I looked in the pantry."

"Thought they were your department."

"I bought them, but that doesn't mean I knew where anybody'd *put* them."

"Well, now what? Can you get the auxiliary generator going?"

"Maybe, but I'll need some help." Denny looked at me.

I said, "I think I'd better stay here with Angela."

Denny's expression grew puzzled, but before he could ask why, Sam said, "I'll help you. You want to come too, Neal?"

"Sure." He sounded as if he only half meant it.

The three of them left the library. I turned to Angela. She was still sitting in the big leather chair, legs crossed, swinging one foot nervously. Her long fingernails bit into the chair's arms.

I said, "We should go check on your grandfather."

Her eyes narrowed and she opened her mouth to retort. Then she seemed to think better of it. After bit she said, "Yes. All right," and stood up.

I picked up the candle, spilling a drop of hot wax on my hand, and kept close behind her. I wasn't really worried that she would try to get away from me, and it didn't particularly matter if she did. As Sam had said, Angela wasn't going anyplace—at least not anyplace she wanted to go—for a long time.

We went through the deserted living room. The wind gusted down the chimney and blew ashes from the grate; the rain sheeted against the windows. In the reception area, the light from the candle bounced off the prisms of the chandelier and reflected in thousands of tiny flickers off the silver fleurs-de-lys of the wallpaper. Angela led the way down the stairs and into the lower hallway, her footing sure in spite of the scant visibility.

From the far end of the hall I could hear a child—possibly Jessamyn—crying in a monotonous rhythm that quickly rasped at my nerves. The wind howled around the mansion. It battered the doors in the barroom, as if it would rip them from their hinges. The child's cries escalated into screams, and then Patsy's voice shouted, "Shut up, damn you!" and there was the sound of a slap.

I stopped. It wasn't any of my business—or was it?

Silence. Then Patsy said, "Oh God, I'm sorry!" and started to cry.

Over her sobs I heard Andrew say, "It's all right, Mom. I'll find the flashlight, and everything'll be all right."

My nephew, I thought, forced into the role of man of the family once more. Where was Evans, when they needed him?

Angela had stopped too, and was looking at me. I half expected her to make a caustic remark about how tacky my sister was acting, but she only said, "Do you want to go down there?"

"No, they're dealing with it."

She nodded and moved toward the room where Tin Choy Won was. As she looked inside, she gasped and said, "Where is he?"

I realized she didn't know I'd moved his bed. "To the left of the door. When I checked on him, it seemed too cold under the window, so I pushed the bed to where it was warmer."

She looked at me, her eyes shiny and unreadable in the candlelight. Then she turned toward the bed. And stopped.

I said, "What's wrong?"

Her hand gripped my forearm. The fingers were like metal clamps, and her nails pressed clear through my heavy sweater.

"Angela—"

"Look at him!"

I moved around her and held the candle higher. Tin Choy Won lay on his back as before, but his covers were disarranged, the bedspread I'd placed there half on the floor, and his arms were flung out wide on top of them. His head was turned to the side, and trickles of spittle traced paths along his cheeks and chin. He was very still.

I disentangled myself from Angela's grip and handed her the candle. When she took a couple of steps backward, I said, "Follow me! I need to see."

I bent over the bed and looked closely at the old man. His skin had a bluish tinge. I reached for his wrist and tried to find a pulse, then put my fingers on his neck and felt for the artery. His flesh was still warm, but the blood no longer coursed through his body.

Behind me Angela seemed frozen. The candle flame fluttered in the draft from the window.

I pulled back my hand and straightened, staring at Tin Choy Won. How had it happened? A stroke? A fit of choking as he drowned in the fluids that build up when one has contracted pneumonia? The man had been old and weak. He should have received medical attention.

And while we had argued about money in the library, he had lived out the last moments of his life down here—alone and helpless.

I reached for the sheet and pulled it over his face, then turned to Angela. "I'm sorry."

She stared at me, her eyes as black and unreadable as before. Then she blinked and a tear slid down either cheek. The hand in which she held the candle wavered, and hot wax spattered to the floor. I took the candle away from her and cupped my hand around the guttering flame, shielding it from the draft until it burned strongly again.

Angela turned away and pressed her forehead against the door-jamb, crying silently. I didn't offer any comfort; it wouldn't have been accepted. I was about to suggest we go upstairs when I saw the pillow on the floor next to the bed.

I glanced at the foot of the mattress where I'd previously left the fallen pillow. It was gone. This one resembled it—in a case printed with tiny red tulips. I stooped to pick it up and examined it more closely. The side that had been turned to the floor was creased and indented. In the middle of the indentation was a wet spot—one that might have been left by the same spittle that stained Tin Choy Won's face.

I stared at the pillow. Then looked at the covered body of Mr. Won. Who? I thought. How long ago? And why?

A coldness that had nothing to do with the rain or the wind or the draft began to crawl over me. I continued to look at the covered form on the bed while I struggled to remain calm. For many years I'd hyperventilated when confronted with the victims of violent death. I didn't do that anymore, but I'd never become indifferent. My impulse now—because I was keyed up by the storm and the darkness and the earlier ugly scene with Angela—was to shriek or hurl the candle across the room. But I couldn't do any of those things. They would panic Angela, and her fear would infect everyone she came in contact with.

Everyone, that was, except the murderer of Max Shorkey and now Tin Choy Won.

22

My next thought was that it was Angela who had killed her grandfather. After all, when I'd visited him at his house in Locke, he'd said, "I think she's trying to kill me." Right away he'd made it out to be a joke, but there might have been some element of truth—of *fear*—in the statement. Besides, he'd known of her embezzlement, had come here uninvited and unwelcome, and they'd quarreled.

But if she'd done it, why had she waited so long? She'd had multiple opportunities since he'd arrived on the island. He could have supposedly passed away in the middle of last night; she could have removed all traces of evidence and summoned the doctor; by the time most of the others had risen, Tin Choy Won's body could have been on the way to the mortuary. Why would she have chosen to do it in such a hasty, clumsy way?

But she *couldn't* have killed him. She'd been closeted in the library with Neal since before Sam and I came down here to use the computer, and Mr. Won had been alive when I'd looked in on him after we'd finished in the office.

It was now clear to me that we'd unintentionally provided the murderer with his opportunity with our scheme to keep Angela away from the lower level, and I deeply regretted that. Until then she'd stayed close by Tin Choy Won's side in case he needed something. Someone had waited until Sam and I had gone upstairs, then slipped in here. . . .

But why? Because Mr. Won knew something more than just about the embezzling? Because he'd seen something while he was here? It seemed unlikely; he'd had very little contact with anyone except Angela.

Angela. Was I *sure* she'd been in the library the whole time? For that matter, I couldn't be certain about Neal, either. And Sam? I didn't know for a fact that he'd been in his room from the time he went upstairs until we confronted Angela.

Stop it, I told myself. You can drive yourself crazy with that kind of speculation. Next thing you know, you'll be suspecting one of the kids.

The one thing I did know was that I ought to get Angela out of that room. I set the pillow on the foot of the bed again, and went to her, putting a hand on her elbow.

"Let's go upstairs. I'll get you a brandy—"

"I don't want a drink."

"Well, coffee, then. The stove is gas; it'll still be working. I'll make some coffee—"

She wrenched from my touch. "I don't want *anything!*"

"Well, at least come upstairs."

"Stop treating me like a child!"

I sighed. Even now, she wouldn't unbend. "I didn't mean to be patronizing. But I'm going upstairs, and I'm taking the candle with me."

I thought she was going to insist on staying here with her grandfather's corpse, but then she said, "Have it your way," and moved toward the door.

I shut it securely behind us and followed her down the hall to the stairway. Everything was quiet in my sister's quarters now. The only sounds were the wind and the rain. Then, upstairs, I heard voices. When we arrived in the reception area, I saw Denny, Sam, and Neal in the living room. Their flashlights were positioned on a coffee table to give maximum light; the beams made their shadows unrecognizable and grotesque. Stephanie knelt on the floor in front of the fireplace, trying to get the flames started.

I said softly to Angela, "Don't say anything about your grandfather just yet. I want to do it when I'm sure none of the kids are around, and in a way so no one will panic."

A line of bewilderment etched itself between her brows. "Why would they panic? He died. People do that all the time."

If I hadn't witnessed her earlier tears, I would have thought her callous. "Some people might react badly to being trapped in a house with a dead body." To say nothing of a *murdered* dead body, I thought. That was a fact I was telling no one.

"Oh. I see." Perhaps she saw too much; I wasn't sure she hadn't begun to suspect her grandfather's death was from something other than natural causes. As we moved into the room, her expression became distracted, as if she were thinking back to the death scene, remembering everything that had been said and done.

Everyone looked toward us as we came in. I asked, "What happened with the generator?"

"Flat out fuckin' nothing," Denny said.

"It won't start?"

"Nope. It's a hunk of junk that should have been replaced right away. But would anyone listen to me?"

There wasn't time to get off on that subject now. "So what do you suggest we do?"

"We make a fire and hope the sheriff's launch comes back soon."

Stephanie stood, dusting her hands on her jeans. Behind her the fire began to flare. "Don't count on that," she said. "I was listening to the radio a while ago. There's a bridge out near Rio Vista, and a big pileup on the levee road near Isleton. They're not gonna come back for us when they've got things like that to contend with."

Denny sighed heavily. Neal began his hand-wringing routine. Sam was watching him—carefully.

I said, "Where are the others?"

"In the kitchen," Stephanie said. "At least, I heard the kids' voices out there a few minutes ago."

"We need to hold a conference—of the adults only. The kids will have to . . ." I hesitated. I'd been about to say they should go downstairs to their quarters, but I didn't want to chance them finding Tin Choy Won's body. On the other hand, little ears were capable of hearing all sorts of things they weren't supposed to. "They can go upstairs to my room," I finished. "The novelty of it should keep them occupied."

The others looked puzzled at the need for getting the kids so far out of the way, but no one questioned me.

I left them and went to the kitchen. Evans, Patsy, and the kids were seated around the table. The candelabra from the dining room burned on it, and the kids were having milk and cheese and crackers. Evans and Patsy clutched big glasses of red wine. From the clutter on the counters, I guessed preparations for dinner had been under way when the electricity went out.

Patsy raised her glass to me. "Nice weather we're having. I bet you're sorry I got you into this."

I was, but like Denny's lament, this wasn't the time to go into it. "The adults are having a conference in the living room," I said with more of an edge to my voice than I'd intended. "We can't get the generator going, and we need to discuss how to handle the emergency."

Evans stood up immediately. "Okay," he said to the kids, "you guys stay here and finish eating. And don't touch those candles."

I said, "I'd rather they took their snack upstairs, to my room."

Patsy said, "It's cold and dark up there."

"It's cold here, too. They can take a light."

"I won't have them carrying lighted candles around."

The kids were watching us curiously. Andrew's lips were about to form a question. "There are extra flashlights in the pantry." I went in there and, by the light of the candle I still carried, found a few flashes in an open drawer. I took the largest and gave it to Andrew.

"You're in charge," I told him. "We'll call you when we want you to come back down."

Oddly enough, he didn't meet my eyes, just herded his sisters from the room. As the door swung shut, Kelley said, "Just 'cause you've got the flashlight doesn't mean you're any big deal." Jessamyn contented herself with adopting her sister's favorite epithet and calling him a "poop."

As soon as they were out of earshot, Patsy turned angrily to me. "Look, I don't like you telling my kids what to do."

Her prickly independence had started to wear on me. Also, I had begun to doubt its authenticity. When it suited my sister, she played the archetypal strong woman; when things got rough she leaned on whoever was handy—including her young son. "Shut up," I said. "This is an emergency, and we don't have time to bicker over lines of parental authority."

"Sharon!"

"Go into the living room."

"Now wait a minute—" Evans began.

"The others are waiting, dammit."

They looked indecisively at each other, then went. I snuffed out the candles and followed. In the living room Patsy and Evans took seats on the periphery of the group by the fireplace. I stood with my back to the flames, taking perverse pleasure in getting the lion's share of the warmth. The faces that confronted me were all tense, except for Angela's. She seemed to have drifted away, possibly was in shock.

Rain drummed against the high windows, and the cypress branches thumped against the outer wall. There was a loud cracking sound, and Denny said, "Tree limb, probably from the big sycamore. It's half rotten, I wouldn't be surprised if we lose it. Plus a whole lot of the ones in the old orchard."

No one seemed to want to comment on that, so after a bit I said, "We have another problem in addition to the storm. Angela's grandfather has died."

A murmur went up, and they all looked at her. Angela stared into the distance, not acknowledging the attention.

"I don't think the children should know about this," I went on. "Is there a key to that room?"

Patsy cleared her throat before she spoke. "I think the same one works all the doors down there. It's on a ring in the pantry."

"Good. After we're done here, will you see the door is locked?"

"Of course." Her glance apologized for her earlier harsh words. I smiled faintly in return.

"Now," I said, "it's fairly obvious that the sheriff's launch won't be back for us—"

"Why?" Evans asked.

Stephanie repeated what she had told us earlier. Evans's mouth tightened and he put his arm around Patsy, rubbing her shoulder as if to warm her. She patted his hand, but kept her eyes on me.

"Since that's the case," I said, "I think we should assign different people to look after different things until the storm is over."

Neal stood up. His fists were clenched, his face contorted with rage. "Who told you you could make these decisions?" he demanded. "You're not in charge here. This is my island—"

"Sit down, Neal," Sam said.

Neal glared at him. "I'm not going to back off and let her run my show—"

"*Sit down!*"

Neal sat, still glaring at his brother.

I said, "Actually, I think Denny should take over from here on out. He's the one who's made most of the preparations for an emergency." It was another of those decisions that depended on my gut-level instincts. I hoped to God they were correct.

Denny looked around the room at the others. Sam and Stephanie nodded encouragingly. Patsy and Evans also nodded, a beat later. Neal looked down, clenching and unclenching his fists. Angela remained in her private world. Finally Denny pushed up from his chair and took my place in front of the fire. I moved to a hassock a couple of feet away.

Denny proved to be a calm, capable leader. Immediately he suggested that I should provide security and call on either Sam or Stephanie or himself if I needed backup. To my relief, no one questioned why we needed security. It wouldn't do for them to panic, thinking of a killer prowling the island—much less a killer sitting in our midst.

Repairs to any damage the storm might do the mansion, Denny went on, would be best handled by Stephanie, Sam, and himself. Would Neal tend the fire and make sure matches and candles and medical supplies were on hand? Yes, Neal said after a moment, he would.

"We should try to use candles as much as possible, to conserve the flashlight batteries," Denny said, "and also not use up too much wood. Why don't you gather up all the blankets and quilts and pillows and bring them down here? There's no point in us freezing in separate rooms when we can keep each other warm in front of the fire."

Neal nodded, and I silently commended Denny for the idea. It suited my purposes, but for a different reason: I wanted them all together, where I could keep an eye on them.

Denny went on, "Evans, of course, will be responsible for the food. Keep it simple, and don't use the stove; I'm not sure about the gas lines, and we don't want to risk an explosion. Patsy, you can help him when you're not looking after those kids. Give us lots of food and coffee. No booze."

Patsy looked at her unfinished glass of wine, then set it on the table beside her. Evans did the same.

Denny glanced at Angela, concern in his eyes.

Sam said quickly, "Angela's had a shock. I don't think we can expect her to do anything—at least not right away."

Angela didn't so much as twitch an eyelid.

"Okay," Denny said, "is everybody clear on what they're to do?"

There were assorted murmurs.

"Good. Let's ride this one out and show the sheriff's deputy we're not citified fools after all."

Evans and Stephanie clapped, and I had the absurd sensation that we were football players coming out of the huddle.

The group dispersed quickly. Denny and Stephanie went to the third floor where, she said, there was a leak in the roof that needed immediate attention. Neal went to gather the bedclothes. Patsy said she would lock the room where Tin Choy Won's body lay and then bring the kids down from my room. Evans hurried off to the kitchen. I watched as Sam went over to Angela's chair and knelt down, speaking reassuringly to her. She gave no response. He took her hands in his, kneaded them, and continued talking. After a moment she tipped her head forward and began to cry.

I left them and went to the pantry for a flashlight. Denny's enormous slicker was hanging from a peg; I put it on and went out into the gale to get my gun from the MG. When I tried to close the heavy front door the wind almost tore it from my grasp. I had to pull with both hands to get it shut. The rain stung my face, and I could barely make out the vehicles parked along the drive. The asphalt was buried under mud and branches; I had difficulty walking in the icy wind. A VW van belonging to Evans and my sister rocked back and forth and I was afraid it might be blown over. The MG looked all right, though. Or at least I thought it did, until I saw the broken wing window on the passenger's side.

I rushed over there, bent down, looked in. When I touched the door handle, I realized it wasn't fully latched. And the door to the glove box lay on the seat, pried off its hinges. The compartment's contents were scattered on the floor—all of them except for one thing.

The .38 was gone.

I stood beside the car, heedless of the torrential rain. The wind slammed into me so hard I almost staggered, but still I stared along the flashlight's beam at the violated glove box.

It was the murderer who had broken in there and taken the gun. I was sure of that. But how had he or she known the .38 was there? Even my sister wasn't aware of my practice of keeping the gun in the car. And I'd been careful to conceal it while it had been on my person that morning.

Quickly I thought over my movements since I'd taken the gun from the car. It was possible the person I'd surprised in the library had doubled back and watched me fetch it, but I somewhat doubted that. He'd probably put as much distance between us as he could. Evans might have noticed the way my robe sagged as I talked with him in the kitchen, but even if he'd figured out what was causing it, that still wouldn't have told him where I'd put the gun later. The rest of the time I'd kept it in my purse, and the purse had been hanging from my shoulder. Had Denny noticed it as I sat next to him in the boathouse? Or . . .

Of course. I'd replaced the gun in full sight of the mansion after we'd returned from our trip to Max's shack. Anyone might have observed that from one of the high windows. And while I'd been careful to get inside the car before removing the .38 from my bag, someone with good eyesight might conceivably have realized what I was doing.

I leaned forward, my arms and face against the cold, wet roof of the MG. Frustration and rage rose up, and I pounded my fist against the metal until I'd expunged it all. Finally I straightened and fought my way back to the house.

Sam was coming out of the living room. Beyond him, I could see Neal piling blankets and pillows on the floor in front of the fireplace. Angela lay on the sofa, covered with one of the quilts, her eyes closed. I stopped in front of Sam and stared at him, evaluating what I knew of the man. Could I trust him? I had before, but that had been merely a financial matter, his area of expertise. This was life or death, and I wasn't sure how he'd respond, if he'd panic or, worse, refuse to believe me.

He said, "I've seen eyes like that across a boardroom during a takeover attempt."

Once again, I opted for trust. "We have to talk."

He was silent, waiting.

"Not here. Some place private."

"The library."

The room was colder than it had been before. I pulled off Denny's slicker and dropped it on one of the chairs. A rivulet of rainwater ran from the towel at the base of the doors and disappeared under the desk. There had been no ashes on the grate for the wind to toss around the room, but a pungent smell of former fires pervaded. I shut the door behind me as Sam set his large flashlight on the desk.

"What is it?" he said.

"We have a problem here. Worse than Mr. Won, or the storm."

"Yeah, Angela's in pretty bad shape—"

"No, not that. Sam . . . Tin Choy Won was murdered. Smothered with a pillow."

A pause. He put his fingers to his mustache and rubbed it. "Jesus. Does she know?"

"No one does but you and me. But it gets worse: Someone's taken my gun from my car."

He drew in his breath, held it for a few seconds, then let it out explosively.

"Sam, whoever killed Mr. Won and took my gun—"

"Is one of us."

"Yes. And I have no idea who it is."

He rubbed his mustache again. The wind baffled around the house, gusted down the chimney, filled the room with its chill. Finally he said, "What can I do to help you?"

Relief at not being alone in this spread through me. "Watch—all of them. Try to figure out who has that gun. If you see anything that looks at all suspicious, tell me."

"What else?"

"Pay particular attention to the kids. Don't let anybody harm them."

"Of course. There must be something else, though."

But there wasn't. Beyond that I was alone. "That's all either of us can do." I paused, feeling foolish. "Sam?"

"Yes?"

"Do you believe in God? Do you pray?"

"I never pray. And I'm not too sure about the God business."

"Damn," I said. "Neither am I."

23

By eleven o'clock that night I knew how a reasonably peaceable animal would feel if caged with members of various other, not-altogether-friendly species.

At first the occupants of our self-constructed cage had acted as if the storm were an adventure. For the kids' sakes, Patsy said, but I sensed the pretense was also being upheld for their own peace of mind. Evans made sandwiches and fresh vegetables with dip; there was pop, and coffee that he boiled over the logs in the fireplace. Since he'd brought it out too early, the ice cream was half melted and soupy, but that was how the kids liked it, and most of the adults allowed as how they'd mushed up their own ice cream a time or two in their lives. Finally Evans unveiled marshmallows to be roasted over the fire.

Once the meal was finished, Patsy settled Kelley and Jessamyn in quilts on the floor. Sticky-faced and sated, they demanded a story. It evolved into a long, round-robin affair, initiated by Denny, about a bad-tempered duck who operated a drawbridge somewhere near Rio Vista.

I sat slightly apart from the rest of them, on a cushion near the door to the reception area. The scene that was being enacted before me struck me as bizarre and somewhat unreal, considering the undercurrents of fear that flowed through the room. Of course I was more sensitive to them, knowing that one of these storytellers—who were all working so hard to amuse the children—was a killer whose early actions indicated he or she considered those kids mere pawns in a vicious campaign of terror. Someone here had a very good facade, and as I watched the group I was at a loss to penetrate it.

At my request, Sam had positioned himself next to the door to the library, and every time I met his eyes, they were as vigilant and wary as I supposed my own to be. Whenever anyone wanted to leave—to go to the bathroom or the kitchen—I insisted on going along. For their own protection, I claimed, since no one knew if the murderer was on the island or not. The first few times I did this, it was greeted with good humor, but after a while I sensed their tolerance of this invasion of privacy was wearing thin.

By midnight, Andrew was the only one of the kids still awake. He had taken his pillows and quilts to the far side of the room, against a section of wall between two windows. When Patsy had protested that he'd be too cold there, he should come over near the fire, Andrew had pointedly ignored her. Evans had come to his defense, telling Patsy to let the kid be, but Andrew hadn't acknowledged his support with so much as a glance. Instead he propped his sketch pad on his knees and drew. Every now and then I caught him looking my way, his expression cold and complex. I wondered what was wrong, but I didn't want to question him in front of the others. He'd have to go to the bathroom sooner or later, and I decided I'd talk with him when he left the room.

After a while the conversation lagged. Patsy suggested we all could use a drink, but Denny nixed the idea. She didn't really seem to care, and in minutes she leaned against Evans's shoulder and dozed off. Evans pressed his cheek against her hair and stared at the fire, his face sagging into tired, sad lines. Perhaps, I thought, he was seeing the ruin of his dreams for the future.

Angela still lay on the couch; she'd refused any food or drink and had merely rolled over so she faced the high back of the sofa. Denny lay supine on the floor, eyes closed, hands folded on the mound of his belly. Next to him Neal reclined on his side, head propped on his fist, reading one of the books from the library. I suspected he was having trouble concentrating, because there were long intervals between turned pages. Stephanie had taken over his responsibility for the fire; she crouched near the hearth, monitoring the flames, able to remain in one position for a long time without shifting or stretching. Her transistor was beside her, tuned to the weather channel, and its mutterings were a strangely calm contrast to the raging storm outside.

The storm, the announcer said, showed no signs of abating. The National Guard had been called out, and the Delta had officially been declared a disaster area. There was a major break in the levee at Isleton; homes were being inundated at an alarming rate. The bridge washout near Rio Vista had left many motorists stranded, and at least a dozen vehicles had been blown or skidded into the sloughs. Porkpie Tract was mostly underwater, and shelters in Walnut Grove and Rio Vista were making pleas for supplies and assistance. In Sonoma County, the streets of Petaluma were flooding and evacuation of homes on the east side was under way. The Russian River area was hard-hit, with waters rising above the hundred-year flood level. Fatalities—

Angela suddenly rolled onto her back, sat up, and screamed. She put her hands to her ears and thrashed her head back and forth, and shrieked again and again. Sam's eyes grew wide and he started to go to her. I motioned him back; Patsy was closest to the sofa, and she was already on her way. Both girls woke and started crying. Andrew's eyes were black holes in his ashen face.

Patsy put her arms around Angela and tried to calm her, but she thrashed harder. Her cries were largely incoherent, but what was decipherable told enough.

"Make them shut up . . . fatalities . . . my grandfather's *dead*. . . ."

At last she had spent her frenzy and leaned against Patsy, whimpering. The room was very quiet. Even the girls stopped crying.

Then Andrew spoke, looking directly at me. "*Is* Mr. Won dead?"

I'd considered it fortunate that the kids had been so preoccupied with this novel situation that they hadn't thought to ask about the old man downstairs. Now I wasn't so sure it wouldn't have been better to have brought his death out in the open. I considered saying Angela was simply off her head, but I knew Andrew, at least, wouldn't buy it. And I also knew that whatever I said right now would make or break our future relationship—as well as determine how he handled himself in this crisis.

I looked at Patsy, but she had her hands full with Angela. Evans had moved closer to the girls, but it didn't look as if he was going to take charge, either.

I said, "Mr. Won died a few hours ago."

Kelley and Jessamyn exchanged glances and became even more quiet.

Andrew said, "How did he die?"

In that matter, I was forced to lie; the truth was knowledge only Sam and I shared. "He was old and very sick. He'd probably caught pneumonia when he came over here in the rain."

My nephew's face changed. It was as if the skin had pulled back, accentuating the sharpness of his features. His eyes narrowed, his jaw firmed, and he glared at me.

"Bullshit," he said.

I couldn't speak. Everyone stared at him.

"Bullshit," he said again. "Mr. Won was murdered."

Bedlam.

Kelley and Jessamyn started screaming. Angela began thrashing again, crying, "Oh no no no no. . . ." The other adults turned to one another, gasping and exclaiming. Sam was on his feet, moving toward Andrew, but I got to the kid first. I dragged him upright, got a firm grip on his good arm, and hustled him out of the room. I didn't stop until we were in the pantry, and then I shoved him into a corner and shone my flashlight in his face.

"All right," I said, "where do you get off saying a thing like that?"

His eyes were blinded, but his lips curled with hostility.

I wanted to grab him by his shoulders and shake him. Instead I set the light on the counter and laced my fingers together until they hurt.

"Why did you say it, Andrew?"

"Because it's true!"

"Come on, you didn't even know he was dead."

"I knew. Why do you think I didn't give you any trouble when you wanted me to keep those girls upstairs? So you and your *adults* could have their goddamned *adult* conference."

I was silent, my fingers still gripped painfully.

Andrew said, "Where do *you* get off, thinking I'm stupid?"

I ignored the question. "Did Kelley and Jessamyn know, too?"

"I didn't tell them. I didn't tell anybody."

"Why not?"

"I was protecting them."

"Well, I was protecting *you*."

Andrew didn't look convinced, but his hostility faded somewhat. I said, "Let's go in the kitchen and talk."

We went out there and sat at the table, which was covered with the detritus of dinner. Noisy conversation came from the living room; it combined with the sound of the storm to send echoes through the vast dining hall. "Okay," I said, "exactly why do you think Mr. Won was murdered?"

"Because I saw the murderer."

I tensed. "When?"

"Right after the storm got really bad. Maybe around five or five-thirty."

"Where?"

"Coming out of Mr. Won's room. I'd done some of those sketches you wanted and I was on my way up to your room. This person came out the door—"

"Who was it?"

"The same one I followed before."

I paused, wondering if Andrew were merely the victim of an overactive imagination which I had unwisely stimulated by enlisting his drawing skill in my investigation.

"Really," he said. "I saw him, but not too clear. It's awful dark in that hallway. He went into the barroom."

"Did you follow?"

"Not this time. Whoever it is, he knows his way around. And besides, look what happened to me the last time I did that." He tapped his finger on his cast.

"So what did you do next?"

"Went into Mr. Won's room. I was gonna get you, like you told me to, but Mr. Won is . . . was a nice old man, and I wanted to see if he was okay. Before he got really sick, Evans had me take him down some tea, and he talked with me and told me he'd help me learn to draw Chinese characters. I liked him. . . ." Andrew's mouth began to quiver.

Quickly I said, "Tell me what you found in his room."

"He was lying there and there was this pillow over his face. I took it off, and he was dead. A friend of Mom's died at our house once, so I know what dead people look like."

Patsy had never told me about that, but then, I'd discovered there were a lot of things I didn't know about my sister. "Go on."

"Well, right away I knew what had happened. I've watched enough cop shows to know you can smother a person with a pillow."

"So what did you do then?"

"I was going to get you. But when I went into the hall, Mom was there. She wanted me to watch the girls. I didn't want to scare her . . . well, like you, I always think I should protect people."

"So you went and watched your sisters?"

"Yeah. Mom came back right before the lights went out. After that she wasn't in such great shape for a while."

"Where was Evans?"

"The kitchen, I guess."

"Did your mother say where she went while you watched the girls?"

"No."

"Did you see anyone else downstairs?"

"No one."

"Hear anything?"

"No."

"What about the drawings you were going to show me?"

He looked blank for a moment. "That's funny. I had them with me when I went into Mr. Won's room, but I don't remember them after that. I must have dropped them there. I know I dropped the pillow. I was kind of shook up."

There hadn't been any drawings in the room when Angela and I had discovered Tin Choy Won's body. "Can you reproduce the sketches?"

"I guess."

"Try." I hesitated, preparing my last question. "Andrew, why didn't you tell me about Mr. Won later on?"

He looked away. "I guess I was pissed off. I could tell you knew. That was the only reason I could figure for the great big adult conference. It made me mad that you were treating me like a little kid."

"Please don't take any more chances again. If you see anything odd—anything at all—come to me."

"Okay." He glanced over his shoulder, toward the door to the dining room and the loud conversation beyond. "What about them? I've really upset everybody, huh?"

"Yes. And now you're going to go out there and apologize for making up a story about Mr. Won."

"Oh, Aunt Sharon, no!"

"Don't regress."

"What's that?"

"Go back to acting like a child."

"Well, you want me to go out there and act like an *asshole*."

"I wouldn't ask if it wasn't necessary. You don't want everybody to panic, do you?"

"No."

"Then do it."

He sighed, then said with all the world-weariness of age eleven, "Well, I've acted like an asshole before. I guess I can do it again."

24

When Andrew and I went back to the living room, the group in front of the fireplace appeared as black silhouettes against a flickering gold-and-orange backdrop. The flames roared high on the hearth, sucked into the chimney by a sudden updraft. Just as quickly, the wind whistled back down and made the fire sputter. A billow of smoke wafted out into the room, and one of the silhouettes—Stephanie—went over and began to move the logs around with the poker.

Beside me, Andrew stiffened and grabbed at my arm. "Come on," I said.

"No, you don't—"

"Yes. Now." I nudged him forward.

Then I noticed there were not as many people in the room as before. Denny sat hunched on a hassock; Evans and Patsy were on the floor, each cuddling one of the girls; Neal paced back and forth, hands clasped behind him. But Sam and Angela were gone.

When I asked where they were, Stephanie said, "Angela got hysterical and ran out. Sam followed her."

"Followed her where?"

She shrugged and straightened, replacing the poker in its stand. Then she crossed to the bar cart. "Downstairs. She had some crazed notion that her grandfather needed her."

I turned to Patsy. "That room's locked, right?"

"Yes, and I have the only key. Sam probably took her to her own room to try and calm her down."

It would have seemed odd behavior for one who intended to have

Angela arrested, had I not known Sam. But as it was, his actions were perfectly consistent. He was easily hurt, quick to anger, but also compassionate. And he knew he was the only person here whose attentions Angela would accept.

Stephanie had uncorked a bottle of brandy and poured herself a generous dollop. She held the bottle aloft and looked inquiringly at the others.

Denny said, "We agreed, no booze."

"*You* said no booze; nobody agreed. And it's too damned cold not to have a drink."

He turned his head toward the fireplace.

"Anyone?" Stephanie asked.

"I'll take some," Patsy said.

"Me, too." Evans turned Jessamyn over to my sister and went to fetch the drinks.

I declined with a shake of my head. Neal kept pacing.

Andrew still stood rigidly at my side. I said, "Andrew has an apology to make."

He didn't speak.

"Go on."

"I'm-sorry-I-said-what-I-did-about-Mr.-Won."

"And?"

"He-wasn't-murdered-I-made-that-up."

It was about as convincing as a weather forecaster would have been telling us the night was clear and dry.

Denny said, "To use your own word, son—bullshit."

Patsy glared at him. "My son's not a liar!"

Evans tapped her on the arm and put a brandy snifter into her hand. "He's not telling the truth, Pats. I'd say he's been coached by his Aunt Sharon."

Andrew gave me a look that said, *Well, I tried.* The others' eyes were all on me now—accusingly. I felt a tightening in my stomach as I had to concede the failure of my idea. After a moment I said, "You're right, Evans. I asked him to say what he did because I didn't want any of you to panic."

There was a silence that lengthened as each of them absorbed the truth: Tin Choy Won *had* been murdered, and his killer was here on the island.

The wind baffled around the chimney, then swooped down it. The flames made a fluttering sound, like sails caught in a sudden breeze. The bottom log broke in half, and the ones on top caved in, sending out a shower of sparks.

Stephanie reached mechanically for the poker. When she spoke her voice was huskier than usual. "How was the old man killed?"

I decided to use the old device of giving out false information in the hope the killer will trip himself up by revealing he knows it isn't so. "Strangulation. It wasn't difficult. He was very weak."

Beside me Andrew made a strange sound in his throat. I pinched his arm, keeping my eyes on the faces in front of me. They showed varying degrees of anxiety, from Denny's wariness to Neal's near-panic. But I saw no evidence of disbelief.

Patsy cleared her throat. "Who . . . ?"

"I don't know."

She looked around, raising a hand to her neck. For a moment I was afraid she would scream, but she merely said in a hushed voice, "One of us?"

I couldn't reply.

"Oh Shari, it's one of us, isn't it? All the time you've talked about somebody coming onto the island and doing all those things. And all the time you've known it was one of us. You kept it from us, and all the time the murderer's been right here—"

Evans grabbed her and put his hand firmly over her mouth. She tried to pull away, but he held fast. Kelley and Jessamyn began to cry again. I gave Andrew a little push. "Go to your sisters. Evans needs to look after your mom."

"But I have to—"

"Go!"

He went, got down on the floor between them, and hugged them. They cried harder.

Neal rolled his eyes and put his hands over his ears. "Shut them up, Evans, for God's sake shut them up!"

Patsy had stopped struggling. Tears ran down her face and onto Evans's hand. He said, "Neal, there's nothing I can do right now."

"Just shut them up, they drive me crazy, the little bastards, shut them *up*!"

Stephanie stood up and took a step toward Neal. "*You* shut up! They're just little kids; you're supposed to be an adult!"

He turned on her and smacked her on the cheek with the palm of his hand. She stepped back, fingers flying up to where he'd hit her.

Neal's voice was as high-pitched and breathy as the scream of a steam whistle. "I am an adult, don't you tell me I'm not an adult!"

"You're acting like a three-year-old. What's wrong with you anyway, are you out of your mind?"

"Don't you say that to me, don't you say I'm crazy!"

"Oh, shove it, Neal." Stephanie moved toward the door. I blocked her.

She looked down at me with narrowed eyes. Up close I could see the red mark across her cheek. "Now don't you go trying to tell me what to do."

"Please, Steff," Denny said. "She's only thinking of your safety."

She shrugged and went to a chair on the far side of the room, turning away from all of us.

Evans said, "Neal, sit down. I'll try to get the kids under control. They're quieter already, see?"

Ironically, Neal's outburst had made Kelley and Jessamyn stop crying. They had, I was sure, seen a great deal of bizarre adult behavior in their lives, but Neal's seemed to fascinate them. They stared at him, mouths open, eyes shiny in the firelight. Even Andrew seemed intrigued.

Neal saw the way they were looking at him and glared. "Make them stop that!"

"They're not doing anything," Evans said. "You're blowing everything out of proportion—"

"Don't you talk down to me!"

"I wasn't—"

"You were. You've always talked down to me. Even in the bin—"

"Neal, take it easy." There was a covert warning in Evans's words.

"Even in the bin you had to act superior, didn't you? 'Neal, I'm not as bad off as you. I'm only here for a rest. *You're* the crazy one. You've been fucked up all your life.' Oh yeah, even then—"

Evans stood up. "Take it easy. You know what happens—"

Patsy said, "What bin?"

They both swung their heads toward her.

"What bin?" she said again, louder.

A nasty, triumphant smile spread across Neal's face. "Of course. Evans didn't tell you about that."

"About *what*?"

"The bin. The Michigan Home for the Slightly Deranged, as we used to call it. They sent me there after my parents . . . died. And then Evans joined me. After he killed his wife."

"Wife?" Patsy looked from Neal to Evans. Evans spread his hands toward her—placating, helpless.

Neal's smile became more of a sneer. "Oh my dear, he hasn't told you a thing! His wife, Emily. A lovely girl. He married her after his first year at Yale Law. And five months later he killed her—"

Evans started toward him. "You son of a bitch—"

"No!" Patsy's voice was as cold as the wind that battered the mansion. "No, Evans, I want to hear this."

Evans froze; his hands, which had been reaching for Neal's throat, fell rigid at his sides.

"Evans killed his wife in an auto accident," Neal said. "After a party on an icy Saturday night in December. He was drunk, but the other driver was drunker. And he was so *heartbroken* and *guilt-ridden* that they let him off with probation. So he came home and got sent to the bin for a rest."

Neal's face was mottled, his arms waved about manically, spit flecked his lips. "I suppose he handed you the line about how he'd studied in Europe with all the best chefs. Well, Evans has only been to Europe once, on the trip we took together after we graduated from high school. He's never been closer to a great chef than the Julia Child cooking show on TV. Where he learned his so-called culinary skills was from books in the bin library, plus the cooking classes they held for therapy. He's a fraud, Patsy, a complete and utter fraud, and I'm sick of covering up for—"

"Stop it!" Sam's voice boomed over my shoulder. He stood in the archway to the reception area, his face hard with anger. As he went to restrain his brother, Patsy jumped to her feet. Evans reached for her, but she pushed him away and ran from the room. When she shouldered me aside, I heard her sob. All three kids sat stunned.

Denny got up quickly and put his arm around Evans, but Evans knocked it away and went after Patsy. Denny then turned to

Stephanie. She sat watching, her face unreadable. I caught a fleeting expresson there: interest, or satisfaction, or perhaps even grim pleasure. But it was gone as quickly as I'd half observed it.

Neal's hysteria had passed. Sam led him to a chair and pushed him into it. Neal seemed limp and dazed, as if he were recovering from some sort of physical fit.

Sam came over to me. I asked, "You knew about Evans?"

"Yes."

"Why didn't you tell me?"

"It was his business."

"It was my sister's business, too."

"He was planning to tell her."

"When? Five years frome now? Ten? Do you realize what she's going through?"

"I can't play God. Neither can you."

I sighed and put a hand to my cheek, then ran it down over my chin and throat. In spite of the cold, I was sweating; my skin felt raw and prickly. "Maybe you're right. But what else are we going to find out before this storm lets up?"

He was silent.

"How's Angela?"

"Okay, for now. She had some sleeping pills. I gave her two and waited until she dropped off. What's the situation here?"

"Bad. I had to tell them about Tin Choy Won."

"How'd they take it?"

"Hard to say. Revealing it provoked the outburst you just saw. Is he"—I motioned at Neal—"going to be all right?"

"He'll be docile for days."

"It's a manic-depressive condition, isn't it?"

"So they've told me. I don't understand those labels. I never have."

"Neither do I. I probably never will."

"So what now?"

I hesitated, trying to clear my mind. Outside the wind howled, seemed to be compacting the house, pressing down on me. I put my fingers to my temples and thought, *How the hell can I be sweating when it's this cold?*

"Sharon?" Sam took hold of my arm, then grasped my right hand

in both of his. His were dry and cold. Mine was hot and clammy.
"Are you all right—"

And then there was a thunderous crash. The mansion seemed to
crack, the way a house does in the throes of an earthquake. But this
wasn't a quake; something had slammed high up into the facade.

Denny and Stephanie cried out. The kids screamed. Sam said,
"Jesus Christ!" and threw himself to the floor, pulling me with him.

A great shattering sound came from above us. I raised my eyes and
looked toward the ceiling as shards of glass pelted down somewhere
on the second floor.

25

The glass finally stopped falling. We all remained silent. Sam lay in front of me, his hands still on my shoulders where he'd put them when he'd dragged me to the floor. At first I thought it was only his breath coming ragged and fast; then I realized his gasps meshed with my own. The wind-hurled rain beat at the high windows.

Then Denny said, "Jee-sus!"

"Which window?" Stephanie asked.

"The big one over the front door on the second floor, I think."

"What happened?"

"Tree branch blew into it, probably. Shit, for all I know it was the whole tree."

"We'd better get up there. Too much water'll ruin the carpet and the wallpaper."

The two of them scrambled around Sam and me and ran through the archway.

Sam took his hands off my shoulders. I sat up, then helped him up, too. He smiled ruefully. "Sorry. I was in 'Nam, and when I heard that crash, my reflexes—"

"Say no more."

Then I thought of the kids and looked over where they'd been. Andrew was huddled under a blanket, bumps that must be his sisters under either arm. He smiled weakly at me, but his eyes were like cutouts in a Halloween sheet. I crawled over there and touched his shoulder. "You all right?"

"Uh . . . yes."

"Jessamyn? Kelley?" I lifted the blanket and peered at their terrified faces.

Neither responded.

"Not much fun, huh?" I said.

Kelley whimpered. Jessamyn sobbed outright.

"Where's Mom and Evans?" Andrew asked.

"Downstairs, probably. They're having—"

"Trouble," he finished for me. "Mom's always having trouble with somebody or other."

"Andrew—"

"I *hate* Mom. I hate Evans, too. When this storm is all over, Kelley and Jessamyn and I are going to go live with you."

Oh shit, I thought. Felt dismay on two levels: the superficial inconvenience of even temporarily becoming guardian to a young family, and the larger issue of these children feeling so alienated from their mother. I said, "For a while, at any rate. In the meantime, can you guys hang in there?"

Andrew tried to look brave, but his gaze wavered from mine and his eyes filled with tears. "Don't leave us just yet."

I looked over my shoulder at Sam. He stood a few feet away, watching Neal carefully. Neal sat in the same chair as before, in a near-catatonic state.

"Aunt Sharon?"

"I won't go." The fact that Andrew had forgotten to call me by merely my first name—that grown-up privilege he'd been so proud of—told me how truly scared he was. "But I do have to go out to the pantry for a minute. Will you be okay with Sam?"

Andrew hesitated, then nodded.

I got up and said to Sam, "I'll be right back, and then you can help them out upstairs. I'll watch Neal for you."

Sam nodded and sat down beside Andrew, ruffling his hair. In spite of his terror, Andrew smoothed it down and gave him a haughty look that said Sam didn't understand a damned thing about eleven-year-olds. Sam shrugged an apology.

I hurried through the reception area and the dining room to the pantry. There I fumbled in the open drawer and took possession of the last flashlight. Then I went in search of knives. I found some in a rack on the kitchen wall: a nine-inch carving knife, a medium-sized paring knife, and a shorter three-inch one. I took them all back to the living room.

Sam and Andrew were talking about Mr. Won. Andrew was explaining how he'd found him. ". . . so I knew he was dead. I dropped the pillow, and I guess I dropped the sketches I'd made for Aunt . . . for Sharon."

I'd wondered about those sketches, and I felt reasonably sure Tin Choy Won's murderer had returned to his bedside and taken them. Perhaps he hadn't left the barroom, but had seen Andrew go into Mr. Won's room and return minus the drawings. If so, it put Andrew in a precarious position, and meant I must stay close to him and his sisters, defend them. After all, they were the innocent victims of this situation. However dangerous the grown-ups' plight, they had gotten into it by their own volition.

I felt a vast frustration at my inability to put the details I knew together in a cogent pattern. I sensed I was close to a solution, but it still eluded me. I *should* know. If only . . .

Andrew was saying to Sam, "And now I need to redo—"

I cut him off, sitting down on the blanket and telling Sam, "If you want to go upstairs, I'll take over here." There was hammering and cursing and shouting going on up there. Footsteps pounded down the hall, and heavy objects thudded to the floor. They could probably use another hand.

Sam said, "You'll be okay?"

"Don't worry."

When Sam was gone I said to my nephew, "How scared are you?"

"Pretty fuckin' scared, but I think—"

"So am I." I picked up the blanket and looked in under its edge. "Kelley? Jessamyn?"

Kelley said, "You're not *supposed* to be scared. And he's not supposed to use that word."

Jessamyn giggled.

I started, then realized that so much terror heaped on a five-year-old eventually had to have translated to absurdity. It was something I could exploit.

"Jessamyn," I said, "are you as scared as the duck on the drawbridge was when he thought Deputy Ma was going to arrest him for throwing the rotten tomato at the sailboat skipper?" It was a strand of the story they'd earlier woven for the kids.

"Not *that* scared."

"Kelley?"

Always analytical, she thought for a moment. "Scareder."

"But not too scared to want another story?"

Silence.

"Well?"

"I guess."

Andrew said, "Sharon, I need to redo those drawings."

"Later. First we'll give them another story." *And maybe they'll go to sleep*, I mouthed at him.

He looked around at the deep shadows surrounding us, and nodded.

So I began another tale of ducks and drawbridges. Babbled about the lunch pail that Mrs. Agnes Duck always packed for her husband. Chattered about the nasty sailboat skipper—who in my mind's eye had come to resemble Neal—and the good guy in the rowboat—Denny?—and the inevitable flying rotten tomatoes. When Kelley interrupted to ask why Agnes Duck packed rotten vegetables in her husband's lunch pail every day, I knew I had them hooked. And finally there were yawns, more yawns, and no more questions.

All the time, the racket went on upstairs. Another window shattered, and there was a chorus of dismayed and frustrated voices. At first I identified Denny, Sam, and Stephanie. After a while they were joined by Evans. Then Patsy said something, and I felt a flood of relief. Whatever the damage to their relationship, at least for the duration of the storm, my sister and her lover would pull together.

When I was sure Kelley and Jessamyn were asleep, I let my voice trail off and glanced at Neal. His head had fallen back against the chair, and his mouth was open, snoring. Then I looked at Andrew and was shocked at the fear in his eyes.

"It's okay," I mouthed.

He tried unsuccessfully to look brave.

I took the small paring knife from where I'd hidden all three under a nearby pillow. "Here. This should make you feel better. Be careful with it, but use it if you need to defend yourself or your sisters."

He swallowed hard and took it by the hilt, gingerly feeling the sharpness of the blade with his thumb. Then he got up, looking around furtively, and went to the wall where his quilts and pillows lay. When he returned, he had the sketch pad and pens.

"Oh," I whispered, "the drawings."

Again he looked around, as if he was afraid someone was watching us. He put a finger to his lips, sat down closer to the fire, and motioned for me to join him. I scrambled over there and watched as he sketched.

First he drew a figure. Tall, in baggy clothing. A figure like the ones in the drawings he'd done before. Totally unrecognizable. He looked eagerly at me.

I frowned and shrugged.

His face fell. He ripped the page from the pad and drew more carefully.

This time there was something vaguely familiar about the figure. And the background . . . "What are these?" I pointed at some irregular shapes behind the person.

"Sssh!"

Again he ripped the sheet from the pad and drew. This time it was just the background shapes from the last sketch.

"Fire?" I whispered.

"Sssh!"

He tore the sheet off and drew with quick strokes. Now I saw the outline of a hand.

"Is this what you saw—"

"Sharon!"

I lowered my voice. "Through your bedroom window?"

He ignored me, his body trembling with excitement, drawing with a swift, sure intensity that sprang from fear.

I glanced around us, but could see nothing beyond the irregular splash of light from the fire. Andrew was wise to be afraid, I thought. Anyone could be standing just beyond the boundaries of that fire-light—in the shadow of one of the doors, or outside in the storm, looking in through a window.

I tried to identify the various voices above. The hammering obscured them, and they blended into one loud babble.

Andrew continued sketching the hand. I watched. Waited. And

finally I knew. He handed the pad to me and stared intensely into my eyes.

I nodded.

And then I thought—of *why*, rather than of who.

Andrew shivered. I put my arm around him and pulled his head onto my shoulder. "You did good, my friend," I said.

"You know, don't you?"

"Yes."

"I didn't realize until I saw—"

"That's why you were so uptight."

"Uh-huh." He pressed closer to me.

I held him and stared at the sketch. As I continued to work on my theory, the frustration I'd felt earlier vanished. What replaced it was not quite elation, more like a resolve. I added some facts that I now knew, subtracted some others. Discarded this, reclaimed that. And felt an angry certainty build—that kind of certainty that tells you you're about to break a case.

I thought about Max Shorkey, who had operated the ferry for many years, up until Stuart Appleby had died.

Thought about Stuart himself, his tragic heritage.

Alf Zeisler. His "ghost." The plastic effigy of him.

Tin Choy Won. He'd known the legend, listened to rumors of a ghost—and possibly had thought he'd seen one himself.

Sam came into the room and went over to Neal, speaking to him in low tones. Neal shook his head listlessly, but allowed his brother to lead him to a sofa and tuck him in under a blanket. Then Sam joined us. "You guys okay?"

"Yes," I said. "How's it going upstairs?"

"Not too well. Denny was right: A huge branch—looks like from that sycamore—smashed the big window. Caught on the ironwork and took out the windows on either side, too. Water's pouring in, there's not enough plywood, and we're running out of nails." He dropped to the floor next to me.

"Who's upstairs now?"

"Everybody, I guess, except Angela. It's hard to say, because people keep running up and down for tools and supplies."

"Will you stay with the kids for a few minutes?" I got up and handed Sam the long carving knife, keeping the more manageable medium-sized one for myself. He looked surprised, but nodded.

I went straight to the library, to the maritime history section. Somewhere among all those volumes there had to be one that would tell me what I needed to know. It took about ten minutes to find it, using my flashlight to search through the texts—and when I located the reference, it confirmed what I suspected.

When I passed through the living room, Sam and Andrew were speaking seriously with one another. I looked inquiringly at them, and Sam gave me a thumbs-up sign, so I kept going toward the reception area. As I neared the archway, there was a quick motion out there, and then the front door swung back and slammed resoundingly against the wall.

Somebody had gone out into the storm. And I thought I knew who—and why.

I hurried out there, shone my flashlight through the door, had a blurred glimpse of a figure running down the drive. That confirmed it. This was no routine trip to fetch something from one of the vehicles; it was flight.

Sheets of rain blew into the house. The wind swayed the chandelier, making its crystals smash together in a violent cacophony. As I ran after the retreating figure, I thought I heard one of them fall.

26

I raced along the drive, thinking fleetingly that I should have gotten someone to come with me. But Sam couldn't leave the kids, and there hadn't been time to call one of the others from upstairs. And every second mattered: The figure had by now disappeared into the blinding downpour, but I was fairly certain it was headed for the boathouse. The boathouse, where the skiff and its new motor were kept.

The rain pelted my face, obscuring my vision. It soaked my hair, making it a sodden mass against my neck and back. The legs of my jeans quickly became saturated and flapped cumbersomely. With every step my boots sunk into ankle-deep mud. I leaned into the wind, hunched over, and kept running for the levee.

Halfway across the lawn, a cypress branch flew out of the darkness at me and slapped into my face. A piece of it narrowly missed gouging my eye. I swatted it away without breaking stride.

Under the big sycamore, the ground was a graveyard of dead branches. The tree itself leaned crazily toward me, its roots exposed; it shuddered and groaned in the wind. I veered off sharply, afraid it might fall on me. My flashlight bounced wildly over the terrain in front of me, and then I saw the bulk of the levee.

As I drew closer, the levee appeared to be melting. A river of mud and rock sluiced down its side; beneath that a layer of reinforcing sandbags had been stripped bare. I started up it, slipped, and went down on my hands and knees. Stones bit into my flesh through my jeans. The avalanche of mud almost swept me with it, but I clawed at the gritty surface, feeling my nails tear, and dug my boots between the sandbags. And finally gained the top.

In spite of the darkness I could see the water of the slough, whipped to a white foam. The waves had completely inundated the finger pier, perhaps washed it away. They rolled over the remaining boardwalk as if it were a beach. The rectangular hulk of the boathouse was deep in shadow.

I crouched on the top of the levee, panting and curling myself into a ball against the wind. My flashlight sent out an irregular circle of light; I turned it off quickly. I'd stuck the knife in the belt of my jeans, and now I pulled it out and gripped it firmly in my right hand. Its weight was not all that comforting—considering the person I was after must have my gun.

When I'd caught my breath, I pushed the flashlight into the deep pocket of my sopping-wet sweater and slid down the other side of the levee. The oozing mud and loose stones made my feet skid, and halfway down I lost my balance and fell. The ground there was under water and I went in up to my waist. I cried out at the icy shock, then slogged forward toward the steps that led up to the boardwalk alongside the boathouse.

The railing that had stood alongside the steps had toppled over onto them. I grasped it with my left hand and pulled myself up, feeling splinters bite into my palm. For a moment I struggled to free my feet from the muck; they finally came loose and I wriggled up the steps on my stomach and poked my head over their top. A wave broke on the boardwalk, rolled onward, and engulfed me. I flailed and slipped back a couple of feet, water pouring into my mouth and rushing up my nose.

I coughed and choked, clinging to the railing. The knife in my hand was hindering me, so after I'd regained my breath I jammed it into my belt where I'd had it before. Then I pulled myself hand over hand along the broken railing to the top of the steps again. This time I raised my head higher. Water rushed across the boardwalk, but it hit me at shoulder level. I felt the cold, but not as keenly as before, and briefly I worried that I might be losing sensation in my limbs.

Some twenty feet from me was the wall of the boathouse. The small door in it hung open, banging against the corrugated-iron side and clanking loudly. The opening itself was a rectangle of dim, yellowish light, and from time to time an elongated shadow moved across it. I watched, narrowing my eyes against the stinging wind and rain, but could make no sense of the activity going on within.

Fortunately the clanking door and howling storm would cover any sounds I made as I approached. Still in a crouch, I came up off the steps and moved forward.

I took the knife from my belt again and gripped it hard. The boardwalk was slick and waves washed over my feet; I steadied myself without taking my eyes off the door. The light inside the boathouse spread a faint path on the rainwashed surface of the deck. When I got there I skirted it and sprinted up next to the opening, on the opposite side from where the door banged to and fro. My heart was pounding and my breath came hard. I leaned against the wall and felt it vibrate like tinfoil in the wind.

I listened to the sounds coming from inside the boathouse. Rain battered the iron roof. Water sloshed, probably in the boatwell. The wind wailed, trapped in the cavernous space. There was a bumping and a scraping. After a moment I pressed flat against the wall and inched my head sideways until I could see through the door.

The light came from a large battery-powered torch sitting on the floor midway between the well and wooden stand where the skiff's new motor was kept. The door of the boatwell had been cranked up and rain sheeted in and splattered on the concrete. The water in the well itself had risen dangerously high, and rivulets of it ran over the floor. A pair of oars lay next to the steps leading down to the well; the skiff had been lowered into it. It bobbed violently about, slamming into the concrete walls.

A tall, angular figure in an olive-green slicker crouched near the motor, tinkering with its prop. I studied the person, understanding how easily the illusion of the hermit's ghost had been created. The rags, the noose, enough distance to blur details—

Then Stephanie stood up and turned toward the boatwell.

I jerked my head back behind the doorframe. Even though I'd known who the murderer was—from Andrew's sketches, disconnected details I'd observed, and the information I'd found in the library—the confirmation still shook me. Sharp-tongued but agreeable Stephanie who all along had wanted Appleby Island for herself.

My gun, I thought. Where did she have it?

I chanced another look around the doorframe. Stephanie was lifting the motor from its stand. I couldn't see the .38. Most likely it was in her slicker pocket or tucked into the waistband of her jeans. Now would be the time to catch her off-guard. Maybe the only time.

Stephanie began lugging the motor toward the boatwell. I hefted the knife and edged through the door into the shadows beside it. Waited until she was close to the steps into the well. And ran at her back.

She heard my footsteps, or sensed my presence, and glanced over her shoulder. Then she pivoted and dropped the motor. It fell to the floor not two feet from me, with a metallic crash. I dodged and brought the knife up, but Stephanie was already fumbling in her slicker pocket, probably going for the gun. As she tried to pull it out, it caught. I dived at her feet.

Her foot kicked out at my head. I saw it in time and rolled away, then tucked my feet under me. Rose, ready to spring up with the knife.

But she'd freed the gun from her pocket. Was holding it in her right hand, aiming it at me.

I dived to the floor again, sliding sideways on the wet surface and dropping the knife. The bullet whined and clanged into the wall behind me. The shot resounded again and again in the empty space.

Stephanie knew boats, but she didn't know guns. The recoil forced her arm up and knocked her backward.

I slid forward on my stomach, almost bodysurfing in the water on the floor. Grabbed for her ankles again. This time I caught one and held on tight.

She tried to kick out, but staggered. I heard the gun fall to the concrete. As I locked my hands tighter around her ankle, I tried to see where the .38 was. Over on the very edge of the well, far out of my reach.

Stephanie staggered again. Her other foot slipped and she teetered, then fell heavily. On top of me.

My breath was knocked out of me; I gasped, but air didn't seem to reach my lungs. Frantically I sucked my breath in again. But then Stephanie's hands were at my throat and she was straddling me, pinning me to the concrete. I put my hands on hers and raked them with my nails.

She let go of my throat. When I looked up through a haze of water, her face was contorted with pain and rage. Then she grabbed me by the shoulders and began trying to slam my head down against the concrete. I pummeled her anywhere my arms could reach, but she didn't seem to feel it.

My remaining breath was being beaten out of me. Blood roared in my ears. I summoned my last reserves of strength and arched my back. Pushed up with my whole body.

Stephanie slipped to one side, the side where the boatwell was. She grasped my shoulders harder.

I arched my back and bucked again.

She fell off me.

I struggled into a sitting position. She was inches from the edge of the well. Bracing my arms on the floor behind me, I straightened both legs and pushed her with my feet. She started to slide into the well, but at the last instant she grabbed my ankles and pulled me in with her.

The icy water closed over my head. I plummeted downward, fighting panic; then my feet touched bottom and I pushed up, and almost immediately broke the surface. Stephanie was splashing around some three feet away. The skiff bobbed and smashed off the wall. Before I could get my breath, Stephanie came at me, trying to grab my hair.

The skiff came to from the right and missed my head by inches. Stephanie saw it in time and ducked under the water. When she resurfaced she was within an arm's length of me. I swatted at her, my eyes on the skiff.

It slammed into the opposite wall and made a return trip, clipping me on the shoulder. Briefly I was stunned, and then Stephanie was pushing my head underwater. I grabbed one of her hands and wrenched the fingers back, hard. She let go and I dove down deeper.

My lungs felt as if they were bursting. My limbs were numb and heavy. My hands . . .

I tried to raise one and feel for the skiff.

Couldn't.

Kicked my feet, feeling the panic again; my heavy boots were dragging me down.

The wave action was violent. It smashed me into the rough

concrete wall and then shot me to the surface. The skiff was now between me and Stephanie. It had swung away from the wall and was coming back fast. I ducked down again, tried to swim under it. It passed inches above my head.

When I came to the surface, I saw Stephanie clinging to the stern of the skiff, starting to swing it toward me once more. I was backed against the part of the wall where the steps were cut; I raised my hands and tried to pull myself onto them. And slipped.

The skiff was coming closer.

I tried to raise my numb hands again, to drag myself onto the steps out of the skiff's path. As I did I saw the oars lying there, their ends extending over the edge of the well. I lunged out of the water. Missed the oars. Lunged again, and got one of them.

With only feet and seconds to spare, I brought it down lengthwise between the skiff and the wall. It cracked, but it held the skiff at bay.

Stephanie gave a cry of rage and let go of the stern, thrashing toward me. I lunged upward once more, grabbed the other oar, swung it around just as she reached me.

Brought it down on her head.

It was a solid blow that knocked her underwater; when she came up again, she was facedown and inert. I dropped the oar and clung to the steps, breathing hard, getting myself under control again. For a few seconds I comtemplated leaving her to drown, but I was having enough trouble sleeping nights as it was. Finally I paddled over and turned her on her back, then towed her limp body to the steps and dragged it up to the boathouse floor.

27

The storm blew itself out the following afternoon. And the day after that the Delta skies were an untroubled blue, and blinding sunlight bathed the islands and rivers and sloughs.

Bulldozers cleared the roads and work crews shored up the levees. In the towns people shoveled mud and debris out of their homes, and the stores—while poorly stocked—were open for business. Later in the week, many of these folks would begin the arduous process of dealing with state and federal agencies, all of which had expressed great compassion for the flood victims during the disaster—but few of which had come through with badly needed grants and loans in past years when applications had poured in. But for now the people were taking life an hour at a time, valiantly reclaiming what was left of their homes and salvaging a few of their possessions. The region had once again drawn on its immense recuperative powers, and was already on the mend.

On Appleby Island, the evidence of the storm's destruction was everywhere. The finger pier by the boathouse had broken up, and the levee had collapsed near there, inundating a good part of the lawn. The big sycamore tree—the same one from which the Applebys had hung Alf Zeisler—had toppled, as had many of the trees in the orchard—where Stephanie had hung the hermit's effigy. Great patches of slate were missing from the mansion's roof, and there were slabs of plywood over at least a dozen broken windows. The cost in human terms was even greater, the indications of it more subtle.

After the fight in the boathouse, I'd tied Stephanie up and struggled back through the storm to the mansion. There—with minimal explanations—I'd turned responsibility for her over to the others, and collapsed and slept for thirteen hours. It was a restless, troubled sleep, full of ugly visions and occasionally broken by the sounds of the storm, and I'd awoken feeling drugged and depressed. By then the weather had cleared somewhat and the sheriff's launch returned to check on us. After I'd told Benjamin Ma what I knew about Stephanie and her crimes, the launch had left with her and Mr. Won's body. Angela had gone, too; she would have to see to the funeral arrangements and, I assumed, the sheriff would also want to question her about the embezzlement. As the rain turned into a drizzle, a subdued and upset Denny got the ferry working, and I drove to the sheriff's substation to give a formal statement.

Back on the island, the others demanded explanations. I told them why Stephanie had done the things she had, again without going into great detail. When they wanted to know how I had figured it out and what Stephanie had said in her confession (before her lawyer had shown up and advised her not to say any more), I begged off and gave them the letters I'd found in the library. I was just too damned tired to retrace the steps that had led me to my conclusions, too sad to recount the confession that Benjamin Ma had let me read. So I went upstairs to bed and slept twelve hours more.

Now it was time for me to leave. I would have liked to slip away without further explanations and discussion, but it didn't seem right to go without saying my good-byes. So I went about my rounds, beginning with Sam, whom I spotted walking in what was left of the orchard. He moved through the trees and around their fallen companions with his head bent, hands clasped behind his back—a man shouldering far heavier burdens than when he'd arrived at the island.

At my approach, he turned and his face brightened somewhat. I said, "I've come to say good-bye."

"You're going so soon?"

"My job's done."

"I'll miss you."

I fell into step beside him. "How's Neal?" He'd driven his brother to a clinic in Rio Vista as soon as the ferry had been operational.

"Still under observation, still extremely depressed. I'll have to wait until the doctors say it's all right for him to travel."

"You're planning to take him back to Michigan?"

"Yes. He needs me, but obviously I can't give up my work and life to stay here. I want to get him into a good psychiatric program; it's something I should have done long ago. For too many years I've let things slide and just hoped he'd get better on his own. Now I realize that isn't going to happen."

"What about the island?"

"Denny and I will make any necessary repairs, and he's agreed to stay on for a while as caretaker. Denny's a good guy and I know I can trust him with the property."

"Where is he, anyway? I don't want to go without seeing him."

"Over fixing up Max's shack. He says he's going to live there."

I stopped, dismayed. "Oh Sam, that's a terrible place!"

"I know, but he's determined not to live in the mansion. Don't worry—Denny's talented. He'll fix it up to his liking."

"I hope so. Do you plan to sell the island eventually?"

"That's up to Neal. As he's overly fond of saying, it's *his* island. When he's well, he can decide."

We began walking again, toward the levee beyond the orchard. It had fared better than the one by the boathouse, and there was little evidence of damage.

I said, "Denny's taking it pretty hard about Stephanie, isn't he?"

"Yes. He cared for her. They always bickered, but there was a genuine affection under it all."

I thought of Denny and Stephanie as I'd first seen them; and then I thought of the first words I'd heard him say to her, and filed away a question for when I said good-bye to the big contractor.

Sam stopped by a fallen tree. "Let's sit down for a while. I want to ask you a few things."

I sat beside him, remembering the other time we'd sat and talked on a fallen tree trunk. It seemed a year ago. "About Stephanie, you mean?"

"Yes. You haven't seemed willing to talk about it, but I think we all need to know more than what was in those letters."

"Okay, but I want you to pass what I tell you along to the others. I'm not up to going into it with each person when I say good-bye."

"Fair enough."

"As I told everyone last night," I began, "Stephanie was the granddaughter of Louise Appleby's illegitimate son by the hermit, Alf Zeisler. The Applebys inserted clauses in their various wills to ensure that no descendant of Louise's bastard would ever inherit the island. Stephanie knew she had no legal claim, so she came to work here with the intention of driving everyone away and forcing Neal to sell out cheaply. It's all logical once you know that Louise left heirs."

"How did you figure Stephanie's connection to her?"

"I only realized it after I saw Andrew's sketch of the hand he'd seen outside his window. The sketch told me she was the one doing all these things."

"Andrew said he'd drawn dozens for you."

"Yes, but of the person's whole body, not the hand. And he's not that great an artist—at least not yet. The sketches were of Stephanie as he saw her, in disguise. It was a good disguise, too; in those old clothes she found in the junk room, she definitely looked like a man. And the descriptions I kept getting of her . . . well, the semantics had me fooled. For instance, everyone kept saying the hermit's so-called ghost had long hair *for a man*. Stephanie's is average length for a woman. The baggy clothing hid how angular her body is; it was hard to tell how much the person weighed."

"It had to have been a good disguise, because it sure frightened those workers."

"Yes, but even there she took extra precautions. She was afraid they would start thinking about what they'd seen, decide it was a hoax, and come back to work. So she got her lawyer to get them all jobs, out of town."

"This lawyer must be one upstanding member of the bar."

"I think he may have been involved with Stephanie. The first morning I was here, she mentioned she hadn't been home for dinner the night before because she'd gone to see a 'good old boy' in Sacramento. The lawyer, Bob Barnes, is one of those jolly Southerners; he's also the one who had an acquaintance make two blind offers to buy the island for Stephanie, before Neal's offer was accepted."

"And now he's defending her on the murder charges?"

"Yes. I was at the sheriff's substation when he arrived yesterday. He seemed more upset than most attorneys would be in the situation, which bears out my idea they may have had something going between them. Anyway, Stephanie's worst mistake was letting Andrew see her hand through his window. It probably never occurred to her that an eleven-year-old was so observant—or that he would be capable of drawing what he'd seen."

Sam held up his strong, squarish hands and flexed his fingers. "That's one part of the body that's hard to disguise."

I nodded, laying my own fingers flat on my thighs and studying them. My nails were clipped almost to the quick because I'd torn them while scaling the levee in the storm.

"All right," he said, "so after you recognized her hand in the sketch—"

"I put together what I knew about Stephanie with what I knew about the Appleby family. There was a line of that family with Miwok Indian blood. Stephanie has Indian blood; it's plain in her face and coloring—just like it is in mine. When I first met her, I realized we might have that in common and asked her about it. She went to great pains to explain to me that she was Italian, French, Irish, and Scandinavian. Naturally she wouldn't want anyone here to know about her Indian background, in case they found out about Louise Appleby's part-Miwok descendants.

"But there was still a grain of truth in what she told me; most good liars interlard it with their falsehoods. The Scandinavian part was true, would have been hard to hide, considering her last name. So I knew Stephanie was part Scandinavian, and I also knew Louise Appleby had taken her illegitimate son and run off with a Swedish seaman with the Northern Pacific Line.

"One of the few other things Stephanie had told me about herself was that she was from Seattle. I didn't know where Louse and her seaman had gone, but I did know who he worked for. So I went to the library—the maritime history section—and looked up the Northern Pacific Line. It's headquartered in Oakland now, but at the time Louise and her baby disappeared, it was located in Seattle. Stephanie's family operated a boat charter service; it was a natural business for descendants of a seaman to go into."

"And all of that told you why she'd tried to drive everyone away from here."

"Well, in broad outline. All along I'd had a feeling that what was going on might be tied up with the Appleby family history. Someone had displayed an inordinate interest in information about the Applebys—to the point of stealing a book containing a chapter on them off my bedside table and searching the library in the middle of the night. At first I thought the person was after information; later I began to suspect the purpose might be to suppress the story of Louise and the hermit. That was another mistake Stephanie made; if she hadn't raided my room and then the library, chances are I never would have found and read the Appleby letters."

"Do you think she knew they existed?"

"I'm not sure. She must have suspected there was something like that in the library, because she took the first chance possible to search it privately—in the middle of the night right after Neal started leaving it unlocked. I surprised her before she could find them, though, and she ran outside and reentered the house through one of the downstairs doors. Turns out she had all sorts of routes in and out, so she could carry on what now seems like a pretty stupid campaign of harassment."

"Stupid," Sam said, "but terrifying if you didn't know what was going on. Did you say she's made a full confession?"

"Yes. At first she tried to bluff, but her trying to run away during the storm and the fight she had with me in the boathouse were pretty damning. When she realized the authorities knew of her connection to the Applebys, she must have known they would eventually prove their case."

"What else was in the confession? Why did she kill Max and Tin Choy Won?"

"Let me start at the beginning. After Louise Appleby ran away and married the seaman, Jorgenson, the family did well in Seattle. Her husband adopted James, and when he was grown they established a successful charter service together. But in spite of being reasonably comfortable, there was always this family folklore about the great wealth that they thought was their due—the Appleby pear fortune. They found out early on about the wills that disinherited Louise and her heirs, but they still preserved what evidence there was of their connection; when Stephanie's parents died in 1984, she took those documents—letters, baptismal certificates, that sort of thing—and went to see Stuart Appleby here at the island. He turned her away, so she went to the lawyer in Sacramento, who confirmed what Stuart had told her: that she had no legal claim. Stuart shot himself shortly after that. Stephanie sold the charter business and tried to buy the island, but the estate wouldn't accept her bids."

"Where does Max come into this? I know he worked for Stuart—"

"He was part-time ferry operator here at the time Stephanie came to see Stuart. Later, when she came to work on the island, Max remembered her and wondered why she was acting as if she'd never been here before. There's no way of knowing if Stuart Appleby told Max the purpose of her visit or not, but Max implied to Stephanie that he had. And he started blackmailing her. Stephanie claims she killed him accidentally in a struggle while they were arguing over the blackmail, that they were having a quarrel on the ferry ramp and Max attacked her and things got out of hand."

"You sound as if you don't believe that."

"I do—up to a point. But I wonder why they were out there in the rain, rather than in his shack. Especially when he'd been fixing his supper right before he was killed."

"You think she planned it?"

"She planned something. Maybe not to kill him, but she may have lured him out there with the intention of scaring him; she was wearing her disguise. We may never know."

"And then she tried to kill you."

I nodded, remembering that seeming eternity in the drifting, water-filled boat.

"What about Tin Choy Won?" Sam asked.

"You remember when Angela was downstairs shouting at him? And Stephanie went to see if she could help?"

"She came back all white-faced and stalked out of the house."

"In his fever and disorientation Tin Choy Won must have thought she was the hermit's ghost. It had been on his mind, because of my visit and the questions I'd asked him. His reaction was something I'm sure Angela just shrugged off as ravings, but Stephanie was afraid that after he got well Mr. Won would remember—and tell." I paused.

"It's a wonder she didn't try to kill Andrew, after she saw him go into Mr. Won's room and later found the batch of sketches he'd dropped on the floor. But she probably didn't think the kid realized what he had there, or that he would duplicate them. When she saw he'd done that, it was too late."

"She knew he'd redone the sketches?"

"That was why she ran out of the house and tried to get away in the skiff. She had come downstairs and saw Andrew showing me the drawings in front of the fireplace. We couldn't see her because nothing was visible to us outside the light from the fire, but we were brightly illuminated, and she could see the expressions on our faces. She ran back up to her room, packed a few things, and tried to make her escape. Fortunately she used the door closest to the boathouse—and I saw her leave."

Sam shook his head. "Jesus. So what now—do they have enough evidence to convict her?"

"The confession's legal. They'll probably try to use an insanity defense. It's up to a jury." I paused again. "What about Angela? Is Neal going to press charges?"

"At the moment he's not in any shape to. But someone must have tipped the sheriff about what was going on, because they've been questioning her anyway."

"I'm afraid that someone was me."

"I'm not sorry you did; Angela shouldn't be allowed to get away with it." He looked off into the distance. "Maybe I'm a fool, but when the time came I couldn't bring myself to turn her in."

"Probably you are a fool, but I like you all the better for it." Briefly I put my hand on his, then got up. "I'd better go now."

"Have a safe trip. Would you mind if I kept in touch?"

"Mind? I'd be delighted."

I started across the marshy lawn toward the mansion. Halfway there I turned. Sam was watching me. He waved and then started walking toward the levee.

I found Patsy in her bedroom, packing a suitcase. She looked weary and bedraggled in old jeans and a T-shirt, but I sensed a certain peacefulness about her. Her living quarters were peaceful, too; I listened for childish voices, but heard nothing but the tick of an old alarm clock on the bedside table.

"Where're the kids?" I asked.

"Evans took them to Sacramento for lunch and a matinee. They've been depressed, what with all this, and we thought . . ." She sighed and continued folding garments.

Her use of the pronoun "we" seemed a positive sign to me. "I just came down to see you before I take off."

"You're going right away? I'd hoped we'd have one last evening together. You never did explain everything about Stephanie—"

"I've told Sam, and he'll tell the rest to you. And I really have to get back to the city; I've got to prepare for a court date on Friday."

"Oh. Well, there's something Andrew wants you to have." She went into his room and returned with the sketch of Stephanie's hand. I stared at the long, scarred fingers. It was a hand that had twice tried to kill me, and I didn't particularly want this reminder.

"Take it," Patsy said. "He really wants you to have it. You can put it away and only get it out when he comes to visit."

"Maybe I'll put it in my office, sort of like a wanted poster."

Neither of us smiled.

"Patsy," I said, "what are you going to do now?"

"Go back to Ukiah. There're some friends we can live with for a while, until we decide what to do. There's no sense staying in the Delta; the kids hate it. So do we—now."

"Evans is going with you, then?"

"Of course." She noticed my surprised expression and added, "Oh, Shari, that stuff he lied about . . . it was a line he used to use with people he wanted to impress, because he felt inadequate and ashamed. And when it impressed me, he kept getting in deeper and deeper, and he couldn't just admit he'd lied and start over. I don't care if he had a breakdown; he's been all right for years. And I don't care if he deceived me; I love him. All my life I've been running away from the people I love, ducking out of relationships when the going got rough. I'm not going to do that with Evans.

"Besides," she added, "Andrew needs a father. He's turning into an insufferable little smart-ass."

"Yeah, but I like him."

"Me, too. He's McCone all the way."

We smiled at each other for a moment. Then I said, "So what do you think you'll do eventually? Buy another farm?"

"I'm not sure. Ideally, we'd like to get a place we could turn into a bed-and-breakfast, like we planned to here, but not on such a grand scale."

I frowned.

"With private baths," she said hastily. "And I promise—no potpourri."

"A likely story."

I hugged her, thinking I just might have my little sister—the one I had loved—back again. Maybe even a stronger little sister, one I could respect as well as love.

When I released her, I said, "You'd better call Ma. Our mother, I mean, not the deputy. I didn't tell you, but she's worried because your phone was disconnected. She even tried to call me at All Souls."

"Uh-oh. What on earth am I going to tell her?"

"That's up to you."

"No, really, what do you think I should say?"

Some things *never* change. "Tell her you're staying with friends and thinking of buying a B-and-B. It's the truth, more or less."

When I left the room, Patsy turned back to her packing and started humming.

The MG had survived the storm with only a few new scrapes and scratches on its already scabrous paint job. I stuffed my weekend bag onto the passenger's seat and drove over to the ferry landing. When I honked the horn, Denny brought the barge over. On the return trip we stood with our backs to the island, looking forward toward Max's shack.

"I hear you're staying on for a while," I said.

"Yeah, until Neal's in shape to decide what to do with this place. I'll probably be able to pick up a lot of work around here for a while, helping repair flood damage."

"Why are you going to live in the shack, though? You could have the entire mansion."

"Who needs a mansion?"

"Not me."

"Me neither."

We were silent as the ferry moved slowly toward the shore. Just before I knew he would have to go back to the engine house, I said, "Denny, there's one thing I'd like to ask you."

"I don't want to talk about Stephanie," he said flatly. "I . . . cared about her, and I'm pretty bent out of shape. She isn't nearly as bad as all the stuff she did would make her out to be. She just wanted what was rightfully hers, and when she found she couldn't have it, things got out of hand."

"I understand how you feel. But it doesn't have anything to do with that. It's just that I'm curious. The morning I met you, you and Stephanie were arguing. I came into the kitchen, and you said something like, 'It's dangerous, and I won't—'"

He nodded.

"*What* was dangerous?"

"The pier. She was trying to get me to use it as the foundation for the boat slips. I told her it could go at any time—and I was right, wasn't I?"

"Yes, you were." The idea had obviously been another component in Stephanie's plan of fear and destruction, but I wouldn't voice that to Denny. Down deep, he probably already knew.

"Sure I was right," he said. "I'm right a lot of the time. But does anybody ever listen to me? *Fuck, no!*" He turned and went to the engine house.

I drove off the ferry and waved at Denny. He waved back and lumbered toward the shack. As he went inside, I thought of his comment: "Who needs a mansion?"

Who does? I thought. Only those who have nothing else of value in their lives.

My earthquake cottage suited me just fine. My cat and I were comfortable there, and if he had turned into a wanderer—well, in a way so was I.

I realized now that since I'd regained consciousness in the water-filled boat several nights ago, I'd had very little time or inclination to dwell on the details that had plagued me before I'd come to the Delta.

The little things had faded to insignificance while I had been engaged in the kind of work I was meant to do.

I reached the top of the rise, paused, and looked in the rearview mirror at Appleby Island. Then I turned onto the levee road. The pavement was relatively clear of debris, and I knew of no major hazards between here and the bridge to Antioch. With any luck at all, I'd be in San Francisco by three-thirty.

And when I got home—then I would deal with the big things.